MOONSHINE
BY MOONLIGHT

MOONSHINE
BY MOONLIGHT

ANN HANIGAN KOTZ

BookPress®
publishing

Published in Des Moines, Iowa, by:

Bookpress Publishing
P.O. Box 71532
Des Moines, IA 50325
www.BookpressPublishing.com

Publisher's Cataloging-in-Publication Data

Names: Kotz, Ann Hanigan, author.
Title: Moonshine by moonlight / Ann Hanigan Kotz.
Description: Des Moines, IA: Bookpress Publishing, 2024.
Identifiers: LCCN: 2024912891 | ISBN: 978-1-960259-13-4 (hardcover) | 978-1-960259-21-9 (paperback)
Subjects: LCSH Alcohol trafficking--Fiction. | Organized crime--Fiction. | Nineteen twenties--Fiction. | Prohibition--Iowa--Fiction. | Carroll County (Iowa)--Fiction. | Iowa--History--20th century--Fiction. | Historical fiction. | BISAC FICTION / Historical
Classification: LCC PS3611.O74938 M66 2024 | DDC 813.6--dc23

First Edition
Printed in the United States of America
10 9 8 7 6 5 4 3 2 1

For the people of Carroll County
—then and now.

"I violate the Prohibition law—sure. Who doesn't?"

— AL CAPONE, 1927

MOURNERS AT THE WAKE OF BARLEYCORN

BUT LITTLE DRINKING MARKS HIS DYING HOURS.

DRYS CELEBRATE THE PASSING

Chicago Cafes and Hotels Ignore Birth of Dry Nation—"Hinkey Dink's" Famous Saloon May Become a Confectionery Store.

(By the Associated Press.)

Chicago, Jan. 16.—The death of John Barleycorn in Chicago ended at midnight tonight. Uncle Sam was the official undertaker and the decedent was buried deep beneath a grim tombstone inscribed "eighteenth amendment." Government agents acted as pallbearers and will remain to guard the cemetery.

There were few mourners at the "wake." Most of the downtown hotels and cafes ignored the advent of January 16. If a person carried his own in remodeled hip pockets he was allowed to wish John B. goodby, but in reality there was little drinking.

CHAPTER 1

The wicked winter wind whipped the snow into harsh eddies that swirled up and down Templeton's Main Street, creating a white haze. The snow, glowing in the light of the partial moon, clashed with the dark of midnight. Winter's leftovers piled on the streets, against buildings, and on tops of fence posts. It coated business windows and blocked shopping paths along the sidewalks. It accumulated like sand dunes in the roads, blocking side streets. The pine trees bent to the wind's force, showing their deference to the stronger adversary. Signs along businesses, held firmly by thick bolts, rattled their resistance. The wind screamed down deserted streets.

Green pine wreaths decorating front doors caught snowflakes and were now covered in white. Two long, single garlands hanging from the corners of Main Street and First Street, crisscrossing the center of town, swayed in the wind, threatening to rip from their posts and fly away. A lone wreath succumbed to the gale, leaving its door, and cartwheeled down Main like a western tumbleweed. Neither man nor beast wanted to brave the winter battle, instead surrendering to the elements, quartering in some protected area.

Residents of this tiny town known as Templeton snuggled in their beds, resting for the upcoming Christmas festivities. With only three weeks remaining, there was still much to prepare. Individual celebrations, family gatherings, and town festivities kept the citizens bustling by day and planning by evening. Christmas, the holiest of holy days for this German-Catholic community, was organized months ahead. Nuclear families opened gifts Christmas Eve, followed by Midnight Mass. On Christmas day, extended family gatherings celebrated with large meals of roast pork and braised rabbit, apple and sausage stuffing, red cabbage, and potato dumplings. For this most important celebration, women baked stollen, a bread-like cake filled with nuts and dried fruits. Christmas night brought town celebrations of dancing and more eating with long tables loaded with the women's best. The town hall was decorated with greens, and candles dotted the long tables. Men, women, and children congregated and drank beer, even the children allowed a weak mug for this special evening.

Tonight, though, there were no celebrations or large family gatherings.

A small beam of light, showing through the curtain of snow, came from the north end of town, making its way down Main Street, looking like some drunken man as it wove around the piles of snow. As it drew closer to the center of town, the single beam of light became two beams, indicating a vehicle. The lights fought through snow, coming to a stop under the center of the garlands. A husky, tall stranger, bundled in boots, coat, gloves, and hat pulled low, stepped from the Dodge truck. Bent slightly, the face tucked down into the woolen coat to keep it from the bitter wind, the unknown form pushed through the squall and climbed into the bed of the truck. Stepping onto the side of the bed to get a boost up, the figure crawled on top of the cab. Like a wing-walker, this person wobbled against the wind while making their way to the center of the cab. An object of some sort came from the coat as the stranger reached up, pulling the center of the garland down low. Something was being affixed to the decoration.

Each year, on the third Sunday of Advent when the sun went down, the town gathered to fasten the outdoor chandelier to the crossed pieces, which provided the strongest spot. Mugs of hot liquid—be it cider, hot chocolate, or warm whiskey—were held in mittened hands while residents sang traditional German Christmas songs, the first one always "*Stille Nacht.*"

This was not the third Sunday of Advent: it was the first, and whatever was tied to the garland cross was not part of their Christmas traditions.

Once completed, the human bundle carefully sat down on the cab and slid to the bed, tracing the same path back to the end of the truck, and jumped down to land in a pile of snow. Before continuing to the safety of the truck cab, the vandal looked approvingly at their work. Unable to follow the original tracks as they had been closed over again by the wind, the stranger made a new set, not crisp and clear, but muddled and indistinct. Once inside the truck's cab, the driver put the vehicle in gear and continued down the street, the glow of the red taillights becoming faint.

The decoration now affixed to the crossed garlands was not a star or a tree or an angel as one would assume appropriate for the season. It was a flat wooden piece in the shape of a jug, a jug used to store the illegal liquor made and sold by bootleggers. Across the middle of it, the unknown vandal had painted **X-Mas Spirits**.

IOWA JEWELERS OPEN SESSION

National President Denounces 'Bootlegging.'

(Tribune-Capital's Iowa News Service.)

CEDAR RAPIDS—W. G. Frasier of Dunham, N. C., president of the American National Retail Jewelers association and Lafe Major of Perry, president of the Iowa jewelers group, were the principal speakers at the opening session of the annual convention of the Iowa State Retail Jewelers association here.

Mr. Frasier denounced "bootlegging" among jewelers, saying that the price cutting "makes the public feel that the jewelers have

been overcharging because the bootlegger may sell the merchandise for what it may, cost him."

Mr. Major declared that support of the Capper-Kelly bill was a means of combatting the "bootlegging" evil.

Monday's activities were closed by a banquet at Hotel Montrose.

ANITA CHILD DEAD; ATE POISON LEAVES

(Tribune-Capital's Iowa News Service.)

ANITA—The 21-month-old son of Mr. and Mrs. Harry Johnson, farmers near here, died Sunday as a result of eating poison oak leaves. Funeral services will be at the home Wednesday.

CHAPTER 2

The sun broke the morning after the storm, sending the wind on its way. The once-swirling snow was now settled and throwing crystal glints out into the daylight. Birds came from their protective spots to sit on icy tree branches and look about to estimate the length of time until spring would arrive again. One by one, houses began to awaken and show life. Chimneys spouted smoke, sending scents of burning logs into the air. Doors opened, and the work began to clear the snow to form paths. Young boys and fathers, holding solid shovels, dug into the deep snow and brought up heavy piles of the powdered moisture, throwing them off to the side.

Businessmen also cleared their sidewalks and sprinkled sand to keep their customers safe. Frozen door locks, jammed with ice, had to be melted with hot water until the lock turned again.

The townspeople would take at least a day to recover from their snowy, imprisoned life. The process of digging out after a storm would pass but return, almost ritualistic for the small Iowa town.

Finn Vries, Templeton's only jeweler, sweated through his shirt as he dug his enterprise out of the three inches of new snow. He had promised himself to hire one of the high school boys to scoop his sidewalks this winter, but when the time came to spend the money, his fist curled up into a tight ball; he had declined the business offer when the youths stopped by. Now, he would need to return home and change his shirt to be presentable for his customers.

Back in his store, wearing a dry shirt, Finn began the ritual of shining the glass on his display cases, making them as sparkly as the jewels beneath them. He sprinkled the glass with the vinegar-water solution and made circular patterns with his soft cloth to erase yesterday's smudges. Once the tops of the cases were complete, Finn repeated the process on the fronts except, this time, he put the solution directly on the cloth. Fingerprints took away from the beauty of the brilliant gems laying protected in the case. Customers, wanting a closer look, put their hands on the tops of the displays while their children looked in through the sides, leaving behind nose prints.

The appearance of the store, like its owner, remained pristine throughout the day.

Once Finn finished the inside, he moved to the large windows facing the center of town. Crusted snow blocked the view of his merchandise, and potential buyers would walk by unaware of what they could purchase as Christmas gifts for their loved ones. Finn carefully polished the inside of the window, backing up several times to look for any imperfections in his work. When he found one, he would apply his cloth and cleaner with more effort. Still, the outside would need tending.

Getting into his rubber boots, coat, hat, scarf, and gloves again, Finn went out the front door and started scraping away the snow. He was thankful the winter debris was only powder instead of rain turned to ice. A thorough brushing with his broom removed all remnants of the night's storm. This time, he didn't work up a sweat.

Even though the winter snow created additional work for Finn, he enjoyed the new precipitation. Each layer of white cleaned whatever muddiness or dirt had sullied his town. It became pristine and perfect once again, and Finn appreciated cleanliness and goodness.

Returning to the warmth of the store, Finn went into the back room and removed his coat, replacing it with a fine wool jacket and a matching vest. He took special pride in his shoes, black and tan wing-tipped with rubber soles. They not only looked sharp with all his suits, but the soles were comfortable for those who stood on their feet all day, like Finn.

He kept a small hotplate on his back counter to make his tea. The water on to boil, Finn readied a cup. The water would take time; in the meantime, he went back out and stood behind his counter, looking at the center of town, admiring the work he had done on his windows.

And then he saw it.

Something was hanging from the garlands. He could not see it clearly. Hustling to the window, Finn stared at the object.

None of the other businessmen had opened their shops yet, so Finn was the first to see it. Removing his glasses from his pocket and settling them on his face, his vision cleared, and he saw the object clearly now, recognizing its form. A whiskey jug. His full face curdled in disgust.

As Finn stared at the shape, a small flame ignited in his chest. Once his vision distinguished **X-Mas Spirits** on the wood, the flame turned to a roaring fire, spreading through his chest, down into his stomach, and out from his fists—which were now balled up, ready to fight someone.

"They ruined Christmas! They just had to make it about themselves, didn't they? They had to take their dirty business and ruin something so special—a time of Jesus Christ," he fired off to no one, his thin lips pressed into a grimace and his high cheek bones bright red with rage.

By "they," Finn meant the Wets.

The makers.

The drinkers.

The sellers.

The smugglers.

The Prohibition law breakers.

The vermin, who seemed to have doubled and tripled since the beginning of Iowa's moratorium on alcohol in 1916. Their activities had become worse since the federal enactment of the Volstead Act in 1920. Now in 1923, the liquor making and selling had doubled—perhaps tripled.

Finn had always been a staunch Dry. Not one drop of liquor had touched his lips in his fifty-two years of life. His parents, who had immigrated from Holland, had hammered into him their strict morals and values. No drinking or smoking or lechery. The body was sacred, a gift from God.

Finn's parents, Jan and Ada de Vries, had settled in the Carroll County area in 1878, twenty-seven years after its inception. By their arrival, Iowa's land was settled. Jan paid for his eighty acres and built his family a sturdy house between Templeton and Carroll. Within a year, Jan decided to drop the *de* from their surname, an effort to sound more American.

Templeton, settled by German Catholics, did not appeal to his parents' sensibility. Their religion seemed cult-like, pretending to eat the body and drink the blood of Christ. They mumbled foreign words not even they understood and watched their priest's back as he performed unknown ceremonies. Their love of beer also disgusted his parents. The Vries stayed tucked inside their home during Octoberfest while the townspeople celebrated for days, guzzling vast quantities of the alcoholic beverage.

Nevertheless, they sent their children to the country school full of German students, a few miles from their home. Finn and his siblings were teased often, the children mocking their thick Dutch accents and laughing at their Dutch attire. Finn received the worst of it, his voluminous trousers standing out among the other boys' clothing. They pointed at him and asked him if he could fly when the air filled his pants.

As a Protestant, Finn did not participate in the Catholic ceremonies that marked adulthood in his peers' lives: First Communion and Confirmation. During each of those times, Finn found himself on the outside of conversations as his peers discussed the upcoming rites of passage. Because of his differences, he often stood on the side of the playground, never being offered to participate in their recess games.

When Finn was twelve, his father died. He had contracted scarlet fever and languished in his bed for three days before finally succumbing, leaving his wife to raise the three children. The farm was heavily mortgaged, and poor corn prices could not save it. The bank repossessed it, bringing an auctioneer to sell off the land and their house.

Ada Vries moved her small family into Templeton and found a job as a seamstress; however, her meager wages could not support the family. They lived on the bottom floor of a two-flat house but were eventually evicted when she lapsed four months behind in their rent. Ada acquired another, smaller flat, one that was rundown and infested with field mice. Their home backed up to a cornfield, so no matter how clean she kept it, Ada could not keep the rodents away.

To help his mother with their living expenses, fifteen-year-old Finn took a position at the Templeton jewelry store. Even though he knew nothing about jewelry making or selling, his kind-hearted boss had known his family needed the extra income and had hired him anyway. Finn worked on Saturdays, keeping the store spotless. He spent hours polishing the jewelry cases and windows. The owner, Karl Wagner, would stand back and direct Finn to redo any spots where he saw streaks. Finn took pride in his work and enjoyed his time at the store. Even though Karl was German, Finn admired him greatly. He treated Finn like a son and taught him everything he knew about the jewelry business, always preceding his lesson with "when you own the business." Karl had no sons of his own, and his one daughter had married and moved to South Dakota.

In the last half of Finn's sixteenth year, his mother married another widower, Charles Krupp. Krupp owned the local hardware store and had three children of his own who needed a mother to help raise them since he too had lost his wife to the same outbreak of scarlet fever that took Finn's father.

Charles was a good man and treated Finn's mother and her children well. In return, she tolerated Charles' love of beer. On Saturdays, he walked to the community center and sat for hours, chewing the fat with other men his age. Somehow, there were always pints of home-brewed beer for all to enjoy. He often returned with his cheeks flushed from alcohol and his speech slurred. Finn hated his drinking but could do nothing to stop him.

Charles' oldest son John was a year younger than Finn. John and Finn shared a bedroom, but the two boys did not get along. John was angry his father had married again, bringing more children into the house, and Finn hated John for being one of the children who had mercilessly tormented him in school. The boys physically fought often, showing up at the supper table with swollen eyes and bloody noses. To punish them as well as try to make them get along better, Charles sentenced the boys to complete chores together. The teenagers rose early and scooped snow or restocked the store. They carried out house chores when they came home from school. The boys even walked the same path to the high school, mornings and afternoons, one walking in front of the other instead of side by side. Even though they were together fifteen hours a day, it did nothing to improve their relationship. Finn's only reprieve from his stepbrother were his Saturdays at the jewelry store.

Several years out of high school, Finn married a Protestant girl, a Swede from Deloit, and settled in Templeton. He began working for Karl five days a week until Karl retired. Finn then borrowed money to buy the jewelry store and grew it into a prosperous business.

While in school, Finn had promised himself he would move out of the area and into one that practiced his own beliefs. But the opportunity of the jewelry store had tethered him to the Carroll area.

Now, he and his family involved themselves in the community, but only to the point needed to avoid gossip. Finn, a savvy businessman, knew his participation in the community's doings was important to his success. He dragged his wife to the town's annual Fourth of July parades, the Christmas festivities, and he had even given money for the priest's new vestments.

While he never spoke it, Finn, like his parents, was greatly bothered by Germans. He considered them loud and slovenly. He thought Germans ate like gluttons and drank like swine. Finn's nose was so far above them he could smell the food on God's dinner table.

Finn sent his own two children to Manning and taught them to hold their heads high and remember they were better than the other children.

Staring at the wooden whiskey jug, Finn was brought back to his decision to stay in Templeton. Once the Volstead Act had passed, he had been certain the town would become a decent Christian home for all the Drys like himself. The beer drinking and liquor making would cease, and the God-fearing people would have won out.

That was not the case.

Instead of a few quarts for personal use and gifts for friends, bootlegging had become a profession. More whiskey flowed out of Templeton than water flowed out of the mouth of the Mississippi River. Dozens of men cooked the stuff and dozens more drove it out of town, most of it going to Des Moines, Sioux City, or Omaha to be distributed to other parts of the Midwest. Rye whiskey from Templeton, Iowa, was as well-known as the Great Bambino.

The tea kettle began to scream, bringing Finn back to his present trouble. He returned to his back room, poured water into his cup, and dropped a tea bag into the hot liquid. He sat down at his desk to warm himself with the tea and think about the unknown person who ruined the town's decorations.

Finn didn't know who specifically made the alcohol, but he had his suspicions. His stepbrother John, he thought, was one of them.

John, never a good student in school, did not take over his father's hardware store when he passed. It went to one of his younger brothers. John had worked on various farms until he was eventually dismissed for missing too many days of work. John was never happy working for another man who could tell him what to do, when to do it, and how to do it. Finn had heard he had been fired a few times for threatening his boss. Eventually John married and now farmed his wife's family's land. If one could call what he did farming.

His stepbrother was just the kind of man for whom the bootlegging business seemed to be made. He worked his own hours, always at night, and could drink as much of his product as he wished.

How he could be distilling whiskey was the question Finn hadn't yet worked out. John's farm didn't make enough money to get an operation going. It took money to buy the supplies for the still and then more money to buy the ingredients. With many buildings, he had the perfect place to make and store the stuff. Whiskey needed to be aged for at least six months. The capital it would take before seeing any kind of return would be out of his brother's reach.

On the other hand, perhaps John worked for someone else. Someone who would provide him with all he needed yet allow him to work his own hours in his own way. Finn, along with the rest of the community, had heard there were many Carroll County residents making whiskey. They bandied about many names, but none knew for certain the exact identities.

This desecration of their Christmas decorations was the final hit for Finn. It would make the Carroll newspaper as did everything that happened in Templeton. And the deed would surely be picked up by both the Sioux City and Des Moines newspapers. Their town's reputation was already sullied, but this made it a joke. And even though Finn kept himself apart from all the illegal activities, just being a resident put him in with everyone else. He no longer told people where he was from when he went out of the area. Templeton was synonymous with bootlegging. It was as if everyone and everything in this town were entwined into one illegal enterprise. Every resident was a bootlegger, whether they wanted to be or not.

Finn had done nothing about all the illegal activity around him. He pretended he saw nothing and knew nothing.

In a small part this was true. He didn't know anything specific, but he had heard the talk and guessed some of it had to be true. Instead of keeping to his own business, Finn picked up the telephone in the back of his store and asked the operator to connect him to the Carroll County Sheriff's Office, sixteen miles north of Templeton.

"Sheriff's Office. How may I help you?"

"Hello. My name is…well, I would prefer not to give my name. Is the sheriff available?"

"No sir. He's out for the morning. Would you like to leave a message or have him call you? He should be back around noon. He's always here to eat his lunch."

"Yes, I'll leave you my number. I'm the only one answering the phone, so he won't need my name. It's 4542. Thank you."

Finn was thankful he did not have a party line. Most did. No one's conversation was private, and even with his own line, Finn couldn't be certain the operator wouldn't stay on to listen. Doing what he was about to do would not be appreciated by the town's residents.

Finn hung up the telephone and went back to straightening his store. While it didn't need it—his morning chores were already completed—cleaning or organizing always calmed his mind. He had become so irate he could feel his heart pumping faster and knew his cheeks were still flushed with anger.

The morning's business was nonexistent. The storm had kept people at home, digging themselves out of the piles. Not a single soul could be seen along the main business street. Once he finished recleaning, Finn sat down with another cup of tea and completed some bookwork.

Even though he tried to clear his mind of the hanging desecration outside his window, eventually the image of the jug swinging in the breeze invaded the space. Finn was certain he knew the person who would perpetrate such a stunt. Once again, his suspicions landed on his stepbrother.

More than once, Finn had found a dead garter snake under his blankets when he had crawled into his bed. Several times John had pushed him forward toward a group of young ladies, knowing Finn became tongue tied around females, and stood back and laughed while Finn struggled for conversation. Once, John had set him up with a local girl for the town's fall dance at the high school. When Finn arrived with a wrist bouquet in hand, his stepbrother had nearly wet himself with laughter. There had been no girl for him. John wanted to entertain himself watching Finn gussy up for his supposed date.

Finn pulled out his pocket watch, a silver heirloom from his father. As a child, Finn remembered the watch tucked inside his father's vest pocket, the matching fob swinging from its chain. As a little boy, Finn enjoyed looking at the watch face when his father popped open the front lid. It would be another hour before the sheriff was available.

At exactly 12:05, the phone rang. Normally, Finn answered with "Templeton Jewelry," but he wanted to remain anonymous if it were the sheriff calling. "Hello," he answered.

"Uhh. Yes. I was told to call this number. This is Sheriff Katz. What can I do for you?"

"Hello, yes. I would prefer to remain anonymous. I have some information for you about some illegal activity."

"I'm listening," the sheriff responded. "What do you know?"

"You ought to keep an eye on John Krupp. I'm pretty certain he's making illegal liquor."

"You're pretty certain or you're certain?" the sheriff asked with doubt in his voice. "What evidence do you have? Have you bought liquor from him or seen him selling liquor?" The sheriff's voice sounded bored like he had heard these allegations a hundred times before.

"No. I've not seen anything, but I know him. It's just like him to do something like this. He's lazy and shifty," Finn said with conviction.

"Sir, I don't know who you are, but I can't go around arresting people without evidence. You don't have any reason other than reputation to suspect him, and a bad reputation is not a crime." The sheriff's voice had a sharp edge to it. Clearly, he was frustrated with Finn for calling. "Have a good day." Without waiting for Finn's reply, he hung up.

Finn went back to his front window and stood looking up and down the street. There were now townspeople standing on the sidewalk, across from the decorations. They were pointing at the jug and laughing.

Finn couldn't believe they weren't as disgusted as he was; instead, they found the whole situation amusing. He thought he even detected a small amount of pride on their faces.

This repulsive business needed to be stopped before no one in town could hold their heads high. Finn made up his mind to become more involved. If the sheriff needed proof, then he would find proof.

CHAPTER 3

I couldn't see the effigy from my home, but I certainly heard about it. The whole town was talking, laughing, pointing. Speculation of the doer ran through the streets for many days, but no one was sure of the answer. Its existence was nothing more than someone's 'screw you' to the federal government. Its position in the middle of town signaled a defiance of the law, a 'come-get-us-if-you-can' attitude about making illegal booze. It was done for sheer pride, and that made us proud.

Our people's pride had been taken piece by piece. First came Iowa's prohibition. While that was not directed at Germans specifically, it took an important piece of our culture. Germans have been drinking beer made by monks since the tenth century. Octoberfest, originally started to celebrate the union of two monarchs, was a little over one hundred years old. Our people come together each autumn in celebration of a piece of our culture. With Prohibition, we were made to celebrate in secret, alone or in small groups.

During the war, our most difficult years, our pride was purposely ripped from us. Our birthright was spit upon and hated. Our language, our traditions--even our blood—was loathed. So much so that the Governor made it forbidden to speak our language in public. We could be arrested for doing so. Non-Germans wanted us to crawl upon the dirt, ashamed of ourselves.

First generation emigrants were told they were 'alien enemies' and not allowed to fight for their adopted country. We were called spies, Krauts, Kaiser lovers. The love we felt for America was doubted. Yes, we are German, but we are American, too. Our families came to this country because we wanted to be American, but during the war we were thrown aside, made to feel like outsiders. We were expected to denounce our heritage, but what man can cast aside his past? His roots?

When you take away a man's pride and tell him his heritage— the very thing that makes him who he is—must be given up, that he must walk away from his very self, he will eventually rebel and fight back. He will cleave to what you try to kill. In secret, he will sear his memories into his brain and horde every scrap of his past like someone who is starving. And when the time is right, he will lash out against those who tried to shame him.

Our land, our traditions, our language—these we fought to protect. It was not a physical fight, like the war. It was a secret fight, one only we knew was being waged.

We spoke our language only among ourselves and continued to teach our children the sounds of our mother country. We clung to the land our fathers broke even if it meant going against the law to secure the means to keep it and continued to pass down our traditions generation after generation.

The vandal's rogue act foolishly brings our fight into the open, drawing attention to our small community. The newspapermen will come and take their pictures, splashing our defiance across the state's dailies and weeklies. Instead of quietly going about our illegal business under the light of the moon, this act shouts it from Sacred Heart's steeple.

The eyes of the federal and local lawmen saw those pictures and turned their attention our way. They would not abide by our pride. They wanted to put their boot heels on our necks and push us back to the dust. They broke through our doors and demolished our stills. They locked up our citizens and made examples of them, sending the message of their superiority and our inferiority.

I knew who did this thing. I knew who couldn't defy the government in secret, who had to show them he was defying them. A man who fought against his own countrymen and came home to be told he is inferior because he is German. This patriot came to hate America even though he was born American. Every gallon he distilled defied a law he did not accept by a country he no longer wanted to call his own.

There was retribution for his pride. We all paid the price.

23 DIE FROM HOLIDAY BOOZE

Government Denies Its Poisoning of Liquor Responible.

New York, Dec. 28 (A.P.)—The death toll from Christmas liquor drinking in Greater New York today had risen to twenty-three, with scores, perhaps more than 100 of persons under treatment in hospitals for alcoholism.

In Chicago seven deaths have been reported; in Detroit, five; in Des Moines, two; in Milwaukee, three, and Omaha, two.

Dr. Charles G. Norris, New York City medical examiner, declares that extensive chemical analysis would have to be made before it could be determined whether the deaths here were due to poisoned liquor or excessive drinking.

To Investigate Supply.

The government declines to accept any responsibility for any deaths due to drinking alcohol which passed through its hands. Federal agents in Washington declare that, although 2 per cent wood alcohol was placed in most of the industrial alcohol, this is not sufficient to cause death. Washington officials indicate, however, that the prohibition unit will investigate closely the source of supply of the liquor that caused the deaths.

CHAPTER 4

Will Katz received at least two 'suspected bootlegger' calls a month. They were always anonymous, and they never had any solid information. He often felt like a schoolteacher with children who wanted to tattle on one another. Like the teacher, he didn't want to hear it. These phone calls took up far more time than he liked.

Will had been sheriff of Carroll County since 1921, the year after the Volstead Act and five years after Iowa's prohibition law went into effect. He had a small office on Fifth Avenue in Carroll but was responsible for all 570 square miles and 16 townships that encompassed his county. The people under his care were mostly German and mostly Catholic.

As soon as he hung up the phone receiver, he ran his hands through his short, dark hair. His piercing, dark eyes stared at the picture of a blue jay sitting on a tree limb as he thought about what he needed to do regarding the report. Although he had told the caller there was nothing to be done, the information could not be ignored. He had a name given to him. He would at least drive out to Krupp's place and speak with him.

Will waited three more days before he made the trip. By then, he figured, the farmers would have the roads cleared. Fortunately, the last storm had not brought more than three inches. He probably could have gotten through, but with the bitter cold, he hated to chance getting stuck.

Farmers labored together, hitching up their work horses to snow blades, and cleared the road in front of their house all the way to the next one. If the next house was more than a mile, the farmer next on the chain of snow removal would meet him halfway. If the snow were too deep, only those with horse-drawn sleds could get out. It might take weeks to get dug out. Until then, country folk were prisoners of the weather.

Will loaded his physically-fit body into his 1919 Ford truck. At thirty years old, he was as lean as a panther. Other counties provided a sheriff's car, but Carroll County had never done so. Will knew as long as he was willing to make do, they would never offer to purchase one for him. He didn't mind, though. He felt the official car made him more inaccessible to the public. His old pickup signaled he was just one of them. Just neighborly Will Katz.

As he drove down West Fifth Street, people on the sidewalks gave a friendly wave, and Will reciprocated. Sometimes a small beep from his truck accompanied his lifted hand. As with all small towns, there were no strangers. A true stranger would be noticed within hours. And if the stranger were visiting a relative, an entire write up in the local paper would describe everything they ate and spoke.

Will turned on Fifth Street, headed south, and drove the fourteen miles on newly created Highway 71, his mind replacing the barren, snowy fields with ones of corn, beans, and rye. Carroll County boasted miles of fertile farmland with rolling hills, the bulk of its residents being farmers. Templeton, situated at the southern end of the county, was born from the building of the Milwaukee, Chicago, and St. Paul

Railroads in 1881. The 1920 census had counted 320 inhabitants, expanding by 95 people from the 1910 census. Templetonians were sure the 1930 count would be higher as many new faces settled in each year.

John Krupp lived on his wife's family farm. As their only child, she had inherited the land when they passed. She and John currently farmed the 120 acres. The farm had never made them much money, sometimes just enough to pay the interest on their loans. If John had put more care and effort into his occupation, Will thought, he could have made a better go of it. However, he wasn't interested in farming. His corn was often sitting in fields covered with the first snow before he got out there to pick it. John was a good guy, but he was lazy and didn't always follow the law.

Driving south, Will took note of the fallow fields. Leftover stalks of corn or beans poked through the white snow, reminding farmers of their upcoming season. Barbed wire decorated the fields like rustic necklaces. It would be four months before they would be breaking ground for the spring season. In the last few years, though, it wasn't worth putting seed into the ground. Commodity prices had fallen, and the men spent money and time with little in return. Yet a fallow field during the season seemed like a sin.

This agricultural distress and the price of illegal liquor swirled together to create the tornado of bootlegging. Farmers could either lose their farms—some of them passed down from their immigrant families—or find another way to provide for their families and pay their bank notes. Will couldn't really fault them for choosing the latter.

A pheasant flew out of the ditch, startling Will and bringing him back to his task. He carried a rifle in his truck, mounted behind his seat, but he was not fast enough to take it down to shoot the bird. Will had only used his gun on animals: a cow that had broken a leg and needed to be put down, a deer grazing on unpicked corn, a dog gone rabid. He had a pistol, but it never left his desk.

Will was a crack shot; however, he hated guns. When he was a kid, his father took him hunting. It was precious time spent together, and Will learned most of his manly duties from quiet conversations high up in a tree stand. He shot his first deer when he was fifteen, and with his father's guidance, gutted it in the field and hauled it home. The family ate deer meat that winter, and Will was proud of his contribution.

His hatred of guns came from his time in the military. Feeling patriotic and wanting to do his duty for his country, Will volunteered during the war but quickly found himself in the worst situation of his life. He and his platoon were ordered to storm a large field, shooting as they ran. Will saw a German soldier fall to the ground after being shot in the shoulder. Still holding his gun, the enemy lifted his rifle and aimed it at Will, assuming Will was planning to finish the job. Faced with a gun pointed directly at him from only several yards away, Will shot first, killing the enemy. When he looked at the man's face, he saw not a man, but a boy. Maybe fifteen or sixteen years old. He was someone's son. He could have been Will's brother. Will even considered the possibility of the boy being his cousin, a relative left behind when his family emigrated. Even though he had shot to save his own life, Will never wanted to shoot that gun again. They were not faceless Krauts; they were family men and young boys, and relatives of German Americans. He supposed they hated the war as much as he and had been conscripted. For the remainder of his time fighting, Will never intentionally aimed his rifle at another human being. He shot into the void, and as far as he knew, he never hit anyone else.

When Will returned from the war, he went home to Willey where his parents farmed. Instead of working with his father, he chose a different profession, blacksmithing. He pounded his aggression into the metal. He spent most of his days in solitary work, thinking about his life and the boy he had killed. Will eventually worked his soul so hard it had little time to think. His upper body grew thick muscles, which didn't match his soft voice. His community had known him since boyhood and wasn't afraid of this burly, tortured man.

The war had also taken his suitability for close companionship. Night terrors and days of moodiness did not render him a fit husband. Instead, Will inhabited a small house, choosing an old tom cat as a housemate.

A year and a half after his return from war, Will decided to run for county sheriff. No one else seemed to want the job, and he had been asked directly by the outgoing sheriff to serve. Will had been convinced when the former sheriff had talked of his calm head, well-respected reputation, and the ability to do something good for his fellow man. He had never considered such a position but being able to make people's lives better appealed to his guilty conscience.

Pulling into John Krupp's lane, Will followed a flock of ducks running ahead of him while a dog ran alongside his truck, barking furiously. Alerted by the barking, John came from behind his barn. Krupp's frame, short and stocky, looked even more so bundled in layers of winter gear and gloves. He threw up a friendly hand and waited for Will to pull up alongside him. "How's it going, Will?" John asked as soon as Will stepped from his truck.

"Pretty well, I'd say," Will replied. "Got somethin' to talk to you about. You got a little time?"

"Is this a barn talk or a standing-here talk?" John asked.

Barn talks took more time, haybales providing places to sit and a jar of whiskey being shared between men. "Naw. We can do it right here."

"So what's this all about? Am I in trouble?" John inquired.

"Trouble? John, why would you think you're in trouble?" Will asked with a grin. "I got a phone call this morning," he continued.

"About me, I'm presuming," John said. "Something I've been doing? Maybe something on the wrong side of legal?"

"I think you know what this is about. The caller was anonymous. Didn't have any specific information. Just some speculation. I thought you should know."

"I'm sure I know who it was. My ass of a stepbrother, I'm sure. He's just dying to get something on me. He'd like nothing better than to see my backside in jail," John said with bitterness in his voice.

To change the subject and make it worth his trip, Will said, "How's the family, John? How's Betsy?" Will stayed half an hour just catching up. He thought well of John's family and enjoyed shooting the breeze with him.

As Will returned to town, he passed several farms, his mind pointing out which ones he suspected were distilling. They were small-time operations, a few gallons at a time. Will saw no harm in selling a few pints for a few dollars. It made paying the grocery bill a little easier.

Will knew for certain of one operation. Earl Miller was definitely distilling. In fact, he was one of the originals. Skeet, as he preferred to be called, had been hired as a farmhand for Saul Schneider back in the late teens, a few years after Iowa's prohibition became law. Skeet and another laborer put together their own still by retrofitting a copper wash boiler. They bought copper coiling from the local hardware store. Saul's farm ran along a stream, providing the cooling component needed to turn the steam in the coil back into liquid. The boys hid their operation from Saul until word got around the youths were selling illegal hooch. Saul followed them one night across his fields, right to the edge of them. There, he found their still and the men with fifty gallons of mash.

Saul was gentleman enough to allow them to finish their cook, but he demanded they pack up and move somewhere else. He also fired both men for using his land without permission, putting him at risk of being arrested along with the two of them.

Will didn't know where they relocated and didn't want to know. Skeet's name had not come up again, but Will was sure he was still making booze.

Skeet was favored by everyone and seemed to know every resident in Carroll County. He could talk the leg off a stranger as well as convince anyone of anything. He was a smart man but liked to live on his own terms. A seven-to-five job wasn't his preference. Farm work didn't excite him enough. Outfoxing the law during the dead of night, with only the moon shining to show him the way, fulfilled his need for adventure.

Back at his desk, Will returned to his regimented paperwork. Unlike Skeet, he liked a quiet, predictable life. Running for sheriff wouldn't seem like a quiet life, but things in Carroll County were generally calm. Other than bootlegging, this was a farming community with residents who minded their own business, worked hard, and went to church. An occasional scrap between men required him to mediate. An occasional drunk slept it off in the jail, the cell door wide open. Will always had a respect for the law and found satisfaction in keeping his community safe.

When the Volstead Act went into effect, Will knew he would need to make a decision: either he was going to actively pursue his fellow community members, or he was going to look the other way. He had taken an oath to uphold the law. When Iowa went dry, only a few men made whiskey, generally just enough to drink at home and share with friends. What a man did in his own home was his own business, according to Will's way of thinking. But when the federal law was enacted, the demand for alcohol went tenfold. Now, three times as many stills were being operated, and whiskey making was big business. It wasn't a few quarts or a gallon or two; it was thousands of gallons. It wasn't a drink or two in the house; it was barrels being hauled to Des Moines to be sold to states across the United States.

If Will went after the distillers, he was not just putting the men making the alcohol in jail. He was hurting the farmers who rented them land. He was hurting the local banks who had loans with those farmers. He was hurting the grocers and merchants who sold goods to the distillers and farmers and bankers. The whole town benefitted from this industry. Will's job was to protect and serve, not ruin and starve. As long as the activities stayed out of the public's eye and no true lawlessness happened, Will didn't plan to do any arresting.

His conscience was also partly nullified by the quality of the product. Not all whiskey was safe. There were bootleggers out there who didn't care about the consequences of their product. They would add embalming fluid to make it 100 proof. Some added iodine to make it look aged.

The worst offense was selling industrial alcohol. The federal government had not made industrial alcohol part of the Volstead Act because they felt confident no one would drink it. To make it undrinkable, the manufacturers were required to infuse additives, like gasoline or wood alcohol, which was the most common. If wood alcohol were consumed, the drinker became blind. Unfortunately, though, the human desire to make money was stronger than the government had planned. Unethical bootleggers bought the legal alcohol and redistilled it, trying to remove the toxic elements. They were not always successful. Drinking bootleg whiskey was like playing Russian Roulette. One never knew if one drink was the bullet.

The *Des Moines Tribune* reported on New Year's Eve festivities, which brought about a disaster from denatured alcohol. Forty-one people died on New Year's Day in New York's Bellevue Hospital. In that year, nearly 50,000 people died from imbibing industrial alcohol, prompting the government to replace wood alcohol with other foul smelling and tasting additives like kerosene, which would not kill the drinker.

People also drank something called Ginger Jake, a revised version of Jamaica Ginger. Jamaica Ginger was sold as a patent medication for stomach aches, malaria, and colds. Even before Prohibition, many drank it in dry counties for its alcoholic effects. It continued to be legal under the Volstead Act as long as the manufacturers added enough bitters to the concoction to make it very unpleasant. Brothers-in-law, Harry Gross and Jack Reisman, devised the knock-off by adding Lindon, an odorless and tasteless additive used to make plasticine, which kept the liquor in compliance with the law. Plasticine made celluloid film and explosives and affected drinkers' nerves, rendering the imbibers with paralysis, later referred to as "Jake leg."

Carroll County bootleggers distilled with nothing but everyday ingredients: water, sugar, rye, and yeast. No harm came to those who spent a few dollars on their whiskey. If Will had ever discovered one of them adding harmful ingredients, he would be there lightning quick with his handcuffs to haul away the offender.

A few weeks after New Year's, Will received a call from Alvin Truly, Audubon County's sheriff. Audubon County adjoined Carroll County to the south. There was no visual line anyone could see with the naked eye; there was only a knowledge of where one county ended and the other began. Bootleggers kept their stills safely in Carroll County.

"Alvin, good to hear from you. How are things in Audubon County?"

"Will, we've got a situation." Alvin had never been a friendly man, and as much as Will tried to create a relationship based on their similar jobs, Alvin never reciprocated. He stuck to business and kept his opinions close to his vest. "I got information about some illegal stills in your county. A farmer by the name of John Krupp has been making illegal liquor on his farm."

So, the anonymous caller had gone elsewhere with his complaint when Will didn't give him the action he desired, Will thought. "Alvin, I've already dealt with this. I got a phone call and went out to investigate. I didn't find anything. The caller didn't have any specifics, so there wasn't much more I could do. I didn't have a search warrant. I talked to Krupp and didn't think anything was suspicious."

"Huh," was his only reply to the information. Will could tell by that response he wasn't happy with Will's work. If there weren't guns blazing and a farm being turned upside down and inside out, a proper job had not been done.

"I got another name for you, then. Roy Harmon. I arrested a man who claimed he bought the whiskey from Harmon. I think we should do this one together. My guy is in Audubon County, and the distiller is in your county."

Will knew Roy Harmon. He farmed between Templeton and Carroll. He was a young guy, only twenty-eight, with a young wife and family. He didn't own the land; his father did. Roy was only the tenant. Last summer, a freak windstorm ruined his crop. The hurricane winds flattened the corn stalks to the ground. The best he could do was gather the ruined stalks and feed them to his cattle.

With nothing to sustain them over the winter, Roy had to sell his cattle at the low point in the market. Will was not surprised Roy was using his farm to make booze. He had to do something to make ends meet.

"I appreciate the offer, Alvin. But since Harmon is in my county, I think I'll take care of this one myself. I thank you for the information and your time. You have a good day." Will knew he was cutting the sheriff off, an offense in polite society, but he needed to get out to the farm and warn Roy.

As Will drove to Harmon's place, his mind landed again on the Audubon County Sheriff. While he didn't agree with Alvin's staunch beliefs regarding Prohibition, he respected him as a lawman. Like Will, Alvin had a high opinion of the law and applied it fairly. Unlike Will, he was a Dry—and even if he wasn't—Alvin would enforce a law to the letter. If he ever caught his best friend breaking the law, Alvin would surely throw the friend in jail. There was no turning and looking the other way.

This had been chewing on Will for the last few months. Through the lawmen's grapevine, Will had heard the federal agent post was possibly being vacated. The current agent was Howard Vollmecke, who lived in Le Mars, a town north of Sioux City and over a hundred miles from Carroll County. Howard was more interested in wearing the uniform than traveling too far to pursue bootleggers. He and his men stayed mostly north and east, never working too hard in keeping illegal whiskey making under control.

If Howard did retire, Will was sure Alvin Truly would put himself up for the position. A Federal Prohibition Agent for the northern portion of Iowa could go into any county in his area and arrest any man for making, selling, or distributing booze. Will could no longer hold him out of Carroll County.

And Will's county would be Alvin's first mission. He would assign himself to the Templeton area and sniff out every still until Carroll County would become as dry as last summer's cornfields.

Will was worried for his people. There would be nothing he could do to stop them from being arrested. Husbands and fathers would spend time in prison while their wives and children would lose their land, their houses, their food. Sometimes, Will thought, the good guys were the actual bad guys.

CHAPTER 5

Alvin Truly spent two more years as sheriff before he was promoted to Federal Prohibition Agent for the Northern District. By 1925, whiskey making in his district had gone from bad to worse-than-worse. Agent Truly could waste no time in getting his district back to Dry.

As Audubon County Sheriff, Alvin had been limited to his own area, penned in by imaginary lines. Reporting crimes to other sheriffs, like Will Katz, felt like carrying water from a leaking bucket. Each time Alvin reported illegal whiskey making in Carroll County, Will Katz did nothing. Zero. Bootlegging continued to thrive under his lawmanship.

Alvin's last piece of information passed to Katz, about a bootlegging operation run by a guy named Roy Harmon, brought nothing. And the information he had given him was solid. Katz only needed to go out to the farm and make an arrest. It was as easy as netting fish in a water barrel. That was two years ago, and not only was Roy Harmon still distilling, but so were the other twelve or so Alvin had reported to Will. Alvin had begun to become suspicious Sheriff Katz was on the take.

Alvin might have remained satisfied as a county sheriff, but the lack of arrests and the number of crimes would have driven him to drink if he had been a drinking man. When the position of federal agent opened, he jumped at it. He would have authority over the sheriffs in a quarter of Iowa's counties. If he received a tip, he didn't need to wait for a sheriff to do something; he would go in on his own and make arrests. Alvin directed eight agents under him.

Alvin was a lawman at heart. The occupation coursed through his veins; his father and grandfather had both been lawmen. He often went in the truck with his father when he went out on a call. As a little boy, he had made rifles out of the tree branches from his yard and shot bad guys. For a few years, he had considered becoming a Methodist minister because he became close to his own clergyman, but the law had called even more loudly. Alvin couldn't resist that call.

Alvin's parents still lived in his boyhood home. They attended the Methodist church and participated in all its activities. Their only source of entertainment was through their church.

Alvin, still a bachelor at forty-two, had never found the right woman. He had lived with his parents until it was unseemly to do so. Renting a house only a block from them, Alvin still saw his parents every evening and ate supper with them, pouring out his frustrations with the lack of lawing from his neighboring county.

Donning his new federal uniform, the federal agent looked at himself in the mirror. Trading the grey for blue suited him better. His dark hair and beard had always faded into the grey. And at 6'4" and 200 pounds, Alvin stood out. His blue uniform made him seem more imposing, he thought.

Today was an exciting day for him. He had been holding on to some information about distilling in Carroll County. Knowing he was likely to get the federal job, Alvin had sat on the details and guarded them like a mother hen. For the first time, he had not passed along anything to Sheriff Katz. He had his eight federal boys joining him in a multi-farm bust. He was sure he would be hauling in the biggest distiller. Goosebumps rose on his arms and legs as he imagined arresting his first bootlegger as a federal agent.

Alvin proudly folded himself into his Ford Flathead V8, midnight black. Henry Ford had finally made a car fast enough to catch rumrunners and cheap enough to be afforded by the law. When he was sheriff, he had driven another Ford provided by the county, but it was on its last legs and couldn't catch an old lady riding a bicycle. The larger motor in his federal car, which was also used by the rumrunners, could at least keep up with them. And Alvin considered himself a crafty driver. He didn't need to be faster, just as fast.

Their first bust would be at the home of Jack Weber. He lived in Templeton and had a garage out back of his house, which is where he did his distilling. Alvin would meet one of his agents a few blocks away from Weber's home before making the raid. The remaining seven agents were spread out, catching their own lawbreakers. Alvin knew the element of surprise was essential. If they raided bootleggers in chronological order, by the time they pulled up to the last place, the man would be long gone and the evidence taken with him. No, multiple raids needed to happen at exactly the same time. There would then be no time for word to get passed along the telephone.

The mid-July day flamed, which wasn't unusual for Iowa. The temperature was usually accompanied by humidity, but the pair had been separated for some time. This summer, Iowa's heat preferred the company of drought. The corn's dark green leaves were curled up, protecting itself from the sun. Women's flowers wilted in the afternoons and folded over, lying limply along the ground. Farm animals found shelter under large trees; town dogs panted under porches.

Alvin parked his Ford a few blocks away from Weber's house.

He pulled a rifle out of his trunk, adjusted his hat, and started creeping through backyards toward the home. Hanging laundry afforded him concealment, and when one woman popped out from behind her wet sheets, Alvin put a finger to his lips and slowly removed his badge. He signaled for her to return to her home, knowing as soon as the door was closed, she would be on the party line telling her neighbors what she just saw.

Alvin came up behind Weber's garage and waited for his counterpart. The other agent soon arrived and sidled up alongside him. "On the count of three," Alvin whispered, "you go through the garage side door and tell him to put up his hands. He'll run, thinking it's only you, and I'll catch him when he comes out. Got it?"

The other agent nodded and walked quietly up to the door, gun firmly held in his hands, barrel pointed to the sky. Alvin had his gun aimed at the door, waiting for Weber. His left eye closed, his right eye sighted on the door. With his index finger ready to squeeze the trigger, he heard, "Hands up! Federal agents!"

Just as Alvin predicted, Weber went for an escape. The federal agent heard a crash, presuming Weber had knocked over his still, probably to keep his counterpart from being able to rush at him. Alvin's heart was pumping fast, and beads of sweat stood out on his forehead. Suddenly, he saw Weber exploding out the door, a shotgun in his hands. Alvin yelled, "Stop! Federal Agent!" Weber turned toward Alvin, and Alvin assumed he was going to raise his gun and shoot. Without thinking, Alvin squeezed the trigger, and a loud explosion erupted from the barrel. Weber blew back and landed on his backside, the gun still in his hands, his eyes wide open.

Alvin rushed to the criminal and kicked the gun from his hand, putting it out of reach. The body did not move. A red stain started to seep through Weber's shirt, right over his heart. Alvin, a crack shot, had hit the target exactly, killing Jack Weber.

Weber's wife, hearing the gunshot, rushed through the back door and saw her husband on the ground. A wild scream came from her as she rushed to his body. Alvin stood off to the side and gave her possession of her husband. As she hovered over the body, she looked up at Alvin and cried, "Why did you do this? Why?"

Uncomfortable with a shocked and distraught woman, Alvin did not answer her but went into the garage to take inventory of the setup. Just as he had been told, Alvin found fifty gallons of mash, ready to be distilled when nightfall came, but only a few gallons of whiskey. There had to be more, he thought. If it weren't in the garage, then it would be in the house. And money from his whiskey operation.

Turning to Weber's widow, he laid the search warrant on her husband's chest and said, "We have a warrant to search the entire property. We'll be searching your house next. Is there anyone in the house?"

"My children. Keep your guns out of my house!"

While Alvin went to search the residence, his counterpart radioed for backup. The Carroll County Sheriff would be their only help. He remained outside to flag down the sheriff's truck and keep an eye on the widow.

Alvin knocked on the back door before entering the home. Once inside, he saw four young children in the parlor. They looked shocked when he put his face into the room. "Children," he said, "It's O.K. I'm a policeman. I'm a good guy. You don't need to be afraid of me. I need you to go to a neighbor's house. Your mother will come and get you when she can. Do you understand?" The children said nothing, but the oldest got up, and the rest of them followed her.

With the house cleared, Alvin started his search. He was methodical about it, starting on the top floor in the bedrooms. No place was too sacred or too obvious. Bootleggers hid their booze and cash in any small space they could fit a bottle or a stack of bills. He went through dresser drawers, carefully replacing the items as they had been. He looked under beds and mattresses, including the children's room. Nothing. Alvin rifled through closets, removing small shoes in the event there was a hidden space under the floorboards. Nothing. He searched the kitchen cupboards, under the davenport. Nothing. Then he went out to the outhouse and looked down the hole. He was looking for a rope of some kind. Maybe Weber kept the bottles in the muck? Nothing there either.

Alvin went back to the garage and entered the dim building. By this time, Will Katz had joined Alvin's partner. Jack Weber's body had been covered, and the wife was sobbing on Will's shoulder. When she caught sight of Alvin, she removed her arm, which had been wrapped around Will, and pointed with her index finger at Alvin and screamed, "Him! He's the one who shot my husband!" Will escorted her to the front yard and recommended she go find her children. When he returned, his face was blood red. "What the hell were you thinking?" he demanded. "You killed a man for a few quarts of whiskey? And then you searched his house while his body was lying here getting cold?"

"Sheriff, just calm down. I had good intel this man was brewing hundreds of gallons of whiskey. I was told he was a dangerous man. He came at me with a gun!"

"Yes, he came at you with a gun, but did you bother to see that the safety was still on? He wasn't intending to shoot you!"

"I had every right to shoot him. He had a gun!" Alvin protested loudly.

"You killed a man with four children and then searched his house? Did you find anything?"

"Nothing. But I'm sure he's got more hidden somewhere. I had good intel on this!" Alvin Truly's tone and body language were defensive. He admitted to himself things had not gone as planned, but he felt completely within the boundaries of the law.

CHAPTER 6

Father Joe Klein sat in the dim light of his confessional chamber, the quiet of the church always so soothing to his soul. Saturday afternoons were his favorite time of day. He was thinking about Cora Weber and her children; she had just lost her husband, Jack. The priest was concerned she would not be able to take care of her family without her husband's income. Joe was trying to think of a favor he could collect to get Cora a job.

As he sat contemplating her predicament, he could hear Templeton's Sacred Heart parishioners entering the church with the loud bang of the door closing and then finding their way to a pew and kneeling, the pew wood squeaking in protest. His confessional box literally kept him in the dark, but the familiarity of the church sounds told him every move being made outside of the small compartment.

Father Joe waited for his next parishioner, his rosary beads soft against his fingers as he moved from one to the next in prayer. He thought about his community and his congregation.

The previous year, 1925, had assaulted their senses and tried their belief in God. Crops had withered and died in the fields with punishing heat and no rain. Jack Weber's death that summer laid heavy on him and the members of Sacred Heart. It was followed by the death of little Sam Fosselman, a six-month-old baby. The parents found their only son dead in his crib with no reason for his passing. Death came as an uninvited guest, skulking around their community and visiting without warning. When January of '26 marched through the door, all welcomed its presence, hoping for better weather and better times.

Sitting in the dimness of the confessional, the priest recognized Mrs. Bevar beginning her rosary, given away by the rattle of her beads against the pew back as she knelt up against it. She came weekly to give penance for her sins. As he listened, the confessional door on the other side of his screen opened, and a male entered and knelt, facing a seated Father Joe.

Joe blessed him and listened as he began, "Bless me, Father, for I have sinned. My last confession was three months ago. Since then, I have told lies. Father? You mind if I just get to the big one?"

Startled by the break in the ritual of the confession, Joe sat up and focused on his parishioner. "Please," he said. "Go on. You needn't be formal. God just wants to forgive you for your sins."

"Well, Father," said the anonymous voice, "I've been making moonshine. I've been lying to my wife where I go at night. She thinks I've taken another job, which is kind of true. It just isn't a normal job, if you know what I mean."

The voice stopped and waited for his scolding and penance.

This was certainly not the first time Joe had heard this confession, nor would it be the last. Many of his flock had taken the same path.

"My son," he began, "you'll need to say ten Hail Mary's for lying to your wife. There is no penance for making whiskey. As I've said in my sermons, even Jesus appreciated alcohol. He turned water into wine at the wedding. Our Trappist Brothers make beer. There is no sin in alcohol."

After two more hours of listening to the failings of his congregation, Father Joe exited the confessional stall. The church, completely
empty, echoed the sound of his shoes on the stone floor. He went back
to the sanctuary and removed his stole and white under-cassock. He
was looking forward to a good meal made by his housekeeper, Mrs.
Smith. He had seen her putting a roast in the oven when he left for
confession, and he knew she would have all the fixings with it. Mrs.
Smith always made a big Saturday night meal, giving Joe leftovers
for his Sunday dinner because she didn't work on Sundays.

His housekeeper had been with the rectory since well before Joe
had arrived. He wasn't sure how long she had been serving in her
position. She was a widow, and Joe had only briefly asked her about
her husband and how he died. He spent most of his time either in his
office or out in the town, ministering to the sick and dying. When he
arrived at the end of each day, she had supper on the table for him
and left as soon as she saw he had everything he needed.

Once he was finished with his meal, Joe put the dishes in the
sink for his housekeeper to clean the following morning. He sat down
in his favorite chair, wide and comfortable; lit his pipe, the sweet
cherry tobacco smoke swirling around his head; poured a tumbler
half full of whiskey; and thought about the funeral of Jack Weber.

Seven months had passed since Jack's funeral, and the priest
couldn't put it out of his mind. Jack's widow was now struggling to
raise their four children. After Jack's death, Cora's kitchen had been
filled with food, each family in the church community taking a turn
in bringing something. She had offers of "anything you need, just let
me know." All of that was sincere, but inevitably the food and help
dwindled as everyone went back to their lives and their own problems.

The funeral expenses had been anonymously paid. Joe had gone
out to his front stoop the morning after the shooting and found an
envelope. When he opened it, he saw five one-hundred-dollar, crisp,

green bills with the face of Benjamin Franklin peeking out from the pouch. A note was included: **For Jack's funeral. The rest, for Cora**. The altruist wasn't a church member. No one used one-hundred-dollar bills; in fact, it was very rare to see one.

Father Joe felt certain he knew the do-gooder. It had to be one of the bootleggers. The group of them took care of one another. Perhaps they had even pitched in together, one hundred each, to help their friend's widow.

The priest's troubled mind went beyond Jack's death. The tragedy laid solely on Alvin Truly's shoulders, a supposed good guy. The Law was there to protect and serve, not disrupt and kill. And Joe was told through the town's rumor mill Truly had searched the house after he had killed Jack. Truly wasn't Catholic, but he certainly called himself a church-going Christian. What kind of Christian committed these heinous acts? Joe was surprised Truly hadn't rifled through Jack's pockets while he lay in a pool of his own blood.

For the last six years, since the introduction of Prohibition, Father Joe had minded the business of the church. He comforted the dying, gave Christ's nourishment to his parishioners, and counseled through the confession box. He guided them through the real rights and wrongs of life, but now it didn't seem enough. He was a community leader, and he had sat by while one of his own was legally murdered.

Father Joe thought about the dictates from the Des Moines Diocese's Bishop. Priests were to stay out of political affairs and stick to their priestly duties, which revolved around the sacraments. Bishop Duly would disapprove of any activities outside of that.

To follow his conscience or to follow the bishop's orders: that was the question that had been plaguing him since the funeral.

Joe had always been fond of the Jesuit monks. Of the many orders of priests, the Jesuits were the most radical. The monks were forward-thinking and acted when they saw fit. The Jesuits were

considered almost militant by priestly standards. They practiced service, which was rooted in justice and love. It was the word *justice* that
often gave them notoriety. As a parish priest, Joe was focused on his
community of followers rather than the outside world. He had never
considered himself a radical.

The actions of Alvin Truly had sparked an inner flame of anger.
Father Joe took a deep breath as if he were about to jump from a cliff.
And he decided to jump.

Joe rose from his chair and went into the hallway, the black telephone sitting on a small table. He picked up the receiver and clicked
the switch hook twice to alert the operator. "Lucy," he said, "connect
me to the sheriff's office, please." He looked up at the clock: 6:00
p.m. He wasn't sure the sheriff would still be in his office.

"Hello. This is Sheriff Katz," the voice on the other end said.

"Sheriff, Father Klein here. Do you have time to stop by the rectory before you go home this evening?"

Will was surprised to receive a call from Father Klein. He knew
the priest well. Father Joe had been his parish priest when he was a
boy, and when Father was assigned to Sacred Heart, Will had
attended mass there instead of Holy Angels. He had nothing against
the Carroll church, but he just felt more at home in Sacred Heart.

After having received confirmation from the sheriff, the priest
took another tumbler from the china hutch. He rummaged around in
the kitchen pie safe for a sweet. Mrs. Smith generally kept some kind
of dessert on hand. Joe's sweet tooth often acted up around eight in
the evening. Two pieces of a cherry pie and a few chocolate chip
cookies. Joe wondered which one would taste better with whiskey?
He grabbed the plate of cookies and carried them into his study.

Will knocked on Father Joe's door at 7:25 p.m. He looked worn
through, his eyes drooping with exhaustion and his mouth a straight
line of tension. Joe invited Will inside and led him into the study.

Joe poured two fingers of whiskey into Will's glass and offered the cookies, which Will declined. Each man sat quietly, sipping the whiskey. Both appreciated its rye notes and velvety smoothness.

After ten minutes of sipping and discussing the weather, Will said, "Father, I know you didn't ask me here to discuss weather with you. What can I do for you?"

Father Joe cleared his throat, a sign of an uncomfortable conversation coming, and said, "Will, I've known you most of your life. I was there when the Bishop confirmed you. And I think you know what kind of man I am."

"Sure, Joe. You're one of the good ones."

"And I feel the same way about you," Father Klein responded. It was time to take the step off the cliff. What he said next would either work or ruin his reputation with someone he admired. "I've been just sick about Jack Weber's death. Alvin Truly is dangerous, and he's out to take down our community. I think it's time to do something about this before more people die."

Will did not respond. He sat there, looking into his whiskey glass, thinking about the priest's words. After an uncomfortable silence, he finally responded, "I agree, Father. Did you have something in mind?"

Joe realized he had been holding his breath, waiting for his future. He released his air slowly. "I don't have anything specific, but I was hoping we could come up with something together."

The two men conferred past midnight, creating and throwing out plans. Their main goal was to shut down Truly without getting either of them on his radar.

Several problems existed: one, the bootleggers needed warning before Truly conducted a raid; two, they needed a place to age their whiskey off their own property so that if they were caught, the amount of whiskey would be a few quarts, which would get them a fine rather than jail time.

"If Jack Weber had known Truly was coming, he could have cleared out his garage, making Truly look like a rube," Joe said.

Will knew Truly didn't trust him and hadn't been including him in any of his raids. If he had known about Jack Weber, he could have warned him ahead of time. Will didn't know the answer to this problem, but he would think on it and let the priest know of his plan.

Both men agreed Truly would not lessen his desire to bust every still in Carroll County. If anything, he would become like a hungry wolf, looking for even the smallest rabbit to eat. They just needed to protect even the smallest of rabbits.

Father Joe had the idea of how to fix the second problem. The bootleggers could use the church basement to age their barrels.

"What about the angel's share?" Will asked with concern in his voice.

"Ah, the angel's share," Joe said knowingly. "Yes, that would be a concern." As whiskey aged, a small portion of each barrel evaporated into the air, known as the angel's share. The scent of whiskey would not stay within the confines of the basement. It would wander upstairs and perfume the nave. Unless congregants had lost their sense of smell, anyone entering the church would immediately know the scent.

"I would have to burn incense all day every day to cover that scent. And all Catholics know incense is burned only for specific events. But as a parishioner yourself, Will, do you know anyone who agrees with Prohibition?"

It was true. The parish, made up of Germans, appreciated their beer. As Catholics, they had heard the many sermons about the Church's history of alcohol, not to mention the Bible stories involving celebrations with alcohol.

"I can't think of one," Will admitted. "Some of them are involved in the business, and the rest of them either supply or purchase from those involved."

"I think a sermon on brotherly love and helping your neighbors would be appropriate in the next couple of Sundays," the priest said. Those two topics were his favorites, and he already had some strong phrases in mind.

The men shook hands in partnership, promising to find new ways to out-think their opponent, and parted.

Lying in bed, Joe's mind raced with ideas. His priest friends enjoyed their alcohol, and he could volunteer to host the annual Des Moines Diocese conference at his parish. A small bottle of whiskey as a gift would be in perfect order, and the reputation of a quality product would be spread farther.

Tomorrow, he would make a list of all those he suspected of distilling and invite them to age their liquor on church property. Alvin Truly could look high and low for the hundreds of gallons, but he would never think to look in a church. Father Joe smiled in the dark. His conscience felt clean.

Templeton Distillery Was Raided Recently

Templeton rye, quoted in New York dispatches as the $10 a gallon "Iowa special," came into public light several months ago with the raid by state prohibition agents on a large distillery at Templeton, Ia., a small town in Carroll county.

State agents confiscated a large quantity of whisky, along with manufacturing equipment, and made arrests.

It has been on the market extensively throughout Iowa for the last few years, and has been mentioned as one of the liquor products sold in Chicago.

James Risden, head of the state bureau of investigation, stated Wednesday that he had had no report or complaint on the Templeton case from county officials since the raid.

CHAPTER 7

Sheriff Katz planned to put an abundant number of miles on his old truck after he met with Father Joe. He had a list of known and suspected men who were distilling whiskey, and he had plotted out his route, trying to hit three farms a day. At each farm, he would know for sure who was distilling and who wasn't. In the event he did receive some information, he could warn them of Alvin Truly's actions.

Each stop meant at least a half-hour conversation at the side of his truck. Each stop he was offered a drink or two, which he declined. He never drank on duty.

By the end of the first week, he headed to John Krupp's. Given John had already been outed by the anonymous caller—whether it was John's stepbrother or not—John was in the crosshairs. No telling when Alvin Truly would come crashing in, guns blazing. Will kept the picture of Jack Weber in his mind, so any time he thought about stringing out his visits and heading home early, he was pushed forward instead.

When the sheriff pulled into John's lane, he felt something was wrong. There were no dogs running beside his truck or ducks scattering in front of him. The place looked deserted. He parked his vehicle in front of the house and knocked on the door. John's wife Betsy answered, her face a sign something was amiss. "Betsy, what's going on? Where's John?"

With fresh tears, Betsy said, "They got him, Sheriff. That federal agent came here last night, sneakin' in. He shot our dog, Will! That's why John didn't hear him. He was arrested with fifty gallons of whiskey and a hundred gallons of mash." Betsy's face was aquiver, and her eyes were puffy and red from a worried night of weeping. "I don't know what I'm going to do!"

Will reached out and laid a steady hand on Betsy's shoulder. "Do you know where they took him?"

"Fort Dodge!" she cried.

Fort Dodge, seventy-seven miles northeast of Templeton, housed the U.S. Federal Court, which had been set up in 1924 after federal agents couldn't get any of the bootleggers convicted in their own counties, the men's neighbors unwilling to send them to jail based on an unwanted law. Fort Dodge had federal judges, sworn to uphold federal laws. Better still, those robed in black did not know the defendants.

Betsy told Will she intended to go to Fort Dodge and needed a way to get there. The sheriff knew she would also need money for whatever would come. Perhaps it would be a fine. Perhaps John would spend time in prison, and she would need to pay bills. Will needed help, and he needed it fast. "Betsy, where are the children?"

"With my mother. I just couldn't let them see me crying. I've been in such a panic since John was dragged off. If my head weren't attached to my shoulders, I wouldn't know where to find it."

"Tell your mother you are going to Fort Dodge. She'll need to mind the children for a few days. Someone will drive you."

Without waiting for her reply, Will got into his truck and headed back to Templeton. He knew with certainty where he was going.

There was only one person who could raise money and find a vehicle this fast.

Will found Father Joe in his office, working on Sunday's sermon, one of brotherly love. "Father, we have a bit of an emergency. John Krupp's been arrested and hauled to Fort Dodge. Betsy needs to get there, and we need money. Can you help?"

Without answering, Joe stood up and went into the hall. Will could hear him on the telephone. "Get me Daryl Jantz," he said to the operator. Daryl Jantz, a local farmer, was always in church, front pew, with his wife and children. He gave generously to the collection basket and could be counted on whenever the parish needed a project completed, whether that was his time or his money.

"Daryl, Father Joe here. What are you doing today? I need a favor."

Within a few hours, the priest had rounded up transportation and a few hundred dollars, hoping it would cover whatever they needed. And he was promised more if the need arose. He would also be driving Betsy to Fort Dodge, leaving the Sunday mass to one of the priests in Carroll. Brotherly love would have to wait for another time. In fact, this would be a good addition to the sermon.

John's hearing didn't happen for another ten days. Once in Fort Dodge, after they had checked on his well-being, Father Joe and Betsy were graciously ensconced in Holy Trinity's rectory, guests of a pair of Irish priests. For propriety, their housekeeper stayed nights. If it hadn't been for such a serious matter, the group of them would remember the stay as a 'fine time.'

Delicious meals were followed with Templeton whiskey, brought by Father Joe. While the priests were enjoying the libations, the housekeeper and Betsy knitted in another part of the house and listened to the radio.

Spring weather is always fickle in Iowa; the day could start cloudless but end with a tornado. One day eighty degrees and the next day light snow. The day of John's trial, the sky was overcast with ominous clouds. Did the clouds signal a bad outcome? Betsy wondered.

When the pair entered the windowless courtroom, the clomp of their feet on the oak floor echoed in the room. The large space, filled with benches, smelled of old books, floor wax, and the law. Father Joe guided Betsy to the bench behind the defense's table. There were no other people in the courtroom except a young man, sitting halfway back on the prosecution side. He was wearing a fedora, a white shirt with collar and cuffs, a pair of suspenders, and a bow tie. Betsy noticed he started to write something on a pad of paper as soon as they sat down. Father Joe leaned toward her and whispered, "The press. Probably from Des Moines." Betsy hated the idea of her husband's name in the paper for illegal doings, but she needed to confess something to the priest before the trial began.

Leaning over, Betsy put her mouth to Joe's ear and whispered, "The still was mine, Father. John wouldn't hear of my going to jail, so he covered for me."

Joe didn't move, didn't turn to look at her. He was taken aback by her confession, but he had heard many tales worse than hers. He gave a light nod to indicate he had heard her.

After forty minutes of sitting, they finally saw what they had come for. John was led into the courtroom by a man in a uniform. He was seated at the table in front of Betsy and Father Joe. John was in overalls, the pair he was wearing when they arrested him. Another man sat down beside him.

Someone had gotten John an attorney, but Betsy didn't know who. The attorney, a nondescript man with brown hair and eyes and a well-worn suit, came from Webster City. He looked more like the man who sorted mail in the post office than a lion ready to attack. Both Father Joe and Betsy had little hope for John.

Several other men entered the room, sitting on the opposite side, one of them at the prosecution's table and the rest of them behind him.

The prosecuting attorney, a young man in his early thirties, had eager eyes, a fresh haircut, and a brand-new suit. He was sitting at his table, a pile of papers in front of him, and trying to look very officious. Occasionally, he looked across the aisle at his competitor and smiled.

Behind him sat Alvin Truly and other men who were presumably other federal agents. Alvin looked smug in his pressed uniform and black boots. He was leaning against the back of the bench, his arms crossed over his chest. He occasionally looked at John's side of the room. Sometimes, he leaned forward and whispered something to the prosecuting attorney.

When the black-robed magistrate entered, everyone in the courtroom stood out of respect. The judge was quite elderly, almost too old to be sitting behind the large bench. His face looked pinched, his eyes watery behind silver-rimmed glasses. After doddering to the bench, he sat down and started looking through papers, not even taking note of the people sitting in front of him.

Finally, he looked up. "I see we have a case of illegal distilling. Are both sides ready?" Both lawyers stood up and responded to the judge. Satisfied everything was ready to go, the judge filled his pipe, lit it, and sat comfortably back against his leather chair.

Betsy leaned over to Joe and asked, "Where is the jury? I thought they always had a jury during a trial."

"They both agreed on a bench trial. That means the judge gets to decide," Joe explained to Betsy.

The prosecution went first, starting with the other federal agents. Each one testified to dismantling the still and loading up the whiskey.

When asked who was distilling, each one of them pointed to John. For shock value, the lawyer brought out the jug of whiskey and poured it into a glass, sniffed it, and sent it up to the judge. "It's whiskey, Judge." The judge sniffed it as well and nodded his head. "I'd suggest you take a drink, Your Honor, but that would be illegal—as you well know." He chuckled at his own cleverness.

"I think we can establish the validity of the contents without tasting it," the judge said, apparently not appreciating the joke.

The prosecution put his star witness last, calling Alvin Truly to the stand. Although the preceding witnesses had established the liquor and still, Alvin was asked the same questions. He answered them with seriousness in his voice, sounding like he was taking a murderer out of society. When asked to point out the bootlegger, Alvin stood up and stretched out his arm toward John with his index finger extending like it was going to touch the guilty man. "That man!" Alvin shouted. "He's the guilty one. He's the whiskey maker. He's the breaker of federal laws. He's a menace to our Christian society!" Alvin sat down and crossed his arms, punctuating his testimony.

"All right," the judge said in a tired voice. "I think we've established the evidence. Is the prosecuting attorney planning to bring up any other witnesses?"

"No, Your Honor. The prosecution rests." The attorney shot a triumphant look to his enemy and sat down again behind his table. The evidence was hard to argue, especially when the prosecuting attorney brought out a jug of whiskey.

The defense attorney did his best, trying to convince the judge the liquor was for private consumption only, still illegal, but less so. With the testimony of various law enforcement officers, clearly John was guilty, and no one could be drinking that much whiskey by himself. Desperate, the attorney asked if he could bring up a character witness. The prosecutor objected based on having no knowledge of this witness, but the judge said he would give him twenty minutes to prepare before he would cross examine. The lawyer agreed but did so begrudgingly.

"I call to the stand… Joe Klein." Father Joe was startled but collected himself quickly and walked up to the witness box. Once sworn in, the attorney started his questioning. First, he established Joe's occupation, residence, and relationship to John. "Father Klein, tell me what kind of man John Krupp is."

"He's a good man," Joe said with certainty. "He's a family man, a man with children. A man who farms and tries to provide for his loved ones. A man who regularly attends church." The term *regularly* meant *weekly* to most everyone. But Joe reasoned *regularly* meant a pattern in a time frame. John and his family went every few months and always at Christmas and Easter.

"Is he a bootlegger, Father?" Joe could not lie, especially after he had placed his hand on the Bible. "I can't say for certain," Joe responded. "I've never seen him distill or sell alcohol. I've never had anyone tell me he had sold them alcohol." Father Joe was telling the truth but skirting around it. John had sat in his confession box every month, often confessing things that pertained to his illegal activities. However, Joe had never seen anything, and no one ever mentioned John's name to him as a bootlegger. The confessions within his confessional were privileged, just as any doctor's would be about his patient's health.

After a short recess, the prosecutor got his turn. "Father," he asked, "are you sure you're telling us the truth about this man? Surely as a leader in your church, you know what goes on with your parishioners."

"Are you calling me a liar?" Joe asked. Amused at Joe's response, the judge leaned forward and looked from one man to the other.

"No sir. I'm not saying you are lying; I'm just asking if you're telling me the whole truth." The lawyer knew he was in dangerous territory and was trying to weasel his way out.

"Let me tell you something, my son." Father Joe loved calling men *son*, suggesting they were somehow less wise than he. It always put them in a more humble position. And he was right. The attorney's voice changed, and he looked at his shoes instead of looking at the judge or Joe. "I know plenty of good men who are losing their farms, who are struggling to make it day-to-day, who are making decisions about breaking a law or watching their children and wives starve. If you were they, what would you do to save the ones you love? I'm not sure how I feel about Prohibition, but I don't know anyone who has died from a glass of whiskey. I do know someone who has died by the hands of the law." With that last statement, he looked directly at Alvin Truly, who shifted in his seat and looked down.

"Do you drink whiskey, Father?" The question brought John's attorney to his feet.

"I object, Your Honor. This priest is not on trial." The judge sustained. With that last question, Joe was released back to his seat.

Wanting to wrap the trial up in one day, the judge ordered each lawyer to quickly present his closing arguments.

The prosecution went first, expounding on Christian values and the evils of drink. He went into the foreseeable future where all men lived clean and sober lives, attended church, and worked hard for their families. He then switched direction, and foretold a different future, one with drunkenness and debauchery: men drinking up their earnings, men beating their wives and children, men not knowing even the simplest Bible stories. "If men like John Krupp continue to make their evil brew," he said, "the second world will become our reality. John Krupp needs the most severe punishment available. Two years in prison. Take this menace off our streets, Judge."

Once the lawyer turned around to return to his chair, Father Joe thought he detected a slight eye roll from the judge. He hoped he had.

John's attorney would finish the trial with his rebuttal. Instead of declaring John's innocence, he started by reminding the judge of John's good character and his desire to feed his children. Once he had established a reasonable motive for an illegal act, he broadened his argument into the law itself. He talked about freedom of choice, the freedom to put into one's own body what one wished. "The government's protection is overreach," he insisted. "Our Founding Fathers fought for the right to live their lives the way they saw fit. Many of them, including Thomas Jefferson and Ben Franklin, enjoyed alcoholic beverages. Our own Declaration of Independence affords us the 'pursuit of happiness.' Alcohol makes people happy, Judge. Our government is going against our founding beliefs." He finished his speech by quoting Henry David Thoreau: "[I]f the government required people to participate in injustice by obeying 'unjust laws,' then people should 'break the laws.'" He did not finish the remainder of that quote, which stated "even if they ended up in prison."

"As you know," he said, "Thoreau is still admired today. His words inspire us toward that civil disobedience of which he spoke. I think I will end with one of my favorite lines: 'Let every man make known what kind of government would command his respect, and that will be one step toward obtaining it.' Your Honor, I think our society has already made known its disapproval of our government and its Prohibition law by refusing to obey it. Thoreau would tell us our duty is to civilly disobey that law and let our government rule by our desires. Thank you." He then sat down and put his hand on John's shoulder, showing his alignment with his client in disobeying the law.

Father Joe approved. He thought it was fruitless to stand up in front of this intelligent man and try to convince him of John's innocence. Instead, he had appealed to his heart. He was hoping the judge would think about his own family and what he was willing to do to take care of them. As a learned man, the judge would appreciate the Thoreau quotes and possibly feel inspired by them. If by rotten luck the judge was a teetotaler himself, then they were sunk. Even with such an inspiring speech.

The judge said nothing after John's attorney sat down. He looked at the papers on his desk. He cleared his throat a few times. He knocked the ashes from his pipe, having smoked throughout the entire case. "I have my decision," he announced. The attorneys and John rose from their chairs. "Mr. Krupp, you are certainly guilty. There is no doubt in my mind that you have been breaking the Volstead Act. For that, you will be punished." John's face fell, and Betsy's eyes began to leak tears again. Alvin Truly grinned broadly and reached out to shake the prosecutor's hand. The judge continued, "I am fining you one hundred dollars. You will remain in jail until your fine is paid. The court is now adjourned." He rapped his gavel once and returned to his chamber.

The reactions of everyone in the room were audible. Alvin released a gust of air from deep within his stomach as if someone had punched him in the gut. John released air as well, but his came from his chest as if an elephant had finally removed itself from atop him. Handshakes and hugs were given on the defense side, and shaking heads were seen on the prosecution side.

Alvin Truly said to no one, "We were robbed. We just got robbed of justice!"

As the judge walked back to his chambers, he could hear the protests of the federal agent. Disrobed and sitting in his tall-backed leather chair behind his desk, Tom Youngers sighed. He hated these cases. They wasted the court's time. Real crimes were being committed: murder, robbery, embezzlement. And now he was forced to sit and judge men who had made some liquid. Nobody was getting hurt. In some ways, it was keeping some of Iowa's economy going.

Tom reached into his bottom desk drawer, pulled out a bottle, and poured himself some whiskey. It came from Templeton.

PROHIBITION AS AN ISSUE

MR. BRYAN URGES DRYS TO BE ON THE ALERT.

RETURN TO SALOON RUINOUS

Triumph of Prohibition Neither Sudden Nor Incomplete—With Other Questions Pending, Prohibition Should Not Be Paramount Issue.

By William Jennings Bryan.

The activity of the opponents of prohibition comes in the nature of a surprise, but of their activity there is no longer room for doubt. It is a surprise because the triumph of prohibition was neither sudden nor incomplete.

Instead of being sudden it was the result of a prolonged conflict during which those engaged in the liquor business and their patrons had ample information as to what was going on.

The Women's Christian Temperance union, organized nearly fifty years ago, began in a crusade against Ohio's saloons; the women visited the drinking places, pleaded with those in charge and prayed for the abolition of the traffic. From the first, the noble women who marshaled under the banner of the W.C. T. U. proclaimed undying hostility to the saloon, and they have never for one moment lowered their flag or slackened their efforts.

Twenty-six years ago the Anti-Saloon league was organized. It also had its birthplace in Ohio. Its name indicates its relentless opposition to the liquor traffic.

CHAPTER 8

I looked at my family and knew I had to make a bold move. My children were starting to have "the look," the one that announces they aren't getting enough to eat. So far, my method of making money wasn't spreading the butter, so to speak. After holding out while others made money as fast as the federal government could print it, I steeled myself and decided to start up my own liquor operation. However, I knew nothing about making whiskey. Instead, I had been born with business savvy.

Jack Weber, God rest his soul, was my closest friend, and I was his only confidant. When Alvin Truly gunned him down two years ago, he had distilled his last batch, earning him enough money to sustain his family until he could follow through on a bigger idea. Jack had started putting in place the pieces for a large operation. Instead of a side-road business, selling pints and quarts to individuals, he had envisioned a syndicate whereby multiple cookers would cook for him, and he would sell to a distributor.

Jack had gotten as far as making a contact with a large broker in Des Moines, a guy by the name of Harold Thompson; but, behind his back, everyone called him "Sniffy" because he was partial to the white powder. Sniffy wanted better quality whiskey because his clients were Al Capone's syndicate in Chicago and Tom Pendergast's gang in Kansas City.

Al Capone, originally from Brooklyn, came to Chicago in 1917, working for Johnny Torrio's operation of gambling and prostitution. With the passage of Prohibition, Torrio took on bootlegging, eventually making Capone a partner after he had shown his worth. Torrio left the life in '25, moving back to Italy, leaving his partner in full control of the business. Torrio and Capone's outfit started moving into Iowa even before Iowa's prohibition began.

It was no surprise to me or any other Iowan that the business started in Sioux City, a town known for its history of lawlessness. Due to its location on the Missouri River, between 1880 and 1890, its population exploded, bringing with it a nest of crime. Nearly forty years before federal prohibition, Clark's Law—championed by Talton E. Clark, closed down all Iowa saloons with the exception of Sioux City. Saloon owners paid a 'contribution to the municipal treasury' for the town's law to look the other way. The Colosimo Mob, Capone's outfit, started its Iowa business in Sioux City, expanding across the state as prohibition took hold.

Capone bought liquor from Sniffy, who had the Iowa contacts Capone didn't. Jack was counting on Sniffy needing more liquor than ever before to grow his enterprise.

I was a little more comfortable with the Kansas City boss, Tom Pendergast, who was different from Capone in that he had the appearance of an upstanding citizen. Pendergast served one year as an alderman on city council and then chaired the Jackson County Democratic Club, helping politicians get elected—sometimes by way of voter fraud. Unfortunately, he had gambling debts, specifically from horse racing, and needed his illegal activities to fuel his gambling addiction.

Neither of these bosses made me comfortable, and I was sure they were into more than illegal liquor selling, but who am I to judge a man's business at this point in my life—especially since I was going to stand on the other side of the line myself?

Once Jack had established a whiskey schedule with Sniffy, his next move would have been hiring cookers. He thought fifteen operations, making 3,700 gallons a day, or 27,000 gallons a week, would fill Sniffy's needs. He hadn't worked out how to get the liquor to Des Moines or how to satisfy Sniffy until the whiskey had aged for six months—or longer if they wanted better quality.

I would have to start again, and it would begin by using the only piece of information Jack Weber had left behind—Sniffy Thompson's contact information.

I drove my truck east of town, nearly to the county border, just a few miles shy of the Crawford County line. Earl Miller, generally referred to as "Skeet," lived out in those hills. I was probably the only one in western Iowa who called him by his given name. I had known his mother—a fine woman—and knew she hated that nickname, which everyone assumed he had given himself. So, to honor his mama's memory, I liked to remind him of the fine name his parents had bestowed on him at birth.

Earl and his family had been making moonshine in those hills for generations. The man wasn't much good at anything legal, but he could make the best whiskey in the state of Iowa. And he loved to defy the law. He wasn't shy about telling anyone who brought it up he could outfox, outrun, outshoot any lawman ever born. "Just let 'em find out" was his favorite saying.

I needed Earl to help with the product. He was an expert when it came to this end of the business, and I had no intention of putting my name out there. I didn't want Agent Alvin Truly coming after me like he had done with Jack.

I pulled into what appeared to be Earl's driveway; however, it was so full of weeds the term driveway was a politeness. The entire place looked abandoned. The house, which his great grandpa had built, seemed to be leaning a little to the left. Without much paint remaining, the house would surely fall with nothing to keep it together. I didn't even want to think about what the inside of the house looked like. Earl didn't have a wife—or a woman who would stay very long with him—so I figured the inside was probably just like the outside. I killed the engine and beeped the horn. No telling if any mean dogs might jump out of the weeds and attack me.

Earl seemed to come out of nowhere and walked up to my window. He was a man in his mid-sixties, tall and powerfully built—like a football player—and going bald. You never saw Earl without a cap on his head. "Well, this is certainly a surprise," he said. "I didn't think you even knew where I lived. To what do I owe the pleasure?"

"I'd like to talk some business with you. Mind if you just hop in the truck?"

He seemed flabbergasted but did as I asked and sat quietly once inside, waiting for me to begin. His reticence stunned me because Earl Miller loved to talk. My presence must have shocked him into muteness. "There's rumor that someone is making a whole lot of moonshine. Either a big operation or several smaller operations. Is that true and is that you?"

Earl took a deep breath and let it out slowly. He looked out the side window of the truck, took another deep breath, and gave another slow release. Finally he said, "No, it's not me. And I don't think anyone has more than one or two stills. That's just a bunch of baloney we all cooked up to get the Feds looking for someone big. Why?"

I didn't feel the need to answer his question right then. He'd figure out his own answer within time. "I'd like you to go into business with me," I stated in my most officious manner.

"You runnin' a still?" he asked, the shock showing on his face.

"I am," I lied, "but I'd like to grow the business and help others in the same position. Instead of each man running his own operation, I'd like to take it over and offer him a good deal. I provide the supplies and men to make the whiskey. He provides the place to distill it. In return, I'll give him three dollars a barrel. And he gets my protection."

"That's a fair deal." His tone indicated his blessing even though I didn't need it. "Don't get no better than that, I s'pose."

"I'm going to hire the men to do the cooking, and I will ask each farmer to stay out of the way and keep his mouth shut. If he wants to do his own distilling, then he gets four dollars instead of three."

"Sounds pretty good to me. You're takin' all the risk, though. If you get caught…"

"I won't. Whoever goes with me must swear never to confess anything other than the operation, the whiskey—whatever he gets caught with—is his. If he's arrested, I'll supply a good lawyer and pay whatever fine is given to him. If he does jail time, I'll provide for his family and compensate him when he gets out."

"And what's my part in this?" Earl wanted to know. He was like a bulldog about to be fed.

"You are the front man. You sign up the landowners, you talk to the merchants for supplies, you hire anyone needed to make the product. They and anyone else who knows about the business will believe you are the kingpin, the boss. They won't know a thing about me. You will never reveal my identity. Not now, not a hundred years from now. Understand?"

"The kingpin. I like that. And what do I get for doing this? What's my cut?" I realized he had not answered my question. But that was fine. He was focused on being the big man, and he wouldn't reveal my identity because then he wasn't really the boss.

"You get ten percent of my earnings. It doesn't sound like a lot,

but the more men we get to go into business with us, the more you earn. Call it an incentive."

"Where you sellin' all that whiskey? Nobody round here can drink that much. And we're gonna need a whole bunch of men on the ground to sell it a gallon at a time. I don't see how you can keep that many men in employment, making that much whiskey, without having a different way to sell it."

Earl was quick to poke holes into my business plan, but I didn't intend to divulge my connection to Des Moines.

"I like the plan, but I think you got some problems," he continued. "And I'm not good at keepin' things straight. Heck, I can't even keep the books on my own business. I couldn't tell you how much money I've earned. I just spend the money in my pockets if I have it. And if I do this thing, I'll take twenty percent."

"Fifteen, and it's a deal. I'll do all the bookwork. I'm good at keeping accounts. Let me worry about getting it sold. Like I said, you're the front man with the mouth. I'll tell you who to talk to, what to say. And you get all the glory." I threw him a grin, and he reciprocated. At that point, I knew I had him.

I left Earl with instructions to start talking to the men he knew who were already in the business. I warned him to keep it as low to the ground without actually eating the dirt. Earl was never one to make statements quietly. His best quality, which was also his weak point, was his ability to draw attention to himself and then proceed to entertain.

Before liquor was illegal, Earl lived at his favorite hangout, the Templeton saloon. He stood at the bar like a king keeping court. Other men would gather around him and listen to his tales, his booming voice and animation keeping them enthralled. Once, Earl became so inebriated he got up on the bar to tell a particular story about a man who stole a hog and left behind his tracks only to be found by the hog's owner. When Earl got to the best part, he lifted his fist in the air to emphasize the owner's punching the thief but lost his balance and fell from the bar, headfirst. He cracked two ribs and broke his arm.

I reminded him he was just as vulnerable to arrest as the rest of the enterprise, and the fact he wasn't actually the kingpin didn't matter to the law. Earl was not the type of man who did well in prison. We shook on the deal, the only means necessary to make it binding.

Back home, after my family had gone to bed, I made a list of everyone I knew who distilled and those I suspected. I also added names of farmers who were in financial trouble. I hated to prey on their need, but sometimes…. Then, I made a list of merchants who would be amenable to making money from illegal activities: the grocers, the hardware store owner, maybe even the undertaker. All the businesses in town were in danger of closing. When there was no money to be spent, everyone suffered. Last, I made a list of every man I thought would want to make some cash by distilling. By the time I finished, my list was long—nearly every man I knew in Carroll County.

My next task was money. Supplies for twenty or so operations would be expensive. Some stills were already made and in place or needed to be moved to the farm. Easy. But the cost of sugar, yeast, and rye—along with a whole lot of barrels—would take everything I had. And I doubted I had enough to get everyone up and running at once. Even if I did, the liquor had to be aged. We had to store it and continue putting money into the making before we could sell anything and get funds coming back in.

Storage—that was my biggest concern. We needed a very large open space. Ideally, it should be inside. A barn would be perfect, but the farmer who owned the barn would get the largest penalty if he was raided because he would have the most volume of illegal whiskey. No man was stupid enough to take the risk. And I wouldn't want him *to. There had to be a place where the Feds would never suspect. An idea fluttered around the corners of my brain and finally landed. It was so far out of the realm of ridiculous it would probably work.*

My planning had taken me far into the night, but before I could go to bed, I needed to ascertain my cash amount. Standing in my living room, crowbar in hand, I rolled up the braided rug and found the spot where the boards had been removed and then reinstalled. They were nailed tight and made a cracking sound as I eased the flat end of the bar under one of them. Suddenly, the board popped up, giving me easier access to the second one, which came away with a little more creaking and cracking. Looking down into the guts of my house, I felt relieved to see the paper bags lying end to end, side by side—snuggled like sleeping babies under the protection of my floor.

I sat at the kitchen table in the dark of night and poured the contents from the bags. The bills were worn but neatly lined up against one another. An old string bound each bundle. I untied the strings and started peeling off bills and laying them on the table. One hundred dollars. I thought about the hands who had held those dollars and had then passed them over for liquor. Were the dollars meant to feed children but fed a Need instead? Our politicians had convinced themselves this was so. There were ten bundles of a hundred dollars each, which was less than I expected, but enough. Enough to now become the Kingpin Bootlegger of Iowa. This was not a title I would have ever dreamed—or even wanted—but it was to be my new life.

CARROLL COUNTY SUFFERED MOST

Crop Losses Up to 25 Per Cent in Some Places.

Two persons were killed, and damage estimated at more than a quarter million dollars was caused by thirty-six floods and wind and hail storms which struck Iowa in July. Charles D. Reed, federal weather observer, said in his monthly storm damage report Thursday.

One person was killed in an electric storm near Manchester, Delaware county, July 6, while the other met death in Des Moines July 9, the report said.

The most devastating storm of the month, with floods and wind combining to cause equal damage, occurred near Glidden, in Carroll county, July 3. Damage due to wind in this storm was estimated at $50,000, while similar damage was charged to floods. Winds and high water combined again July 8, near Rockingham, Scott county, to cause damage estimated at $4,000, while estimated damage of $30,000 was caused by a similar combination in Prairie township in Fremont county July 14.

CHAPTER 9

Two years before Earl "Skeet" Miller was made kingpin of a bootlegging operation, another man, Alphonse "Scarface" Capone, was also made kingpin. One man in Iowa, and the other in Illinois. One German; the other, Italian. Both were from modest backgrounds. Both would make a pile of money.

Skeet, like his counterpart, was not generally a man who liked to have another man's thumb on top of him. His adult life had been his own: he decided when he worked, for how long, and what tasks he accomplished. However, two events had shaken him enough to consider a new life view: the death of Jack Weber and the arrest of John Krupp. These were serious happenings with serious consequences. The federal law was now training its eye on Carroll County and was determined to bring it down. A raid only a few months past had convinced Skeet that business as usual was no longer effective. Each man making his product and minding his own business left them all vulnerable.

The raid had happened in the dead of night, the clouds covering the moon. Regulators converged on a farm with headlights from their many cars shining in different locations. Men poured from vehicles, rifles and pistols pointed in the air. The leader pounded on the farmer's door, dragging him and his family from their beds. The small household could only watch as they tore apart the outbuildings, pulling boards from walls, digging trenches in the floors of the barn and hog shed. Even though the farmer insisted he was not distilling, the Feds continued to rip through his property with little care for the destruction they caused. When they found no trace of illegal activities, they left without so much as a simple "sorry," the wreckage left behind for the farmer to repair.

The farm they should have raided was only a mile away, owned by the Schmidt family. Both husband and wife distilled and sold their product one jar at a time, bringing in only enough money to make their farm payments. The near-hit of the Feds frightened them so much they dug a large hole and buried their still behind their barn, closing shop for good.

Skeet believed distillers banding together would be safer for everyone. As the boss, he would buy and deliver the supplies for all the cookers, thereby eliminating multiple men going into businesses and buying whiskey materials. If the Feds were watching, instead of gathering multiple names, they would have only one. The farmers who were only providing the cook sites would be partnered with the setters; they would not start up their own stills (they often had no idea what they were doing), putting themselves in a dangerous position. Giving all men involved in the business a lawyer in the event they were caught ensured they had the best representation. Skeet could see no drawback in his new boss's plan.

His first task involved finding setters and locations. Skeet knew everyone in the business. He spent a few weeks traveling throughout the county, selling the benefits of joining the organization. Some of the farmers who were distilling for themselves joined the business, but many of them wanted to remain independent and felt confident because of past successes. Men who didn't have a farm and were cooking in their own homes or out in the woods wanted a more secure location and joined immediately.

Finding more setters was the easier task. Jobless men abounded. With a depressed agricultural economy, plenty of former farm workers were without employment. They didn't want the responsibility or risk of their own operation, so they gladly joined Skeet's.

By the first month, Skeet had five farms. He set up two or three stills on each location and had enough men to make the whiskey. His next task was supplies: yeast, sugar, barrels, and copper.

At two in the afternoon, a beautiful Saturday in downtown Templeton, Skeet walked into Wagner's Bakery. The scent of baked goods hit his nose with his first step inside the door. The glass cases were mostly empty, a few pies and loaves of bread their only occupants. Rich Wagner, the proprietor, came from the back and placed himself behind one of the cases. "Afternoon, Skeet. What's doin'? You come a little late. I get wiped out by eleven. If you want somethin' special, you gotta be here by eight. Any of these pies suit you?"

Skeet chuckled, removed his hat, and scratched his dome. "Not interested in any baked goods today, Rich, not that you don't have the best product around. I need to buy yeast from you."

Wagner furrowed his eyebrows. "Yeast? How much? I've got a few bricks I can sell. I'm assuming you need it for your special project?" Everyone around Carroll County knew Skeet Miller was a moonshiner and used yeast to make his product, buying it from the various bakers in the county. Rich Wagner had sold to him dozens of times, usually a few bricks each visit.

"I'll need a hundred bricks."

Richard Wagner's eyes bulged. Even he didn't order a hundred at a time. One batch of dough used a few tablespoons. He'd have to bake his head off to use a hundred. "Holy cow! A hundred? I've never ordered that much at one time!"

"A hundred," Skeet confirmed. "And I expect you to mark up the price. You buy wholesale and sell to me retail. If I'm making money, then you're making money. That's the way I do business. And this isn't going to be a one-time purchase. I'll need the hundred every other month. Are you in? Can you get me what I need?"

The baker stood mute, thinking about the ordering he would need to do. He wouldn't order a hundred bricks at a time. Instead of his usual three-month order, he would order every month, tripling the amount to make it look like his business had caught fire. He also calculated his profit from each brick. Multiplying that amount by a hundred made it easy to estimate how much money he would make with each purchase. He could start replacing his worn equipment. Maybe do some updates on his building, or pay off his house. The list of possibilities added up quickly. "I can do that," he replied. "When do you need the first batch?"

"Soon as possible. And we need a drop-off site. I can't be coming in here every few months and walk out with armloads of yeast."

"How 'bout the railroad platform? All our supplies get dumped there. I could pick up what I need for the business and leave the rest for you. When the supplies come in, I'll put this small American flag in my window. You'll know to pick up your share that evening. Does that work for you?"

Skeet was impressed by the baker's cleverness. Using a signal, which no one would ever notice, was brilliant. Skeet would remember that from now on. Even if a federal agent were watching the bakery, waiting for someone to come out with yeast—or visit it a little too often—he would see nothing.

Just as Skeet offered his hand to shake on the deal, he had another thought. "You buy a lot of sugar as well, don't you?"

"Pounds of it. You need that as well?" the baker asked, counting more potential earnings.

"I do. Order me five hundred pounds every month."

The baker nearly passed out. He would be ordering railcars full of sugar. Again, he calculated his profits and nodded his head. With that, the men shook on their deal.

Skeet continued his deal making, visiting Ron Fischer, who owned the grocery store. Skeet ordered more sugar from Ron, using the same delivery system he had set up with Rich. He also bought used barrels. Ron would also put a small American flag in his window. The town's businessmen would appear to have become very patriotic. Ron was as easy to convince as had been the baker.

Skeet next visited Louis Jager, the coffin maker, who was a little less eager to become one of their suppliers. Skeet needed wood to make barrels and copper, used to line the coffins, to make stills. The funeral business was never affected by a bad economy. People still died, and their families still wanted to honor them with a decent burial. Jager wasn't a rich man, but he also wasn't a suffering one either.

"Skeet, I've known you a long time, and I know your business. I'm not interested in doing anything illegal. I've got a family to think of, and I don't want to be hauled into court and have to lie for you. I think I'm going to pass."

"Louis, I'm not asking you to do anything illegal. You are selling me raw materials. What I do with them is my business and not your concern. Actually, I need the copper for my cupola. I'd like to make it something special for my house. After that, I think I'm going to put cupolas on each of my outbuildings, and I'm going to need copper for them, too. The oak is for the inside of those cupolas. I want them to last. Does that sound like I'm doing something illegal? And to make this easier for you, double the cost on me."

Louis Jager wasn't a stupid man, but he was a greedy one. Like the other businessmen, he had a list of things he would like to do if he had more money. Louis needed a bigger workspace. His tiny shop had enough room to work on one coffin. If he built a bigger building, he could hire more men who would work on three to four coffins at a time. He could also buy more equipment. "You have a deal on one condition; if I'm ever called to testify, I won't lie for you. I'll tell them exactly how you are using those materials."

"Fair enough," Skeet replied and held out his hand to shake on the deal.

Skeet spent the following weeks setting up more purchases. He ordered sugar from several grocers and dry-goods stores. He ordered more oak from a cabinet maker. Skeet had a guy in Cumberland who made barrels and another in Earling who made stills. Since they were already in the business of making products for illegal activities, Skeet didn't have to convince them to work for him. Once a price was negotiated, Skeet ordered fifteen stills and one hundred barrels. He promised delivery of the necessary materials within a few weeks.

Lying in bed after his last task was completed, his mind whirring from all the business activity, Skeet thought about his boss, who wasn't a bootlegger, who didn't even know how to make the product. Within the last few months, Skeet had done all the work: locations, men, supplies. Once he discovered the distributer's name in Des Moines, he could set up his own deal, take all his work and leave his boss with nothing. What would keep him from seizing the business for himself?

Honor. Skeet didn't go back on his word. His grandfather had taught him a man had only one thing in this world—his name. If Skeet dishonored the Miller name by cheating people, he would ruin it for himself, past generations, and future ones—if there ever were any. Skeet might be many things, but an oath breaker was not one of them. And never would be.

CHAPTER 10

Albert Stange had eight children to feed, and the layer of icy baseballs covering his corn plants just made that responsibility impossible.

Iowa springs were like children: they could never make up their minds. Some days were blue and beautiful with sixty-degree weather; and other days were grey, cloudy, and so cold the winter coat had to be taken out of storage. Farmers drove out to the fields every few days to check the soil. Was it warm enough to germinate seeds? Were the fields dry enough to keep the horses or tractor wheels from sinking in the mud? No farmer wanted to wait too long—the growing season was a limited amount of time—but he also didn't want to start too early for fear of a spring snow, which would freeze his tender plants.

Albert owned a 120-acre farm just north of Templeton and was usually one of the first men in his fields. Up at dawn and working until dark, Albert felt the strong pull of the farm siren, drawing him to his plots of land. When he finished his last acre, he looked across the expanse of fields with satisfaction, the siren's song quiet until harvest.

Early June of 1927 came with sighs of relief. They were past the dangerous time of fickle weather. Albert could watch his corn, now six-inch plants, greedily drink the spring rains and grow with the warmth of the sun.

July came with heat—and often little rain—making it another month to worry over. The beginning of this year's July was a stranger: blistering hot one day, coolish the next. Rain came in downpours for the first few days, which likely meant a drought in the second half of the month.

On July 12, the day opened with a fifty-degree morning, climbing to eighty by ten o'clock; young summer wore her best blue dress with white puffy clouds. By noon, she had layered a thick cloudy sweater, the temperature dropping to seventy degrees. Then, it was as if someone had escorted summer to the door and invited winter to return. The warmth fell. First is was fifty, then forty, then twenty-eight. Foreboding, dark clouds covered the sun and settled over the area. The wind pushed in brutishly. Then, the first icy drop fell with more following. The pea-sized ball grew until its baseball-sized heft pummeled the land. The hail flattened corn and broke house and car windows. Everything looked as if someone had come in with an angry bat and smashed everything in sight. The hail took its leave and ushered in torrents of rain. Puddles grew to lakes, sitting in ditches and fields. Roads became rivers, and men were stranded when their trucks flooded out.

Albert Stange stood without words, looking at the lakes rather than his fields. His hours of hard work had been tromped down by Mother Nature. Scraping together the money for the seed had been difficult. Albert had sat up nights, going through accounts, figuring how he would sustain his family until harvest. If he could get past harvest, he thought he would have enough money to make it until the next harvest. Providing the corn did well and brought a bountiful crop and providing the corn prices remained good.

Albert didn't see a single green plant poking through the water, and he didn't have the funds to replant. And, even if he did, it was too late in the season. The corn would ripen, but his yield would be low. He ran his hands through his cropped hair in frustration.

Mark Decker, Albert's neighbor to the west, drove by in his Ford pickup. He, too, had been out assessing his crop damage. Seeing Albert standing at the end of his destroyed row, Mark stopped his truck and beeped his horn. A single wave from Albert brought him out of his vehicle and over to the decimated field. "You got hit too, huh?" Mark asked in sympathy.

"What a mess," Albert replied. "The hail got it all. Yours too?"

"Yep. Mine too. I got one field that might come out of it. The stalks are bent over pretty good, but they might come back up. The rest, though…."

"I can't replant. I don't have the money. And in these times, credit at a seed store is nearly impossible to come by. And I already owe money to the bank. They aren't going to lend me more. I'm plain out of options."

"There is another way to make some cash. Skeet Miller is look-ing for farm buildings. He's starting up a big whiskey operation. I heard tell he's paying good, cash money for your farm, and you don't have to do anything but let 'em use one of your buildings."

"And if I get arrested? What then? How's my wife going to put food on the table if I'm in jail? I just don't know. It's a lot of risk," Albert replied with skepticism in his voice.

"Well, if you decide you're interested, he's always around. You can talk to him and find out the system." With that, Mark jumped back to his truck and drove off.

Albert couldn't stand to look at his ruined crop any longer. He didn't know where to go. If he went home, he'd have to face his wife's questions about 'how we're going make it through' along with looking at the faces of his trusting children. He thought about driving around, assessing the totality of storm damage, but with money so short, wasting gas was just plain stupid. Albert decided to go home but spend his time in the barn, hoping a plan would materialize out of the haybales.

Pulling into the driveway, Albert was met by Rusty, his orange and white collie mix. She was a faithful dog to the family and would attack any stranger who even looked like he might hurt one of the Stange children. Albert opened the pickup door and stepped from the vehicle. Rusty was at his side, wagging her tail, which was full of cockleburs. She followed him across the farmyard and into the barn. Albert settled on an old stool; she settled herself at his feet.

Albert looked around the barn, assessing each item, from farm implements to cows. Could he sell one or two of his cows? If he did, how would they make it through the winter without meat? Could he sell some hay? If he kept all his cows, he would need the hay to feed them through the winter. His farm implements were out of the question. Albert had already sold everything he could to buy seed this spring. He had eaten all the meat off the bone and was now contemplating sucking out the marrow. If he did that, he would have nothing left.

Albert got off the stool and started pacing back and forth. Rusty raised her head and watched him pace. Her dark eyes questioned his mood. No matter how many plans he ran through to get him out of his bind, he could come up with nothing without causing some other problem. Mark Decker's words circled his brain. If he were going to risk his freedom, he needed to talk to Mary.

Mary Stange had also come from a farm family and knew the trials of trying to make a go of it. Her father had lost his farm in the early 20's when the farm markets plunged. Albert's wife still had the internal scars of watching the family's land being auctioned to strangers. Mary was always willing to lend a hand in any of the farm-ing operations. She had helped bale hay and feed animals. She was a sensible, sturdy woman who viewed life through the lens of doing what was needed and what was practical.

After their children were sent to bed, Albert sat in his office and asked his wife to join him. "I suppose you've already realized we're in a pretty tight pinch with the hail and flood damage," Albert began. "I've spent all afternoon trying to come up with a way out of this, and I can't. We've got nothing left to buy seed, and we've got nothing left to sell to raise the money. I've got a way to make money, but you're not going to like it."

Mary had been pondering their financial crisis herself. Like many farm wives, she was a partner rather than an outsider. She knew their finances down to the penny. She, too, had grown plans and hacked them down. She could not cut back on the household expenses anymore unless they started to skip meals. She had planted a large garden, but it had taken the same beating as the crops. She could replant, but produce would take a while to mature. They needed the money in her monthly grocery allowance to get them through until the garden produce could supplant some of their store-bought food. Her egg and cream money could not be used because that was her grocery money. The children's clothing needed replacing, but she could hold off until the next harvest. But by then, they would have outgrown and worn through much of it and would need some replacements. Nothing Mary had, except the brooch her father had passed down to her, was worth anything. And Mary was saving the brooch for a time when they had no money for food. Now was not the time to sell it.

"What am I not going to like?" Mary asked warily.

"Skeet Miller is paying farmers to distill whiskey on their land. He's paying cash money." Albert didn't want to add more because he didn't want to lead Mary astray with speculation.

"How much money? And what happens if you get caught? You'll

go to jail!"

"I don't know the particulars, Mary. But I wanted to come to you first. If you'll allow, I'll go talk to Skeet to find out the details. Before I make any decision, I'll come back and discuss it with you. I won't make this by myself. I figured you're going to be in this as much as I am."

Mary couldn't see any harm in just talking. With no other way to provide, they had no choice but to explore other options. "Just talk!"

Albert left at eight the next morning. He didn't know exactly where Skeet would be at that time of day, but a general guess was the Templeton feed store. Farmers hung around drinking coffee, and where there were farmers there would be Skeet.

Albert had never been one to go to the feedstore for socializing. He went in, bought his feed or seed, paid his bill, and left. A pack of men standing around discussing business was no different than a women's sewing circle, he believed. Albert always said the men gossiped worse than the women. And he wanted no part in gossiping about other people. "It weren't Christian."

When he walked through the door, he could tell by the looks on the men's faces they had been discussing the farms with damaged corn. He smelled brewing coffee along with sacks of corn, beans, and animal feed. Feed and seed stores had a particular smell that could not be duplicated anywhere else. The low rumble of multiple conversations added to the smell. The men were dressed in their work overalls and boots. No need to dress up for one another. The store was the equivalent to a women's beauty parlor. From out of the rumble, Albert heard, "Say there. You got a lot of damage, don't ya, Albert?"

All conversations stopped, and all eyes turned toward him. He walked over to the wood stove and poured himself a cup of coffee from the pot. "I suppose I do. Every stalk of corn was flattened. There's nothing else to do but plow it up; that is, when the water goes down." Albert tried to sound calm about his situation. Protocol called for stoicism, not complaints and fear.

"You planning to replant?" asked a voice from the crowd.

How to answer the question? Should he sound confident and lie? Or should he admit his defeat? He did not see Skeet Miller among the men. But that didn't mean Skeet wouldn't hear of his situation and reach out. He only needed to pass along the opportunity. "Not planting again," he said. "I don't have the cash for it."

The men nodded their heads in camaraderie. There was no shame in not having money. Too many were in Albert's situation or on the verge of it.

"Well, it's a damn shame what's happened. I believe those would have been good crops this year."

Another group nodded, and the topic of conversation was changed. None of the men inquired into his future plans. That question would be prying into a man's business, and it was rude to pry.

Albert finished his coffee and left the store. He had planted a different kind of seed that morning, and now he needed to wait and see if it germinated.

Albert had not been home for longer than four hours before an old truck came rambling down his lane, Rusty the collie announcing the visitor. Mary pulled aside the kitchen curtain and announced, "I believe you've got a visitor. You should probably go out and meet him. The barn's the best place to talk. We don't want anyone driving by and supposing on our business."

Albert walked out of the house and up the driveway. He met Skeet at the truck and waved him and his vehicle into the barn.

Seated on haybales, both men talked of farming business for a few minutes.

"I heard you lost your crop, Albert. I also heard you got no money to replant. You know how you're going to feed your family?" Skeet hit him right in the gut by bringing up his family.

"I don't. But I heard there might be another way." Albert went from looking at his boots to looking Skeet right in the eyes. "You know anything about that?"

Skeet started his sales pitch: the payment for each barrel, the responsibility of the farmer, the legal help if it was needed. "There's one condition," he said. "You have to keep your mouth shut. You can never give my name to the authorities. You'll just have to take what comes if you get busted. You interested?" he asked when he finished.

"I need to talk to Mary. If I go to jail, she's the one who will be taking care of the children. This has to be a joint decision. And if I do this, I've got a condition of my own: You give me your word you'll make sure Mary and the children are financially provided for if I go to prison, for as long as I'm in prison. And you won't be using my barn; I've got my cows in there. But I've got a few other build-ings I don't use. You can do your business in one of those. They're on the other side of the farm, so no smell will be close to the house. If you can agree to that, then I'll let you know."

Skeet didn't have the say so on taking care of farmers' families, but he couldn't admit he didn't have the authority. "I think we can make that happen," he fibbed.

Albert and Mary talked through the night and into the morning. They ran the full scenario of not planting and not putting a still on their property. They would probably lose the farm. They certainly would have little in way of food. The outcome went beyond that one year into many years. They also ran the scenario of hiding a still. The only drawback was prison, and it was a big one. Could Mary run the farm without him? How long might he be away? This was the quintessential rock and hard place. There was no winning. They could only take the one that gave them the best chance for a decent outcome.

Albert Stange called Skeet the following morning and told him to bring the still.

CHAPTER 11

The black Chevy truck squatted in the empty lot beside the train tracks, the Saturday night sky pitch black, the moon and stars covered by a thick layer of clouds. A February storm had dumped wet, heavy snow across western and central Iowa, and it looked like more was on its way. Roads would not be plowed for two days—this being a Saturday—so the vehicle would have to pick its way carefully all the way to Des Moines.

Blowing into his cold hands, Frank Hogan hunkered behind the steering wheel, waiting for the load of whiskey. He didn't risk starting the truck and throwing out tailpipe exhaust. To any lawman, the truck was supposed to look like it had been left behind.

Frank's vehicle was parked behind Templeton's dancehall, giving the appearance someone had perhaps gotten a ride home after the dance and left the truck. Frank knew it wasn't the best diversion, but so far, he had had no issues. His only thoughts at this point were directed toward his frozen hands and feet. He had been waiting behind the building for several hours. Whoever was supposed to drop the load was late. Usually, Frank picked up the merchandise at midnight.

It was never the same man who met him, and Frank never knew their names. And they didn't know his.

Frank worked directly with Skeet Miller, and Skeet liked to keep everyone in the dark about different parts of the operation. The farmers didn't know the cookers, who didn't know the pickup men, who didn't know the delivery men. If anyone were caught, the Feds couldn't go very far up the chain if someone in the organization decided to squeal. Frank didn't know anyone other than Skeet.

Frank came to the business in 1919, the year before the Volstead Act. He sold whiskey for another distiller and sometimes delivered cases of it to the larger distributers around the area. He had learned to keep his mouth shut and his head low, which made him an ideal employee.

Skeet had approached him with this transportation job in 1926 when he was 24, and so far, he had liked it well enough. By the end of that first year, Frank had made good money, which is how he weighed each occupation. This job was not his first foray into illegal businesses, though.

Frank emigrated with his parents, Marc and Angela, and his sister Lucy from Ireland when he was eight years old. They had boarded a ship in County Cork, their meager means purchasing tickets in steerage. The ship was full of hopeful Irish, making the family's accommodations tight, the narrow bunks three across and three deep. Illness spread as quickly as a smoke in the wind. A single passenger with typhus, likely gotten from lice, distributed the disease throughout steerage, especially when strong storms required the hatches closed to keep sea water out.

Frank's father, mother, and sister caught the contagion. They vomited anything put into their body. Frank ran himself so thin one could see through him. He spent most of the voyage fetching water, changing cold cloths in an effort to cool their burning bodies, encouraging them to drink water, and trying to get first in line to receive the freshest food; but anything they consumed was immediately expelled, and nothing he did could lower the temperature of their coal-hot bodies and then no number of blankets—which Frank borrowed or stole—could keep their chills abated. Lucy's tiny body was covered in rash from her chin to her groin. First Frank's mother died, then his father. With only his sister remaining, Frank dedicated himself to Lucy's recovery, never leaving her side other than to bring her water and try to coax her to drink and eat a little. Eventually, Lucy recovered, thin and pale.

Frank was now in charge of his four-year-old sibling. He was determined they stay together once they debarked from the ship. Frank and Lucy stood on the deck of the ship and stared in awe at the Statue of Liberty. Ironically, they did not feel liberation once they reached port, and they never saw Lady Liberty up close.

The passengers in their steerage section were taken directly from the ship to Hoffman Island, quarantining for two weeks. Frank and Lucy were separated and bedded into the men's and women's quarters. Other steerage passengers were ferried to Ellis Island to be processed. First and second-class passengers were released directly from the ship to go whichever way they pleased.

In quarantine, Frank heard languages of all sounds and saw men dressed in all manner of clothing. Some men were kind and looked after the youngest; others were cruel and took what they wanted. Fights broke out among those who were no longer ill. His time in quarantine was Frank's first look at the wideness of the world.

Neither Frank nor Lucy saw Ellis Island, the famed port of American entry. Once cleared of the disease, the Hogan children were transported to a detention center in Elizabeth, New Jersey, and separated again.

They were not the only orphan immigrants. Sometimes children traveled to America alone, sent by their families with the hope of making a new life and sending money for the rest of them. That was only if the child immigrant were sixteen or older. Children under sixteen were sent to a detention center until someone—a church, synagogue, missionary, or private citizen—would step up and take guardianship of them.

Frank gave the immigration officer the name and location of his uncle, who was contacted by the detention center via telegram. Until then, they received an adequate bed, warm meals, and some education, compliments of missionaries and Catholic nuns. Frank was separated from his sister and was required to stay in the boys' dormitory, but he saw her as often as he could to ensure she was safe.

Three months after their arrival to America, they heard from Frank's uncle. He sent the children money for train passage. With notes of identity and destination around their necks, Frank and Lucy were safely put on the train heading west, stopping in Chicago. In Des Moines, they took another train to Denison where their uncle, Michael Hogan, collected them.

Michael Hogan was a bachelor and a rather unsavory character. He ran illegal poker games in the backs of small businesses and sold illegal liquor when Iowa passed prohibition in 1916. He bragged about being one step ahead of the law. Michael consorted with all types of lawbreakers and never intended to settle down with a family. When he received the telegram, he felt an obligation to his dead brother. He didn't know the ages or genders of the children, and he certainly didn't know how to raise them. However, he sent the train fare, thinking he would pass them off once they arrived.

Finally in Denison, Frank and Lucy huddled together on the train platform, holding hands and looking around their new location. Iowa was very different from Ireland. While they had seen snow before, the amount of it along with Iowa's blasts of winter wind, shocked them and froze their bones. The milder climate of Ireland and their poor living conditions had left them woefully underdressed.

The children had never met their uncle and didn't know which of the men walking into the train depot was him, but Michael recognized them immediately. Frank—his tall slender frame, soft brown eyes and hair—looked exactly like his father Marc. Lucy was petite with dark, chestnut hair and eyes. Her curly hair fell in ringlets down her back. She was dressed in a yellow, plain dress, which was too light for the brutal weather. Michael looked at the two orphans in the train depot and shook his head. He was no father and didn't want to be one.

Within a week, Michael had sent Lucy to a distant cousin, Marguerite Hogan, a spinster in Council Bluffs. She had taught school for several years and, when Michael contacted her, she begrudgingly took Lucy into her home.

Frank was furious when he was informed of Lucy's leaving. He hung on to her as tightly as he could, but his slender frame was no match against his uncle's. Lucy, another note around her neck, was transported from Denison to Council Bluffs. Frank never saw his sister again.

Michael decided Frank could be of use to him in his business endeavors. He occasionally sent Frank to school until he reached the end of eighth grade. At fourteen, Frank helped Michael with his poker games, fetching drinks and sandwiches for the men. He learned the strategies of the game from his uncle, but he never played much himself. Michael had warned him about taking his earnings and wasting them on cards, liquor, and women. Sometimes Frank would deliver cases of liquor to Michael's customers. Frank was a good runner because the law would never suspect a boy.

By Frank's seventeenth birthday, he was running some of his own poker games in the small towns surrounding Dunlap. Those games had the same weekly players and were as boring as a church service. Frank's life had seemed to take on a pattern with little vari-ation—until his uncle was pinched.

Michael Hogan was small time but didn't see himself that way. In his mind only, he was a one-man Irish mafia. Small timers pointed to him with respect and parted ways when he came through a crowd. Men asked him for advice and followed it like it was from God Him-self. Michael's self-importance was so large no man could convince him otherwise.

Ignoring his own rules of life, Michael got himself into a poker game in the backroom of a Sioux City establishment. He became drunk and belligerent, insulting the dealer, suggesting that the dealer's wife was fat and ugly.

Michael had no idea the real mafia, a guy by the name of Manny O'Connor, who was connected to Chicago, owned the game. Manny's games were played by gentlemen and well-known Sioux City leaders. This particular game included the sheriff of Woodbury County along with the Sioux City mayor. Following Manny's strict rules of conduct, the game manager decided he had listened to enough of Michael's insults. He tried escorting Michael out the door, like a gentleman, but Michael spit in his face and called his wife a whore. The game manager became enraged when the insults landed on his own house, so he punched Michael in the nose and threw him out the door.

Michael became indignant. "No two-bit son of a whore is going to disrespect me!" he raged to a closed door. He picked himself up off the street and stomped to his car. Under the seat, he carried a Colt U.S. Army model 1915. He had only pointed it once when a Dunlap local had refused to pay his gambling loans, but he had never shot the gun.

Michael went back through the front of the establishment, crashed through the backroom door, and pointed the pistol at the game manager. Another player lunged for the gun, and, in the confusion, Michael pulled the trigger, shooting the game manager in the head. The man fell dead on the floor, blood soaking into the expensive carpet.

Michael was now ensconced in the Iowa State Penitentiary in Fort Madison, for life.

Frank skirted the county home for orphans until he turned eighteen. He then took over his uncle's businesses. Frank discarded some of the two-bit games that brought almost nothing in terms of revenue. He sold them to one of the other small-time game managers. Frank focused on building the pots for the games he retained and took on new territory. Sometimes the new territories came with their own game owners, but Michael Hogan had taught Frank well. It wasn't long before those other game owners sold out to him.

Frank also expanded his alcohol business, buying from a distiller in Carroll County and selling to his poker players and anyone else who knew he had it.

Frank's business sense was excellent, and it wasn't long before he carried a wad of cash in his pocket. Even though Frank could drive a fancy car, his uncle had taught him to keep a low profile. He drove a car fitting for a young man who had little money.

There was only one way in which Frank showed his money. He loved wearing the latest trends. As a youngster in Ireland, Frank wore his father's worn-out clothing, which his mother had cut down and remade for him. His uncle never thought of Frank needing clothing, so Frank had had to buy his own—usually used clothing—from the money his uncle gave him for tending games. As soon as Frank had enough cash to keep his body sheltered and fed, he went to a clothing store in Denison and bought the best of what they had. However, Denison catered to farmers and carried practical, well-made clothing. Frank put the new suit on and looked in the mirror. Dissatisfied with his new purchases, he returned them. After that, Frank shopped exclusively in Sioux City. Along with two stylish suits, he bought shoes, several ties, and a Fedora. The hat made him particularly happy. His father had always worn a beat-up, flat cap. Only the monied men in County Cork had a Fedora on their heads. A new look from head to toe gave Frank confidence.

Frank looked the part of a well-established businessman and could afford anything he desired. He changed girlfriends about as often as he changed his socks. Frank still carried the scars of being ripped from his loved ones and never wanted to experience losing someone who was close to him again.

To complete his business persona, Frank adopted current slang phrases, like 'skirt' or 'babe' or 'Sheila.' To his disappointment, however, most of his clients didn't speak fluent English much less know slang.

Frank met Skeet Miller when he and Skeet formed a business relationship in 1921. Frank was a tender 19, but he and Skeet hit it off right away. Skeet sold Frank whiskey, and Frank resold it. Frank took the risks, and Skeet took the bulk of the profits.

Frank could have continued his poker-playing-whiskey-selling business for many years and been comfortable. But, that was the problem. Frank was comfortable, and comfortable was boring.

His last buy from Skeet confirmed the rumors swirling around the whiskey business. Rumors of a multi-still operation with thousands of gallons of mash and thousands of gallons of whiskey. A boss or kingpin of some sort. Skeet gave Frank an "oh shucks" look, which was totally fake, as he announced himself the kingpin.

Skeet was looking for a reliable delivery man. Barrels of whiskey needed transportation to Des Moines. A major distiller, one who was rumored to work with Al Capone's gang, transported the whiskey across state lines. Would Frank be interested in the job?

"Hell yes!" was Frank's only response. And now he was sitting in an empty lot, freezing off his appendages, and waiting for some 'bird' with a broken watch to bring him the delivery. It wasn't as glamorous as he had imagined.

Two hours late, a pair of lights finally shone through the dark. That must be the one, thought Frank.

Protocol dictated Frank stay in his truck while men loaded him. The fifteen-gallon barrels were loaded first, followed by some kind of agricultural product. Tonight, bales of hay were stacked over and around the barrels. If Frank were stopped, the heaviness of the bales may dissuade some local lawman from unloading them to see if anything were underneath. If it were a Fed, though, the bales would be thrown to the ground without concern for a man's private property.

Loaded, his truck's lights pointed above the ground rather than on it, due to the truck's heavy bed. Frank started his trip to the capital city. The most direct route was 71 through Audubon, Hamlin, Brayton and then take US Highway 32 into Des Moines. Unfortunately, those two routes were major ones in Iowa, and they were heavily watched by the Iowa Highway Safety Patrol. They were also watched by federal agents. If Frank wanted to get caught, taking those two routes would be his fastest way to prison.

Instead, Frank took the back roads, those known to the locals. He had established three tracks and varied his patterns of taking them. By using such a method, Frank added three hours to his trip, but he considered three additional hours nothing compared to the years he could spend in jail if he were caught.

Frank had only gotten as far as Willey when he tried to plow through a pile of snow. The wind had picked up in the night and the snow, piled on the side of the road, was now a barricade across it. Frank hoped hitting the gas would give the old truck the speed to punch through the drift; but once in the midst of it, his vehicle failed to move forward.

Frank was on Main Street directly in front of St. Mary's Catholic Church. "How fitting," Frank muttered angrily when his tires spun ineffectually. The weight of the load did not make matters any better. The hay and barrels sunk him deeper into the drift.

First, Frank tried forward, then reverse, then forward, then reverse. The tires spun but did not move him. The streets were empty at that late hour, so there was no one to help even if he had wanted it—which he didn't. The last thing he needed was some nosy farmer asking him about his load of hay.

Frank stepped out of the truck. He had foolishly dressed as if the weather would be warmer. He had worn his flat cap but had failed to throw a pair of gloves into the truck. His footwear was no match for the fresh snow.

He walked around his truck to assess the situation. He needed some kind of board to put under the wheels. He spent a little time walking the perimeter of the truck, searching for anything he could pull from it to use. But the hay had filled the bed completely, and nothing stuck out. He then walked up and down the street, but to no avail. It was as clean as a sheet on a line. Clearly he needed to venture farther, looking into some yards and in the back of local businesses. Somewhere there had to be something he could put under his wheels.

Two blocks away from his truck, having found nothing to help his situation, Frank was turning around to walk back to the vehicle when a black car pulled alongside his transportation. A man, bundled in winter gear, stepped out and walked up to the truck. He cupped his hands and looked through the side window. Seeing no one, he walked around the back and started pushing on the bales of hay. He was attempting to see if any of them were loose enough to pull free.

This man was no farmer or curious Willey citizen. His car indicated the Law.

Frank ducked into the entrance of a building and watched from afar. He was invisible as he hid within the shadows, but he could clearly view what was happening down the street.

Frank sighed relief as the officer went back to his own vehicle, but instead of getting back inside, he went to the trunk of his car and brought out a long pole.

Frank's stomach turned to water as he realized the stranger's next move. And he was correct. The man walked with the pole to the pile of hay. He began poking it through the bales and into the interior of the load. Frank was certain he would hit a barrel and feel the difference between the compacted bale of hay and the hard wood of oak. Frank watched tensely as the officer hit wood and realized there was something else other than feed for animals.

Frank was now in a bigger dilemma. He could not return to his truck. And he was a long way from home, too far to walk it. Even if he did try to put his feet to work, the chance he would be found walking alongside a road was almost one hundred percent. With an abandoned truck full of bootleg whiskey, no lawman would believe he was out for an evening stroll. The only abandoned vehicle was carrying illegal goods. It didn't take a genius to put together his lack of wheels and a left-behind whiskey carrier.

Frank rarely panicked. He had been in many tight spots and was always able to out-think or out-talk his problem. He was a likable fella, and people generally responded to his charisma and offered help. If he had gotten stuck around suppertime, he would now be seated in front of a hot, delicious meal, telling tales and making friends. However, in the middle of the night, he was more likely to be met at the door with a shotgun than an invitation to the supper table. He needed a place to hide until morning. Then, he could knock on a door and get some help. He looked around, searching for an unlocked building, some place to get him out of the elements. It would be nice if it were warm, but he wasn't going to be picky.

Then, he spied what had been in front of him the whole time, St. Mary's church.

Many Catholic churches left open a side door in the event a member of their congregation needed to converse with God in a time of crisis. The reverence for a house of worship kept any mischievous children from vandalizing the property, the shame and outrage from parents and community members sweeping away any flitting ideas of desecrating the exterior or interior of the building.

Frank kept to the shadows, ducking behind houses, and made it to the side door. He turned the knob and felt relief as it drew the latch back from the doorjamb. He slipped inside, the darkness surrounding him. Frank was unfamiliar with this particular church, but most Catholic churches were designed similarly. He was probably in a small hall, which meant he could go up to the nave or down to the basement. Frank chose the nave.

As he came through the doorway to the worship area, he was met with soft darkness and gentle quiet. Only his boots, making sharp thuds on the stone floor, interrupted the tranquility. Frank headed toward the only light source, the few flickering votive candles in front of the Virgin Mary.

He had not been to mass in several years, and this made Frank feel guilty. His parents had been devout church goers. They made every Sunday mass along with every holy day. They fasted on Fridays and tithed their suggested annual amount even in years when they had little money. Frank had been raised to follow church dictates and had done so until he lived with his uncle.

Michael Hogan went to church when he attended a funeral. He even missed the Christmas and Easter masses. Frank did not know why his uncle had become so lapsed. Perhaps it was his guilt for all the commandments he had broken, or perhaps he had a grudge against God for killing his brother. Because Michael didn't attend mass, he did not make Frank go, either. Frank attended St. Patrick's mass regularly when he first arrived in Dunlap, and then it was only once a month, whittled down to Christmas and Easter, and now he hadn't been for the last three years. Frank felt guilty for letting down his parents.

He treaded as quietly as possible down the outside aisle until he was standing in front of Mary's statue, the soft candles lighting up and warming Frank's face. He took some bills out of his pocket and shoved them through the slot on the collection box. He took the thin sliver of wood and picked up the flame from one of the candles, placing it on the wick of an unlit votive. Frank then knelt on the single kneeler and began the Our Father. He hadn't lit a candle and prayed for his parents since he had last attended church. As the head of his family—what there was left of it—it was his duty to continue prayers for his parents. Guilt washed over him as he thought about the many ways in which he had let them down: he hadn't taken care of Lucy, he hadn't been a good Catholic, and he was not living a righteous life.

Frank continued to pray, wishing he had a rosary, so he could keep track of his prayers. When he finished his first ten Hail Marys, his brain failed to conjure the Second Joyful Mystery. The nuns in Ireland would have wrapped his knuckles bloody if he had stumbled on such an important ritual of his faith in front of them.

Frank said a few more prayers he could remember, crossed himself, and sat down in the first pew. In the quiet, the votive lights playing softly at Mary's feet, he thought about his current life. He was ashamed of himself. He had been the smartest boy in his class in Ireland. His mother bragged to the neighbors how Frankie was going to become an important man someday. The parish priest had blessed him when they left Ireland.

Frank had often thought about his parents' deaths. He didn't know why he had been spared of typhoid. He knew it was not luck, but rather the doings of God. His Maker had saved him for something, but he did not know what that was. For a brief time, he had considered joining the ranks of God's soldiers and become a priest. But his love of money and women had extinguished that idea almost as quickly as he had conjured it.

Instead, what had he become? An important man? No, he was a criminal. Frank could blame his poor upbringing on his uncle, but now he was an adult, and the decisions were his to make. He was choosing a bad life. He sent a promise to his parents he would take the right path and make them proud. But he couldn't do it right now. Frank needed to build his nest with enough resources, so he could survive once he quit. He said a quick prayer to Saint Anthony, the patron saint of lost things, because Frank was lost. He hoped Saint Anthony would help him find his way again.

The solitude of the church overcame him, and Frank laid down on a bench and fell asleep. He dreamt of his parents and his home in Ireland. He dreamt of Lucy, who was now a young woman.

A murmuring awakened Frank. He sat up and looked around. Daylight streamed through the stained-glass windows. Men and women were kneeling in the pews with rosaries woven through their fingers or hanging from their hands. Frank realized he had spent the night, and it was now a half an hour before mass when the congregation prayed the rosary together.

Sunday morning spread its holy wings, and the sinner in the front pew thought only of how to escape his sanctuary. Frank crossed himself and exited the pew, walking down the long aisle, chin down to avoid questioning eyes. He left the church by the back doors.

Frank, cap back on his head and his coat collar up around his ears, looked to where his truck was last parked. Two local law cars were parked in front and behind it, leaving no space for a driver to pull forward or to back up. The snow had been scooped from around the tires. They were waiting for his return, and they were planning to confiscate the vehicle and bring it to the nearest sheriff's office.

Frank pulled his cap lower and walked past the truck, looking only at his feet. He needed a telephone. And a ride.

Devout Catholics passed him, making their way to church. Frank needed to ask someone to use their telephone before they left for church. He could offer cash for the inconvenience. A block down the street, a row of houses sat north of the church, and an older gentleman was outside scooping his front walk.

"Sir, could I trouble you to use your telephone? I can pay for the call," Frank said to the man.

"My telephone? Why do you need that?"

In small towns, strangers were suspicious. This man didn't know him, and Frank was asking to enter the house. Of course, there would be questions, which would necessitate a story.

"I came for a poker game last night and overextended myself. I gambled away my truck. I need to call a friend to come and give me a ride home. And my wife is going to hang me from the barn rafters when she finds out what I've done." Frank's lie slid like oil from his tongue. He added a sheepish look to his lie, hunching his shoulders as he had seen other men do when they had done something stupid. "Can you help me out?"

"I figure that truck sitting with the law surrounding it is yours. That right? You some whiskey runner that got caught and now you need to get out of town?" The gentleman didn't sound threatened or anxious. He was just matter of fact.

Frank's initial reaction was to continue the lie and add to it. However, if he did, then he was breaking trust with this stranger. The truth might actually get him what he wanted. It was a fifty/fifty gamble. "Yep. Got the truck stuck in a snow drift. It's loaded with whiskey, and now I'm in a bit of a bind. I just need to get out of town."

The man only replied, "Figured." And then he pointed toward his house. "Phone's inside the hall on the table. Leave the money next to it." He went back to clearing his path.

There was only one person Frank could call. Skeet Miller. He had Skeet's house extension number, and Frank hoped he would be asleep in bed this early on a Sunday morning.

After the twelfth ring, Skeet's sleepy voice came over the wire. "This better be important."

Frank explained his situation. Several curses came from the other end. He would come to Willey himself to retrieve his employee. "It'll be a while," he said. "Best find some place safe while you wait. Give me an hour or so."

Frank thought about asking the owner of the telephone, but he didn't get the sense the guy wanted to harbor a fugitive. His only choice was to return to St. Mary's and attend mass. "I s'pose it won't hurt me," he grumbled, and headed back toward the church to await his rescue.

CHAPTER 12

"Dammit, Frank!" Skeet was not a pleasant man when he was pulled out of bed on a Sunday morning and made to rescue one of his employees. "Do you have any idea how much money you lost us?"

Frank didn't think it fair Skeet was blaming him for the loss. He hadn't been foolish or reckless; he had done his best to get the load to its destination. It wasn't his fault the weather hadn't cooperated.

Dropping Frank off at his car, still parked close to the drop-off point, Skeet returned home but couldn't return to his Sunday slumber. His brain worked feverishly on his current problem. He would need to replace the fifteen barrels of whiskey while keeping his current production commitments. The Des Moines supplier would forgive his tardiness—run-ins with the law could not be avoided—but he expected a replacement delivery within the week.

His current cookers were working at capacity. Pushing them would only produce a bad product or get someone killed. This liquor business wasn't worth a man's life.

To make more whiskey, Skeet would need to add another location to their enterprise. Someone had passed along a name a few weeks back, but Skeet hadn't investigated. His boss had warned him about growing the business too quickly. Many steps needed to occur with utmost caution, and that took time. No action could be done before the previous one was completed. If the process were rushed, mistakes could be made. However much he had agreed with his superior and promised to follow orders, Skeet broke his promise. He wanted to get a still up and running within a week or two.

Through the grapevine, word had reached Skeet of another farmer, Butch Schwarte, who was interested in having a conversation with him. Butch wasn't a regular at the billiards hall or any of the backroom bars. In fact, Skeet was bowled over when Schwarte invited him out to his farm. The man wasn't a Dry, but he certainly wasn't a drinker either. What little Skeet knew of him were the general rumors surrounding Butch Schwarte, which spoke of a man with piles of cash. Butch owned a large farming operation, one grown from the agricultural boom during the war. The farmer had bought up surrounding land and purchased the newest equipment to plant and harvest his acres. Skeet couldn't think what the farming tycoon wanted with him, but he was intrigued enough to pay him a visit.

Skeet drove his new Chevy out to the Schwarte farm. With his recent earnings, the liquor boss had been able to purchase something befitting his status in the organization. Like his counterpart in Chicago, Skeet liked nice things, and cars were his particular passion. His new vehicle, a coupe, drew eyes wherever he drove it. The body was a buttery yellow with a tan top and brown matching trim. The wheel rims, including the spare, shone a bright orange, contrasting the whitewall tires. Skeet loved the attention his car brought. Children pointed, and men gave him approving looks.

Pulling into the Schwartes' farm lane, Skeet looked around the farm. The house needed some paint, but several newer buildings, housing the farmer's larger implements, surrounded the barn. Skeet took note of the opulence, most farmers having to store their equipment outside or in smaller sheds.

Schwarte met him at the side door and invited him into his kitchen, Mrs. Schwarte serving cups of coffee and slices of apple pie. The men discussed recent farm prices and next year's crop forecast before Schwarte finally gathered the courage to address his intentions. "I was talking to my neighbor, Albert Stange, and he told me about his deal with you." Skeet sat silently, waiting to see how much the farmer already knew. "He told me about allowing you to use his farm to make liquor and how much he gets paid. I was wondering if you need any more places." Butch's eyes directed on Skeet's, his hands clenched together on the table.

"Butch, why would you want to get yourself involved in this? This isn't for the worrying man. You've got your family to think of. Besides, you're a man of plenty. Why would you want to risk all this?" He spread his hand out to include the house and land.

"Don't nobody know this, but I'm in debt, bad. I've got loans on the land and the machinery. I haven't been able to meet my obligations for the last three years. The bank is comin' to take my home, Skeet. It's just a matter of time, and very little of it. I've got no place for my wife and kids. I got no choice."

"Butch, you understand you could end up in jail?"

"My wife and kids are going to end up on the side of the road. Like I said, I've got no choice in the matter. Just tell me what I need to do."

Skeet ran down the list of rules and explained the support the farmer would receive if he were arrested. Could Schwarte agree to these? With a pinched face, like his body was squeezing hard to hold in his ethics lest they leak out and ruin the opportunity, Schwarte shook hands on the deal and showed Skeet three possible locations. The kingpin chose an abandoned chicken coop, the farthest location from the house. Skeet directed Butch to keep his eyes peeled for the equipment and men, which would always be brought in at night. He also instructed the farmer to purchase or adopt a dog, a loud dog. When asked why, Skeet stated it was for protection, from liquor thieves, farm thieves, and most importantly, the Feds. He would train the dog to recognize the men who would work their nightly shifts as well as their cars. Anyone else coming onto the property would alert the animal and, consequently, the farmer and the distillers.

From Schwarte's farm, Skeet went into Carroll to do some purchasing. He had stretched his Templeton businessmen as far as they could go. He needed to reach out to his Carroll contacts to fulfill his orders for the new location.

He stopped first on Simon Avenue and walked into the business of Robert Kasperbauer, the local furniture maker. "What's doin', Skeet?" The two men had been friends for many years, and Skeet could count on Bob to furnish him with much of what he needed. With this new location, fifty barrels were needed as soon as possible.

"Need some wood, Bob. How much you have on hand?"

Kasperbauer thought for a moment, recounting his inventory and sorting out his own needs. "I suppose I could let you have enough for a few barrels. I've got a shipment of wood coming in a week. I can put in an order for more. Oak, I assume."

Skeet nodded his head in agreement. "'Preciate it. I'll need a load every couple of weeks until I tell you otherwise. I also came to order a piece of furniture. I'd like a chest of drawers made from walnut."

Surprised, the furniture maker asked, "You got someone special I'm making this for, Skeet?"

"It's for me. But I want some accommodations made to it." Skeet proceeded to explain his order for a six-drawer chest, but he wanted the drawers shorter than usual. They should be ten inches deep instead of the usual fifteen. The remaining space behind the drawers would have shelves, and the rear of the dresser was to have a hinged back piece, the hinges hidden on the inside. Once opened from the back side, the bedroom furniture became a storage area for stacks of hundred-dollar bills.

Finished at the furniture woodshop, Skeet walked up the street and entered Hahn's Bakery. Timothy Hahn sold him one hundred bricks of yeast.

After the bakery, Skeet stepped next door to the grocer's store. Matthew Hoffman supplied him with the sugar needed to feed the yeast as well as some oak barrels. Many of their dry goods came in large amounts. Skeet bought the barrels, had them cleaned, and then charred on the inside, which gave the whiskey its copper color. Often, Skeet asked the grocer to leave the moniker of the dry good on the side of the barrel. Sometimes, he directed his men to change it to 'vinegar.'

Supplies bought and on their way, Skeet needed to hire some man power. Templeton was the most accommodating town in the county as far as accepting the whiskey business. Therefore, he headed to the local job market. He drove to the edge of town and entered the pool hall. Jobless men hung out there, whiling away their time with games of pool and commiserating with other jobless men. Not all were jobless; some of them just wanted a place to go that was devoid of wife and children. Some were hobos who had jumped from the train to spend some time in town.

When he entered, those who recognized him gave him a respectful nod and continued their business. Those who did not, out-of-towners stopping for a game and a clandestine drink, looked him over and kept him within their sights.

A billiards hall served as the modern jousting tournament. Instead of lances, they held pool sticks. As they battled one another on the playing field of felt, each man sized the other. Their skill in the game earned them respect. The losing man did so with courtesy.

Skeet took off his coat and laid a nickel on the top rail of the table. The coin put him in line for the next game, and he would be playing the winner of the current one. Until then, he would stand off to the side, striking up conversations with other onlookers. Like the rest of the processes, this could not be rushed. Men needed to metaphorically sniff around him to determine his strength and character. His skill and prowess in the game would establish him in the pecking order. His banter and storytelling capabilities would ease their suspicions.

Skeet had no fear of losing any games. He had been taught by his grandfather, a stellar knight of the pool stick. Skeet had not been tall enough to reach the table when he played his first game, so his grandfather—Earl, Senior—had brought a chair for him to perch on while he shot. By his twelfth birthday, Skeet was beating the mid-level players in any hall. By fifteen, there were very few who could outplay him, except his grandfather.

Skeet clearly remembered the day he had won against his idol; he was seventeen years old. Like a noble knight, his grandfather had lost with dignity and grace. After that, the old man never played again, preferring to watch his grandson outplay many a cocky man who thought he was taking money from a child. With each 8-ball dropped into the pocket, the old player slapped his knee and belly laughed. The loser stood looking at the coins on the top rail, which he had just forfeited to a kid.

Skeet could have made a living from pool games; however, he loved something much more—distilling a fine batch of whiskey. At this task, he had also shown great skill for which his grandfather bragged loudly to any other cooker. Skeet knew it was not the process of cooking he enjoyed. It was the time spent with his grandfather and the old man's pride in his skills.

Making a batch of whiskey took time and patience. While they waited, Skeet listened to the stories of the older Earl. He loved that old man more than he loved his father—Earl, Jr.

Here he was, many years later, bent over the felt table, cue stick between his fingers. Skeet broke the pool balls, scattering them across the table. If he had wanted, he could have finished the game in his one turn, but that left no time for conversation. He didn't plan to lose, but he did want to slow it down. With each game, Skeet chatted with his opponents and spectators. He was looking for someone specific.

Strangers passing through towns were not uncommon during these hard times. Men left their families in search of work. Others rode the rails to escape their situations and find better lives. Templeton was close to the rail line, so strangers were noticed and noted, but they were not infrequent.

Skeet struck up a conversation with a spectator at the bar as he was waiting for his next attack on the balls. The young man was passing through town and currently unemployed. He had come to the billiards hall hoping to find some work with either the owner or one of the farmers who was enjoying his day of leisure. He said he had no family and no home. He was looking for a job, and he wasn't picky so long as it paid. He revealed he had been through some rough times but was reluctant to disclose what those were. Skeet respected his privacy but thoroughly read him through his clothing and mannerisms.

Along with the young man, Skeet picked up two more men, whom he assumed had ridden the rails. He felt confident of his hires. He knew he hadn't hired any federal men pretending to be homeless. He also had a sense these men were authentic. Even though he had enough manpower for his new location, Skeet would keep his eyes open for more men. He planned to add another distilling operation within the next six months.

Skeet, his new hires loaded into his vehicle, drove them out to Butch Schwarte's farm. For now, they could sleep in his barn and enjoy the cooking of Mrs. Schwarte.

CHAPTER 13

Alvin Truly was both elated and angry. One of his agents had been cruising the back roads around Templeton, hoping to catch a runner. He had watched both the highway running south to Atlantic and the one running east to Perry. No vehicles. Deciding the runners may have taken a back road, he turned his vehicle and headed into Willey.

The agent told Truly he had a hunch they may be using this out-of-the-way back road. Discovering the truck, loaded with hay, parked—actually stuck—in front of the church, had been sheer luck on the agent's part.

When he first saw it, the agent was suspicious of hay being hauled into town. The hay was going in the wrong direction. The truck should have been trapped on a country road as if the farmer were bringing it to one of his pastures for winter feed. Curious, the agent stopped by the stalled vehicle and discovered the barrels when the rod he inserted into the load hit upon wood instead of hay. The agent parked his car as close to the truck as possible and waited until early morning. Then, he called his boss and requested additional help.

He and the second agent dug the snow away from the truck's

wheels and pulled their vehicles as close as possible. They didn't want the driver to hop in and speed away. The rumrunner never returned.

Alvin scored big with this appropriation. Fifteen barrels were hidden among the hay, each holding fifteen gallons of whiskey. Alvin did the math and came up with 225 gallons or 900 quarts or 1,800 pints.

Several weeks before this score, his counterpart, who had the Des Moines territory, relayed some shocking information. One case was now selling for $250.00. Eighteen cases had been smuggled into Des Moines, and before the agent could bust the driver and seize the liquor, all of it had been sold—in two hours. Prohibition had not stopped people from drinking; it had only driven up the price of it.

Truly did more math and figured the street value of what they impounded: $37,500. The maker of the whiskey certainly didn't get that much, and the seller in his area didn't get that much. Only the dealers in Des Moines were making that much. But whoever had money invested in what was now sitting in a federal government's warehouse was awfully angry at such a valuable loss.

As Alvin sat and thought about the money for the confiscated load, he became angry. The bootleggers made more money than the judges, the local and federal agents, or even himself—people who were all working day in and day out, trying to keep the country from falling into anarchy. The more Alvin allowed his brain to go into the whiskey barrel, so to speak, the more frustrated he became.

Truly had become especially troubled over Carroll County. His anonymous caller had reached out and relayed rumors of a large whiskey operation being run in that area. As with each of this individual's calls, the man did not know specifics, and he did not have any proof. In Truly's experience, small-town rumors generally had a few kernels of truth. According to his source, half the farmers in the area were hiding stills, and one man was running the show. Even if his intel was only partially true, it was enough to motivate the federal agent to divert more of his men to that area to start regularly patrolling the main roads.

The recent confiscation of the whiskey load had proved his instincts correct. Unfortunately, he did not have cuffs around any of the hands who had been involved in that truck being on the road in the middle of the night: the owner of the still, the one providing money for the supplies, the one loading the booze, or the one driving it to Des Moines—which is where he presumed it was heading.

If his men had been able to nab the driver, Truly felt certain he could have squeezed the information out of him. If there really was a boss or kingpin of some sort, he could narrow the possible man down to about ten. Individual men had been making this stuff since 1916. Only a few of them had the ability to put this syndicate of sorts together. The rest of the names were most likely part of the organization in some manner.

The number of men out there committing this crime brought him to his next thoughts, which were about Carroll County Sheriff Will Katz. How much did he really know? And did he know the name of the kingpin? Federal Agent Truly wished he could interrogate this lawman. He was sure Katz knew so much more than he was saying. Instead, every conversation was friendly but evasive.

Since Alvin couldn't interview the sheriff properly, then he would see what his reaction would be when he spoke to him about the abandoned truck.

Truly decided he needed to see the man's face when he gave him details. Every other time, the two had spoken only by telephone. Surprisingly, Alvin had only met Will Katz in person a few times.

The telephone conversations had always been initiated by Truly; the relationship began when he was sheriff of Audubon County. He called with information that had been passed along to him about illegal activity in Carroll County, and Will Katz sounded interested, thanked him, and then sat on it. As a federal agent, Alvin didn't speak nearly as often to Katz. He sat on his leads and informed the sheriff only when necessary. His one regret was his requirement to notify the county sheriff when he stepped onto his territory.

Alvin didn't know Will's true feelings about Prohibition. He had only assumed Will, like the rest of the lawmen, was in favor of enforcing it.

A week after they seized the truck and its contents, Alvin made a trip to Carroll to visit the sheriff in his office. He chose morning, knowing Will probably went to work early, as did most lawmen.

Alvin found the door to the sheriff's office unlocked, so he walked in, not bothering with a quick rap to announce his presence. Will's eyes widened, and his mouth opened just slightly. He was clearly shocked by the federal agent's presence.

"Good morning, Will. I was passing by your office this morning and thought I would stop by for a friendly chat. We haven't spoken much since my seizure of Weber's still. Hope you don't mind my dropping in on you this morning." Alvin could see Will was clearly bothered by his surprise visit.

Will was annoyed but tried to hide it as well as he could. Truly's downplaying the Weber murder into just a 'seizure' raised Will's hackles, but he decided to put forth his best face and see what the agent really wanted. "Gosh, no," he said. "It's always nice to speak with someone who knows the job. What's new? What brings you to our area?"

Alvin looked around Will's office. He spotted the picture of the blue jay and thought it was odd subject matter for a lawman. He would have expected an eagle or some bird of prey. Eagles represented power and nobility; blue jays seemed like a woman's bird. Alvin suddenly developed the opinion Will Katz was a weak man. "Thought I'd see if you had any information you could pass along to me. There always seems to be gossip about who's doing what. Have you heard any bits about the truck we found in Willey?"

Will's eyes flicked quickly to the left and then back center again. His opponent saw it. Every lawman knows the signs of lying, and Alvin was certain Will was about to tell him a big one.

"Heard it was out of Greene County. Apparently, some new operation started up in Jefferson. Heard there were multiple stills in one location." Will wanted nothing more than to send this man far away from his territory and himself.

"Jefferson? Then what in the hell was he doing in Willey? He was goin' the wrong way. That's the opposite way to Des Moines. Don't make no sense." Truly countered. Will Katz was glass, and Alvin Truly could see right through him. Will was trying to move him out of his county, and if he wanted him far away, it was because Will had a part in the operation. He was on the take. Or he was hiding illegal operations.

"Spose they were headed to Omaha," Will continued to lie.

"Probably right. I 'preciate your time, Will. Good to see you. Take care." He shook hands with the sheriff and left the office. Alvin didn't need to hear any more. He had everything he wanted.

Alvin Truly boiled with anger. He didn't understand how a man who had sworn to uphold the law could so callously help criminals break it. The law was black and white. One side of the line or the other. For Alvin, it was easy to know what to do. He followed the law. He stayed on the right side of the line. No temptation of money or friends or family could have changed that. When he laid his head on the pillow each night, he did so with a clear conscience. He wore his uniform with pride and felt worthy to step into it each day.

Alvin didn't understand Sheriff Katz. Will seemed like a good guy. Alvin had never known him to shy away from doing the right thing when it came to everything other than bootlegging. Will had arrested cattle thieves and vandals. He had put men in jail for stealing goods from businesses or their neighbors. Will had never seemed like a man who turned away from wrongdoing. And, because Prohibition was now a federal law, Will's avoidance of enforcing it was doubly wrong.

Alvin couldn't trust Will. If he shared information with him, it would only bring shame to Will's badge and ensure another criminal act would go unpunished. He would have to cut the man out of his circle. If only he didn't have to announce his presence.

If Alvin couldn't trust the man inside the county, then he'd have to get his own man. He needed a snitch, someone loyal to him alone.

He had no rapport with any of the Carroll County people. They were Will's people. He needed someone outside the area. But that brought another problem: they didn't trust strangers. Maybe he could bring a federal agent from another part of the state. The agent could learn how to make whiskey and get a job with one of the distillers, move up in the organization or at least find out the name of the kingpin. However, Alvin knew it wouldn't work: these bootleggers would sniff out a fraud. Federal agents had a certain look, a certain way they talked, and they didn't sound like a criminal. Even if there were a man who had family history in the whiskey business, Alvin couldn't trust him. He might want to protect those like his own family.

An idea dropped from the sky and hit him. He needed a criminal, someone who wasn't too far gone but also someone who was desperate. Snitching among thieves was the lowest of the low. This person needed to be selfish and afraid of prison. It had to be someone Alvin could control.

If this criminal were clever enough to get a job with a bootlegger, he would be asked about his background, and a real story with accurate details would pass the test. For the most part, he would not need to lie. He would only need to keep new details to himself.

Alvin felt certain he could find someone who fit his needs if he quietly kept his ear to the ground. He smiled to himself as he imagined rounding up these bootleggers along with their sheriff.

CHAPTER 14

Jimmy Krantz hated the odor of a jailcell. It smelled like urine and fear. He was no bride in this situation; he had been inside of one more than once in his life. "If you dance the Devil's dance," he liked to say, "you have to pay the Devil's price." It was big talk for someone who evaded the law like a coyote from an armed farmer.

Jimmy's life of crime started when he was seventeen, living in Lake View. On a warm, summer evening, Jimmy—full of his father's illegal whiskey—bragged to his friends he wasn't afraid to steal a car, so he hopped into his neighbor's Studebaker—the keys were under the seat—and took off around Black Hawk Lake. Trying to show off his driving skills, Jimmy drove the car onto a dock; however, his perception of space had never been very good, and the car was wider than the dock. The stolen vehicle's left front tire dropped over the side, leaving it dangling above the water. Jimmy abandoned the car and headed home, crawling into bed to sleep off his drunken evening.

The next morning Jimmy could hear his neighbor speaking to his father in the now-empty driveway. Immediately after the conversation, Jimmy's father strode into the house, pounded up the stairs, and yanked him from his cozy bed. There was no doubt in Mr. Krantz's mind who had stolen the car. Jimmy was to turn himself in to the local lawman and confess his crime. Instead of walking straight to the police, Jimmy ran away, never showing his face to his family or the residents of Lake View again. Since no lawman ever located him, Jimmy assumed his father had found a way to repair the car to save the family's good name.

After his escape, Jimmy made his way to Breda, a tiny town southeast of Lake View, and found a job on a farm. He hated farm work, but without any usable skills there was little choice except hard labor.

When he turned nineteen, Jimmy wanted a better life but had no way to get there. Instead of trying to learn a new skill, he entered local businesses and wrote checks on different accounts. He knew he would eventually be caught, but he planned to be far from Breda by the time the checks landed at the bank.

During his final foray, Jimmy strolled up to the counter, goods in hand, and asked for a counter check, always with the local bank and always signed by the name of a local citizen. This last check was written at Gaul's Lumber Company, using his employer's account and signed with the farmer's name. The young man working the counter was new on the job and didn't look at the signature; but the owner of the lumber company, Joshua Gaul, knew Jimmy's employer very well, recognized the forgery immediately, and alerted the sheriff.

This time, Jimmy did not slip away. The owner of the lumber company, a rather large and burly man, stood in front of the door, detaining Jimmy until the local police arrived. He spent several months in the Carroll County jail.

While there, his knowledge of illegal activities expanded. His cell mate, a small-time thief, stole whatever he could lay his hands on. Primarily, he pilfered from farms because their possessions were often out in the open. The goods were then taken to Woodbury

County or Polk County and sold in the cities. In his bunk at night, Jimmy listened to tales of close calls, of outrunning the local law, of large purchases bought with the profits from the stolen goods. His cellmate made himself the Iowa Robin Hood, except he held onto the money for his own selfish purposes. As he was regaled with humorous exploits, Jimmy pictured himself in the stories.

His cellmate took the young criminal under his wing and tutored him in farm theft. Never steal from a farm with a dog, always scout your location several days in advance, steal the largest vehicle possible so you don't limit yourself in how much of a haul you can make. Jimmy never questioned his new teacher's instructions while also never considering the thief's current predicament. Just exactly how good a burglar was he? The lessons were taught daily until Jimmy was released from jail in 1926.

Free from his confinement, Jimmy did not find the righteous path. He was too anxious to make his own stories. He had made a new friend and, as soon as his cellmate was released, a partner in crime. And for that, he was now sitting in jail once again.

Jimmy stuck around Carroll, taking on odd jobs, waiting for his partner's release; and when it happened, it did not take long for the two of them to start their new enterprise.

From Carroll, the two made their way to Harlan, Iowa, a decently sized town with loads of rich farmers. The two men planned a three-day spree. They would hit as many farms each night as they could. When they were finished, they would drive their stolen vehicle to Sioux City to sell their goods. Jimmy's partner had groomed a friendship with a farm implement dealer who sold used stock and didn't ask questions about the ownership of the items he purchased.

Jimmy and his cohort stole a truck from a farm in Manning and drove it to Harlan. They sat at the local café, ordered big lunches with pie and ice cream, and waited for nightfall. Their first night, they fleeced three farms, taking tools and small implements.

They did the same the second night, but their luck was overflowing when they came upon a whiskey still in one of the barns. Their exuberance took over as they danced around, hugged each other, and slapped one another on the back. They couldn't decide if they would sell the still to someone in Sioux City or if they would use it themselves to start their own whiskey-making operation.

The still had been recently fired up, and along with all its copper glory, thirty, one-gallon jugs of whiskey sat ready for distribution. The two thieves decided to celebrate their good fortune by toasting each other with the alcohol. They toasted their cleverness, their good fortune, their good health, their future wealth, and on and on. They toasted so much they could barely stand with only a few hours of night remaining.

After loading the small goods into the back of their truck, the bandits ran into a problem: they didn't have enough room in the truck for the jugs and the still along with all the other spoils of their nightly raid. Like children with a hand caught in a small jar while taking out a cookie, they neither wanted to leave the still and its contents nor leave their already-stolen loot. This created a dilemma. The men wanted the biggest haul possible, but their vehicle limited their goal. Instead of taking what they had safely stolen and going to Sioux City—leaving the still and liquor behind—they decided to steal the farmer's wagon to pull behind their truck.

With the wagon hitched securely to their vehicle, the men left the farm and headed west toward Harrison County. All their celebrating, though, had left them not only drunk but exceptionally tired. They hadn't gotten more than ten miles from the farm when sleep started to overtake them, so the thieves parked the truck and wagon behind a corncrib for a short nap.

Both men were caught with the wagon and other stolen items

when the owner of the property came upon it the next day. He was driving by a farm and saw his missing possessions stashed behind the corncrib. He reported his stolen goods to the Shelby County sheriff's office and parked, keeping an eye on the truck.

The sheriff confidently walked up to the truck, expecting to find it empty, but was surprised by the two men, mouths hanging open, dead to the world. He rapped on the window with no response. When he realized they were heavily asleep, he opened one of the truck's doors. Jimmy, who was leaning against his door, fell to the ground, only to open his eyes and see the sheriff of Shelby County standing over him.

This is how Jimmy came to be sitting in a jailcell again.

Jimmy's history with the law was not nearly as long as that of his partner, but he knew this event would bring him some quality time in prison rather than a county jailhouse. They had stolen thousands of dollars' worth as well as the three cases of whiskey. Not only had they broken one law, but they were also being charged with distribution of alcohol.

His new home was a 6' by 8' cell, located in the bowels of the Shelby County jailhouse. His lanky, six-foot, two-inch frame was uncomfortable on the cot; the mattress was so thin it had made sleeping unbearable the night before. He hadn't showered or shaved for four days and could smell his own odor through the jailcell perfume. Jimmy wasn't sure when breakfast would arrive, but he was hoping for some eggs, bacon, and coffee. Often these small jails were provisioned by the sheriff's wife or another local woman. He thought if the mattress had been better, he wouldn't mind staying in the county hotel awhile. He had no other abode, and he really appreciated home-cooked meals. It seemed he was the only resident lodging on the county's dime.

Jimmy's stomach complained when a bowl of thin oatmeal and

a glass of water were shoved through the bars. His head was foggy from the whiskey, and a strong cup of coffee was sorely needed. "Hey, would you be so kind as to provide me with a cup of java?" When no one responded, he yelled the request a little louder.

Another tall, lanky man in a uniform unlike those of his captors came down the hall and into the jail room. In his right hand was a large mug of steaming coffee. He stood in front of Jimmy's cell and handed him the brew. In his other hand he carried a short stool, which he placed in front of Jimmy's cell. "Son, you're in a barrel of trouble." Jimmy could tell he thought himself rather clever by using the stolen whiskey to make his metaphor. "You have any idea how many years in prison you're going to spend?" he asked in a serious tone. "The two of you are too stupid to even know what's ahead for you. Maybe ten years?" Jimmy didn't believe him. The lawman was working him by predicting a long prison sentence. Jimmy was thinking maybe a year or two for his crimes.

"What are you after?" Jimmy asked. "There's no way I'm spending ten years, so you must want something from me if you're trying to scare me. You want me to roll on my partner?"

"No, he's got his own mess, and we know all about it. But I do have an offer for you."

Jimmy had never learned to trust. No one in his life had ever given him the opportunity. He was angry his father had not lied to the neighbor for him. He was angry the farmer had not treated him more like son. And he certainly had no doubt his partner had already told his captors everything about him they wanted to know. From his view of the world, people earned your trust by protecting you, even if it meant lying or taking the blame. He did not understand that his own actions had never given anyone a reason to trust him. From Jimmy's perspective, it was Jimmy first and to hell with the rest of the world. "What's your offer?"

"You'll do six months in the county jail and then you go to work for me."

"Who are you? And what authority do you have to get me this deal?"

"My name's Alvin Truly, and I'm a federal agent. I will speak to the county attorney and make the deal for you. I'll have it written out and signed. You'll have a guarantee that when you're finished working for me, you're a free man."

"What do I have to do and for how long?" Jimmy asked suspiciously.

"Since you have such an interest in whiskey, you're going to work in the business. You will distill whiskey for an operation and report back to me. Simple."

Deciding to leave part of the job out of the discussion, Alvin made the deal sound effortless and quick. The agent would add the other part about helping him arrest and prosecute the kingpin to the written agreement. By the time the kid saw it, he would have already imagined his freedom. What's a few more details? Alvin thought. If the kid balked, Alvin would pressure him with additional charges and a longer sentence. He could make it sound like this young man would be serving a life sentence.

"A snitch? You want me to become a snitch for you and then I get let go?" Jimmy didn't have any reticence about becoming a snitch; the deal seemed too easy.

"That's it! The more you give me, the faster I can get convictions. Then you're free. Call it an incentive program."

Jimmy didn't like this man or his face or his smug tone. And he didn't trust any deal he was being offered, but he also had no desire to spend any time in prison. If he did take the deal, perhaps he could just slip away again after he served his six months. He could get the job with these bootleggers, save up some cash, and then hit the road—this time to another state. Someplace this slippery snake didn't have authority. Jimmy didn't know anything about federal laws crossing state lines. "You've got a deal as long as I get it on paper."

"Good choice, Jimmy. First you serve your six months. And we're going to give you a bit of an education. Instead of just knowing how to steal whiskey and drink it, we're going to teach you the fundamentals of making it. These whiskey makers will want a man with some skills. And you don't even know how to be a good thief, so I'm pretty sure they're not going to see much in you. Being able to make the product will put you higher in the organization. Maybe you'll even get your own still. You'll earn their trust, and that's when you get the information."

The thief and the lawman shook on the deal, both already figuring a way to weasel out of it.

As soon as the jail room door clicked shut, Jimmy heard a voice from deep inside the unit across from him. "Hey, you think I could get one of them deals?"

Jimmy's heart lurched in surprise. He stepped up to the bars of his cell and peered across into the voice's cell. He could see a form in the corner of the bottom bunk. If Alvin Truly had known another convict was nearby, he would never have discussed the details of their arrangement. Jimmy wondered if the county sheriff forgot about the other lodger, or had he been too lazy to move the man? No matter the reason, someone now knew Jimmy Krantz was a snitch for the Feds. "I don't know," Jimmy responded. "You want me to ask him to return?" Jimmy did his best to regulate his voice, not wanting to announce his shock.

"Naw. I was just teasin'. I got no reason to make a deal. I'll be out before long," the voice responded.

Jimmy was unsure if he should continue conversing or ignore his neighbor. The convict had a friendly voice, but that didn't mean he wouldn't use the intelligence he now had to get something for himself. Jimmy decided to act friendly, hoping to draw some information. "What are you in for? How long you got left?"

The voice came to the bars and peered across at Jimmy. "This time it was check forging. I been here for a few months. I don't mind, though. I got nowhere else to go. What's your name?" The criminal didn't ask Jimmy's crime because he knew all he needed through his eavesdropping.

Jimmy didn't want to give his name, but he also didn't want to appear unfriendly. "John Smith," he lied. "You?"

The man was pale with white hair and a large forehead. He had a small frame, barely reaching 5'5". "Lyle Lang," he said. "That's my daddy's and grandpa's names as well."

Over the next two weeks, Jimmy and Lyle pulled stools up to their cell bars and whiled away the hours comparing lives and getting to know each other. Jimmy was pleased to have some company but reticent in the beginning to share too many personal details. He eventually came to trust his new friend and unrolled the many layers of his young life, including his real identity. Both men were roughly the same age and came from western Iowa. Jimmy had an ideal childhood, but Lyle had been raised by his grandparents, having been abandoned by an alcoholic father and a dead mother.

Lyle reminded Jimmy of his previous cellmate. He was gregarious and liked the attention focused on himself. The convict had a suitcase full of stories, and he became animated while telling them, his eyes wide and his voice taking on the tone of his hero or heroine.

Lyle bragged about his creativity when it came to making money. He held no compunction in stealing from women, old people, or invalids. He sold children's dogs, stolen from their yards, to dogfighting rings. He bought sacks of sugar or barrels of flour and replaced half the product with sand and sold them to women in need of cheap groceries. He filled whiskey pints with water, coloring them with iodine, hocking them to old men as aged whiskey. As he told each tale, he laughed at his victims' naivete and ignorance, calling them 'rubes' or 'idiots.'

Jimmy felt uncomfortable as Lyle relayed his schemes and antics. Jimmy had no remorse about stealing from the Harlan farmer. In his mind, the farmers were all rich and could replace their pilfered items. The victims of Lyle's crimes were innocents, and Jimmy felt Lyle went too far in his desires for easy money. Even though he liked Lyle, he felt himself above him; Jimmy would never harm someone in a less fortunate situation.

When Lyle was released three weeks after meeting Jimmy, the two men shook hands and promised to keep an eye out for one another, vowing to become partners on the outside; but Jimmy did not plan to keep that promise. If he never saw Lyle Lang again, he would not feel as though he had lost a friend.

CHAPTER 15

Thinking about hopping a train on nearby railroad tracks, Jimmy Krantz stood on one side of Main Street, looking across at the door of the pool hall. He had served his six months and was now in the employ of Alvin Truly. He had come to hate that man. When the paperwork was put before him and he was encouraged to sign without reading—"We've already discussed the terms," Truly said— Jimmy felt certain he needed to read thoroughly, and he would not be rushed.

Jimmy's reading skills had never been good, but he made himself sit and digest the complicated document until he thought he understood it. Truly had paced behind him, trying to intimidate him into giving up and putting his signature on the paper.

Jimmy was sure one part of the agreement had not been discussed. He was to get himself into the bootlegging syndicate (he didn't know what that word meant) and collect evidence on its kingpin. Then, he would be in Truly's service until the end of the trial in which he would be required to testify. That bastard, Jimmy thought, I knew he was going to try and cheat me somehow.

When Jimmy questioned Truly and stated he would not fulfill the final paragraph, Truly threatened him with more charges: evading an officer, use of a deadly weapon, a plot to kidnap. Jimmy knew a jury would believe a federal agent far quicker than a man with a record. He understood he was trapped, so he signed the document.

Jimmy had no intention of testifying against some man he didn't know. He would help make whiskey until he had enough pay to get him out of the state and into a new life, and to hell with Alvin Truly.

After being released from jail, Jimmy was on his own with a few ideas of how to get into the syndicate. He was pointed toward the pool halls and small-time backroom bars. He just needed to spread the seeds and see what grew from them.

Jimmy didn't have to spread those seeds too far when some of them took off and grew. His first stop, Kisgen's pool hall on Carroll's Main Street, opened the door to the world of whiskey.

The dim interior led into a long room, windowless but lit by a single light hanging over each of the three pool tables and a light behind the bar. The three tables stood on an oak floor, ample space around each. Thick square columns held up the ceiling but also served to create a separate space between each table. A long bar, also made of oak, ran down the side of the building, its once-filled bottles now standing like dead sentinels. The barman kept his post but now filled old beer glasses with cola or limeade. Once the drinks left the bar area, gin and whiskey were added. Some men skipped the non-alcoholic beverages and drank straight from their flasks, using their hats to cover their sins.

Jimmy entered this world quietly and preferred to watch a few games from the safety of a bar stool pulled close to a column. Most of the men playing were doing so for sizable sums of money. Jimmy's nickel would get him no games. He wasn't interested any-way; he had never been adept at anything with a ball.

After enjoying a few games, a stranger joined him, leaning against the column instead of pulling up a chair. Jimmy decided it was time to get to work. "Have you put your money on the table?" he asked the stranger.

"Naw. I just come to watch the experts and maybe pick up on any town news. You?"

"Me neither," Jimmy responded. "I've been awful thirsty lately. Haven't had me a good drink in months. You know anyone who might be able to sell me something to wet my throat?" He knew the stranger would recognize this ridiculous banter of thirst for his desire to drink something illegal.

"See that guy sitting at the bar? You tell him what you told me. I'm not saying he's sellin' anything, but he might know a guy who knows a guy." The stranger walked away from him and settled on another column, on the far side of the pool hall.

Jimmy did as he was told. He sat down next to the man at the bar and said he wanted to buy a decent drink, maybe even more than one drink. Did the man know anyone who could help him out?

"Why don't you leave your money with me," he said. "And I'll see if I can find the guy who can help you. It'll be $5.00."

"How am I going to get my drink?" Jimmy asked skeptically. He thought this guy was taking him for a ride. It wasn't his money he was gambling with. Alvin Truly set him up with enough money to buy liquor if he thought he could get to the kingpin. Jimmy didn't know if this man was in the operation or knew the kingpin, but he had to start somewhere."

"You know where Templeton is? There's a cemetery on the west side of town, the Catholic church's cemetery. Not too far into it, you'll see Father Schulte's grave marker. It's tall with a chalice on the front. Just go round back of the marker, and you'll see a place to open it. Your beverage will be inside." He didn't wait for Jimmy's response. He took the outstretched five-dollar bill and walked away. The last Jimmy saw of him was his back lit by the light of day as he walked through the pool hall door.

Had he just handed over a considerable sum of money to a crook? The directions sounded far-fetched. Perhaps he had just been directed to a turkey chase? Panic bubbled up in his throat.

His most immediate problem was how to get to Templeton from Carroll. Jimmy didn't own a vehicle, and Alvin Truly had denied him one when he asked. Jimmy looked around the hall, figuring someone would be headed that way. He decided to stay put and watch pool. Maybe something would come up while he was waiting.

Jimmy watched men win games, lose games, add liquor to their drinks, tell stories, trade gossip. The pool hall, like the barber shop or feed store, was another place for men to bond with one another and display their less-than-noble characteristics.

After a few hours, Jimmy finally found someone who was headed in that direction. He was let off in front of Templeton's pool hall, which wasn't far from the land of the dead.

Coming into the cemetery, Jimmy was greeted by a monument area for those buried beneath its groomed, green grass. One had to choose either right or left to go around the tribute. To the right was Jimmy's path, and he didn't go far before he saw Father Shulte's marker. He must have been well loved, thought Jimmy, as he looked at the dark, grey stone, its height taller than himself. In the center was carved a chalice with IHS, denoting the first three letters of Jesus' name when written in Greek. Ironically, the monument reminded Jimmy of a woman: wide on the bottom, slender in the center, and wide on top. A large cross with a crucified Christ sat atop the marker.

Jimmy slipped around back of the granite and found the small door in the center. Instead of the priest's name and information, the embedded tablet had the name Elizabeth Shulte, b. 1815, d. 1887.

Obviously, this was a family stone, rather than just the priest's stone, Jimmy realized.

Jimmy carefully removed Elizabeth's panel and, putting his hand into the cavern, found a bottle of whiskey. He danced around in excitement and kissed the bottle.

After settling back into a respectable repose, Jimmy read the bottom of Elizabeth's tablet and saw *RIP*. She surely was not resting in peace, he thought. How much booze had been hidden here? How many men had shoved their hands into the cavern and drawn out the drink? He was no Catholic, so it didn't bother him to disturb a Catholic priest's marker, but he did feel a little sorry for the mother. Jimmy neatly fitted the tablet back into its spot and headed for a telephone. He would call Alvin Truly and give him the whiskey. The job was done. His contract completed, Jimmy could then go wherever he pleased. He felt light and giddy. It had been much easier than he thought. The feeling of freedom washed over him and settled into his soul. Even the air seemed to smell sweeter.

Alvin Truly was sitting at his desk when the phone rang. He had said no more than "Truly here" when an excited voice replied.

"I've got him!"

"Who is this?" Truly asked in a gruff and irritated tone.

"Jimmy Krantz. I've got the man for you!" he whispered into Alvin's ear.

"What man? Tell me everything!" Alvin couldn't believe it had been that easy to find the kingpin and get the goods on him.

Jimmy told his story, including the booze being hidden inside a grave marker. "When can I meet you to give you the hooch?" Jimmy asked.

"Let me get this straight," Alvin said, ignoring Jimmy's question. "You met two men in a pool hall. Neither one of them gave you their name. You handed over my money and picked up a quart of whiskey.

What am I supposed to do with a quart of whiskey? Arrest *you* for possession of alcohol?" Alvin's voice had grown in its volume, and his face had taken on a deep red. "That does me no good! Unless you have the man's name, I can't make any arrests. And you don't even know if you bought from the syndicate!"

Jimmy sat silent on the other end of the line. He had been so proud of himself and had smelled and tasted his freedom.

"You go back to that pool hall since it clearly is a place doing illegal business and find me the kingpin. And don't buy another drop of alcohol unless you have the man's real name. In fact, until you have him with gallons of alcohol, don't bother contacting me again."

Alvin abruptly cut off the communication and left Jimmy holding a silent earpiece. "Sonofabitch," Jimmy said to no one and hung up the receiver. He felt the whiskey tucked into his waistband, hidden under his shirt. "Guess I'll put this to good use," he said, patting the hidden bottle.

Jimmy liked the look of Templeton. It was smaller than Carroll, which also made it easier to get from one destination to another. He figured one pool hall was as good as the next, and the seller of the whiskey had directed him to this town, which probably meant the maker of the whiskey lived here.

Jimmy spent the rest of the week in that hall, improving his game with the many hours he hung around the tables, introducing himself and getting to know the locals. Even while he was playing, he kept one eye on the door, waiting for the return of the whiskey seller. He hoped the supplier would recognize him. Jimmy had a whole conversation laid out in his head, which included asking for a job.

On Monday of the second week, just as Jimmy was folded over the table, focusing on the cue ball, the bootlegger walked into the hall and sat at another defunct bar. Jimmy's heartbeat picked up, but he made himself focus on his game, knowing the guy would sit for some time before leaving.

Allowing himself to lose, just so he could finish it faster and get over to the supplier, Jimmy dropped his stick into the communal holder and headed to the bar. He leaned against it and asked for a root beer. He sat drinking without comment. Just as he took a breath to expel his opening line, he heard, "How'd you like your purchase? You want more?"

Jimmy didn't know how to respond, flustered from having to change his practiced conversation. With a few seconds of silence, Jimmy ditched his canned talk and answered off the fly. "I did. Best hooch I've had. You make that?" He held his breath, knowing he had asked a dangerous question.

"I might be able to get you more," the bootlegger replied without looking at Jimmy or answering his question.

This was Jimmy's opening. "Wish I could. Need a job first. Know anybody in the business who needs a good man? I work hard, and I know the process."

"That so? And how you come about that learnin'?"

Careful, Jimmy thought. Be somewhat vague. Even though Jimmy had grown up away from Templeton, that didn't mean somebody didn't know somebody from his area. After all, Iowans can usually make some kind of connection during a conversation.

"My grandpa had a hired man who cooked. I learned from him. He moved out of state before I could get real good myself, but I still got what knowledge he taught." Jimmy hoped the story was believable but untraceable.

The bootlegger finally looked him eye to eye. "Hmm. I might know somebody. I didn't catch your name," he said in a voice that just turned from suspicious to friendly.

"Jimmy Krantz. Grew up in Lake View." Jimmy added his hometown because this time he hoped the stranger would check him out. He would find out Jimmy's disgrace, which would give credence to his character.

The man grinned and held out his hand. "Skeet," he said. "You come back here tomorrow, and I'll let you know if I found anything. In the meantime, you go back and visit Father Schulte." Again, without waiting for a response, Skeet slid off his stool and headed out the door.

Jimmy didn't know if he had struck gold or lead. This time, he wasn't reporting to Alvin Truly. He didn't need another verbal whipping. He would keep to himself until he had enough to make Alvin dance. Or maybe he wouldn't. He didn't know this Skeet fella, but he liked him right away. He hadn't even asked for another five dollars.

CHAPTER 16

My frustration with Earl Miller had come to two-hundred degrees, the distilling point. Not only was he keeping details to himself, but he also just couldn't seem to give up his old habits. He was selling booze, which meant he was putting himself in danger and, thereby, putting me in danger. If he got pinched, and the Regulators had enough on him, he'd give me up to save his own back side. I added it to the discussion topics for our meeting as I sat in my truck, idling outside of Earl's house.

I mentally went through my list. It wasn't long, but the items were important to me. Not sure they were ever important to Earl. He had his own items of importance, and they rarely involved bookkeeping matters.

Sometimes he was like a bull running for the fence. Once he got going, it was hard to stop him. And I could truly see a taste of power only makes a man want the whole meal.

Earl slid into the cab and sat beside me. "You know, I don't have a lot of time. These meetings of yours eat up what precious little I got."

I could sense he was in a foul mood. Earl always smelled of whiskey, which made sense because he was still cooking. His clothing and skin would often smell, but I caught some of it coming from his mouth, which meant he was owly because he was hung over.

Earl suffered through the numbers: product in, product out. Money made, money spent. I could tell he was barely listening and didn't ask any questions or add any comments to make the meeting end as soon as possible.

"I want to talk about transportation," I said. "I'm concerned about that lost load. Our Des Moines contact wants to know exactly when he will get a replacement. It's selling fast, and he still has obligations to fulfill. In short, he wants much more as fast as we can give it to him."

Earl sighed heavily. I could tell I hit a touchy spot with him. "Unless you can come up with another way to ship this stuff, we're going to lose loads. We can't take the main roads because the Regulators watch them like hawks. Now, one of our backroads is busted. The farther out we travel from point A to point B, the longer it takes us. The longer we're on the road, the more dangerous it becomes."

He was right. He knew this part of the business better than I did. But I had been thinking on some ideas. "Let's have a talk with Sheriff Katz and see if he can get more information about the Feds and their movements. That may help. What if we shipped it by train?"

"Train? You want to load barrels on the train? Sure! We'll just heft each 220 pound barrel into an enclosed car and send them off. It shouldn't take more than a small mob of men to get the job done. I'm sure we won't be caught!"

I didn't care for his sarcastic tone. I wasn't an idiot. "Of course not! We ship them inside something on the train." I gave him a smug look.

"Like what?" he asked with disbelief and a pinch of anger.

"Coffins. Except we're not going to ship barrels. We'll ship bot-

tles. The coffins are going from Omaha to Des Moines. They'll stop here at night, and we'll load them. The Des Moines people will unload them into their warehouse, remove the booze, and deliver the coffins to their rightful owners."

"This'll never work. There are too many people involved. The coffin makers have to agree, and the coffin buyers will have to agree. You're talking about getting coffin makers and undertakers to help transport booze. They're not the sort of people who break the law. Our coffin guys are a different sort. One of 'em's family brewed beer from the time they could get their brew kettle set up. He don't agree with the law."

"It's already done. I don't need the Omaha coffin maker to be involved. We have a connection to the train engineer. He'll stop the train and give us time to load the booze into the coffins and then divert it to the right set of tracks once it gets into Des Moines. The Des Moines undertaker has already agreed to wait an extra day for his load. It just took a little monetary incentive."

Earl's mouth was open for so long, I was worried a fly might land on his tongue. He clearly was impressed by my organization and connections. Perhaps this was just the thing to get him in line a little more. I was not just some small-time, dumb bootlegger. I was a force.

"By the way," I continued on a different path, "I'm aware you are selling. Part of our deal included your stepping back from the retail side of the business. You are a manager now. It isn't fitting you should be selling booze on the side of the street. We have people for that. And realistically, if you get caught, this whole operation goes down with you. And for what? A few pints of whiskey? For five dollars? It's beneath you. The boss doesn't sell the product."

I hit something when I said it was beneath him. I had heard enough through the gossip chain to know he was enjoying being the 'boss' of the organization.

"How are our current distillers?" I continued. "Have you picked up any new ones? How much do we have in the basement of the church?" I hated to pummel him with questions, but he hadn't been forthcoming with details. I feared losing control of what I started. If he began his own business, offering the farmers and workers the same deal—or even a better one—there would be nothing I could do about it. This whole empire I was building could come down around my ears as quickly as a snap of my fingers. Up to this point, Earl had been busy getting all the pieces in place, but he would eventually have enough time to start thinking about making money on his own. Keeping him busy would be the answer to my fears.

"We have twelve distillers," he said. "I'm close to adding three more. We currently have…" Earl started adding on his fingers, his brain whirling with figures and people. "We have 115 barrels in the basement, which is 1,725 gallons minus the angel's share. Next year that number drops to 1,425 gallons and then less the following year. The basement is full."

"Are they stacked or single barrel standing? If they aren't stacked, we can build a system so that they can go two high." I could tell by his face he hadn't thought about a different stacking system. I had my answer. It would be difficult to get the barrels, now full of liquid, up on a second level, but I had already thought of a ramp system to roll them up.

"Just how much whiskey you planning to produce?" I could hear condescension dripping from his tone.

"I want forty locations distilling full time." I hadn't thought about his question. So I plucked forty out of the air. That would keep him busy for quite a while.

His face turned red. I couldn't determine if he was angry or confused. "Forty! What 'n the hell you need forty stills runnin' at the same time for? Where are we gonna get rid of that much whiskey?

And how you plannin' to buy supplies for all of that? Not to mention storage. I think you just busted a cog in your brain."

"One still at a time, Earl. You worry about getting them up and running, and I'll worry about the rest of the details. I have some ideas."

I didn't really have any ideas, but I was confident in my abilities. I could handle forty stills. Perhaps my Des Moines connection wanted to grow. I could reach out to Omaha, Sioux City, even Chicago. Our whiskey was good enough to go anywhere. Once customers outside of Carroll County gave our liquid gold a try, they would be ours forever. I imagined Templeton's rye whiskey on the lips and tongues of everyone in the Midwest. We just had to make enough and ship enough to make my vision a reality.

CHAPTER 17

A young boy, maybe eleven or twelve, walked into Sheriff Katz's office and handed him a note. "Meet me in the Templeton cemetery today at 3:00." There was no signature or indication of who had sent the note. "Do you know who gave this to you?" Will asked the boy still standing in front of his desk.

"Dunno," he shrugged. "Just some old guy in a blue jacket." He stood looking at Will until the sheriff reached into his pocket and handed him a penny.

Alone again, Will reread the note. He didn't recognize the handwriting. The sender assumed Will would be able to make it to Templeton to meet him at 3:00. What if he had other duties? What if he were busy at 3:00? What if he just plain didn't want to go? The temerity of the note ruffled Will's pride a bit.

However, none of this line of thinking gave him any further information. If he wanted to know the writer of the note, he would have to make the sixteen-mile trip. At first Will was somewhat obdurate in the face of the demand; it wasn't even a request to meet. As a man who liked to see the good in every situation, however, he decided the trip would be an excuse to get out of his office. He also hadn't been in that part of his county for some time. The spring day was looking to warm up some. Why not? Will thought.

Will drove south on Iowa 202. This part of the state hosted pleasant rolling hills, with stretches of farmland snugged up against the road on both sides. Iowa had some of the richest land in the country.

A strong breeze from the south warmed the air and blew debris into the ditches and down the road. Some farmers strung barbed wire around their fields, which caught garbage thrown from car windows. Other farmers had free entry into their fields from the road. If cows broke through their encampments, they would beeline straight for the tall stalks of green corn, tender plants of beans, or the appealing heads of rye.

That would not be for a few months, though. Now, melted snow created sodden ground that squished with every step, caking vehicles and shoes. Farmers out feeding cattle in the yards slogged through, up to their knees in cow muck and dirt. Late March of 1929 could bring spring rains or leftover winter storms. Iowa temperatures could drop forty degrees in a few hours.

Will came into Templeton and drove through town, turning onto the road that led to the cemetery. He didn't see another car parked within the grounds. Whoever was meeting him had parked somewhere else. Will drove up to the memorial and turned right, wanting to appear as if he were visiting someone. He exited his truck and stood next to it, lighting a cigarette and enjoying the warm day while he waited.

He hadn't even finished his smoke before he heard a voice behind him. "Thanks for coming, Will." The sheriff knew the voice and was relieved to hear a friend. He turned around.

"Skeet, good to see you. I owe you one for getting me out of the office on such a glorious day. What am I doing in the cemetery?"

"Mind if we sit in your truck? Don't want any Regulators to see you talking to me. Maybe even take a short drive?" Skeet was as jumpy as a flea.

Instead of answering, Will folded himself back into his truck while Skeet took the other side of the bench seat. "Anywhere in particular?" he asked.

"Just out of town. I'll let you choose," Skeet replied.

Neither man talked while Will continued his southern path, out of town and into the hilly farmland. They drove a few miles before Skeet finally made the first comment. "Nice day, ain't it? Those farmers'll be in the field before long."

"Suppose so," Will replied, waiting for his guest to bring the conversation to the meat.

"How much does that federal deputy tell you about their plans?" Skeet asked, diving into the purpose of the meeting.

"Not much," Will replied. "But he does have to notify me if they come into my county. Can't have plain-clothes men and cars pulling out guns without my knowing who they are. Good way to get shot. Why? What do you need?"

"Don't know if you heard, but we lost a pretty big haul in Willey a while back. It's nearly impossible to get a load from here to Des Moines. Them Regulators is all over the roads. It's like gittin' ticks off a dog." Skeet took off his hat, a homburg, and put it over his knee. "We need some help, or we're gonna have thousands of gallons of liquor sittin' inside this county with nowhere to go. We don't have that kinda storage. Anything you can do?"

Will sat on the question for a few minutes. He didn't know which roads they were watching, but he did know when they were around. The runners could at least get safely out of his county. The rest of the way would be their problem. "I can tell you when they're coming and when they're leaving," he said. You'll know when to stay put and when to go. But that's about the best I can do. If I hear something, I'll alert you," he offered.

"'Preciate it, Sheriff. Every little bit helps." Skeet felt a little of the weight lifting from his shoulders. Maybe between the sheriff's help and the railroad, they could get the product to its destination. "By and by," he said, "we're gonna start using the railroad to ship. If you see a truck unloading near a train car, just keep driving." Skeet could see a question coming to the lawman's face. "Better if you don't ask questions," he continued. "It would only make you more of an accessory."

"I do have a relevant question," Will said. "How am I to notify you when they come into the county? You don't stay home much, and there's no telling where you'll be."

Skeet thought a bit. Will had a point; it was hard getting ahold of him. "The pool hall," he said. "Ask Joey to turn on the outside light. He's always there, and he has a telephone. You can make the call from your office without needing to come to Templeton. When the Feds are gone, call again, and Joey'll turn off the light."

"You drive by the pool hall every day?" Will asked.

"No, but I got enough of my guys who do. They'll get the word to me. It'll also help our setters—the guys who do our cookin.' We'll know to go underground when the Feds are in the county." Skeet's face broke into a big grin. "I got to ask you a question," Skeet continued. "How come you helpin' us? You're the law and all. Shouldn't you be puttin' the cuffs on us?"

Of course, Skeet wanted to know his motives. It wasn't a complicated question, but Will had a complicated answer. Up to this point, he had only turned his back when he had been given information about the whiskey business. He had an idea of who cooked, who ran the booze, and who was buying. Today, he had crossed the Rubicon, and there was no turning back. He took a deep breath and released it before he answered.

"I saw more death and debauchery than you can imagine when I was in France," he started, his voice soft and low as his mind's eye replayed the horrors of war. "I saw dead bodies, missing limbs and heads. I saw men looting corpses, young girls offering themselves up for food. Women and girls being raped. These are crimes, crimes against humanity. Drinking liquor doesn't even begin to compare. Most of these folks are making it to feed their families. And I can't blame a man for wanting to forget his troubles with a swig or two. As long as he's not harming anyone by doing it, I don't see a crime here. I swore to uphold the law; that's true. And I've been doing it since the day I raised my hand and spoke the words, but times have changed. I swore to protect my fellow man, too, and looking the other way feels like I'm doing that. I'm keeping families together and children fed. Who's to say a law is right and just? Man? Or God? Even Jesus drank wine. The Bible doesn't say liquor is a sin. And I put the Bible above the law of man. Besides, I got a few family members who not only enjoy it, but make it."

Skeet's eyes widened. He didn't know Will Katz very well, but he found a new level of respect for the man. "Which of your family is cookin'?" he asked.

"I'll keep that to myself. They don't live in Templeton. I do have another question," Will said, looking up from his hands to stare straight into Skeet's eyes. "I heard there's a boss running a multi-still operation. Word come to me it's you. Is that true?"

Skeet had never acknowledged his role in the operation before. He let people think what they wanted. Since this man had bared his soul to him, Skeet felt like he owed the truth. "As long as I can get your word that nothing leaves this truck, I'll tell you the truth.

Will nodded his head in agreement.

"It's true about the operation. We've got about sixteen cookin' sites. Some with one still; some with two. And I'm the manager of the operation. Everyone thinks I'm the boss, the kingpin; but I ain't. There's one above me, and I'm sworn to never speak the name. As far as you're concerned, I'm the boss."

Skeet felt good about admitting his role. Even though he enjoyed being pseudo-boss, a piece of him always felt not quite right. It was like getting an A on a test when you knew you had cheated.

"Fair enough," Will said. "Will you keep me informed of your doings? I can't help you if I don't know the operation. If information comes to me about a particular bust, then I can signal the farmer. I'll need to know if he'll be notified by the light or if I need to make a trip to his farm."

The two men shook hands, both feeling good about their arrangement. Will was now on the other side of the Rubicon, but he didn't mind in the least.

CHAPTER 18

Finn Vries shook his head in disgust: his town's lawlessness seemed never to abate. The new year, 1929, had brought more liquor, not less. The new federal agent had done his best to squash the illegal trade, but it was like filling gopher holes. One would get shut down, but another one would appear. Finn knew the man needed help and had done what he could to give it to him.

The first time Finn had reached out to the agent and reported on his fellow Templetonian was shortly after Alvin Truly took the badge. The lawman had been appreciative of his information and encouraged him to report anything he saw or heard. Finn had done just that. He had reported the information he had gleaned about the large operation running out of his town.

However, the Wets had known Finn was a Dry. They did not speak openly about illegal activities if he was within listening distance. Finn was keenly cognizant of quiet hushings when he walked around a group of men. He could only report what he suspected rather than what he knew. And none of what he reported seemed to shut the bootleggers down.

That included his stepbrother, John Krupp. After his arrest, the man went right back to his illegal activities. Now, however, he was more careful.

Finn was certain John continued his illegal enterprise because his children wore new school clothes, and John had been into the jewelry store at Christmas time and purchased a locket for Betsy. He had paid in five-dollar bills.

John hadn't walked more than a few feet away from the jewelry store before Finn was calling Alvin Truly to report the purchase. Instead of his usual appreciation, Truly had seemed angry with the call. Finn thought perhaps it had more to do with the subject of the call rather than the caller himself.

February was always a slow time of year for the businessmen. Customers had spent their hoarded cash in December. Finn couldn't complain about his Christmas sales, especially in a depressed economy.

He spent each lonely day in his store, removing his merchandise, counting each piece, and cleaning the insides of his jewelry cases. Finn enjoyed the work. Putting the store right and proper made him feel like the world itself could be made so as well.

While he was down on his knees, cleaning the bottom shelf of his front case, Finn heard the tinkling of his doorbell. He could see a man's pair of black brogues walking toward his counter. Finn sprung up from his position, unconsciously straightened his tie and smoothed back his hair. A customer on this bitter February day was quite a surprise.

"Welcome, sir," Finn said with enthusiasm. "Is there something special you're looking for?"

The male customer did not respond right away but investigated the front case.

"Perhaps I can help you find something?" Finn was undeterred by the man's silence. "Something special for an anniversary or Valentine's

Day?" he continued. Silence from a customer always made Finn a bit nervous.

Finally, the man looked up at him, smiled, and looked back into the case. Without looking up again, he said, "I'm not sure what I want. I'm just checking out your merchandise."

Relieved to hear a friendly signal, Finn said, "Take your time. Let me know if you would like me to remove anything from the cases." Finn stood sentry-like.

The customer continued to browse, walking around the square of cases with Finn standing in the middle of them. While he was browsing the ropes of pearls, he spoke without giving any eye contact. "This town sure has a bad reputation."

Finn didn't know this man. He certainly wasn't a local or someone from Manning. He didn't attend Finn's church. Before he considered whether this person was a Wet or a Dry, Finn's gut pushed the words out of his mouth, "Unfortunately, so. Yes."

Finn was relieved by the lack of comment. The stranger continued to look at the merchandise, walking around each case, making a wide circle around Finn like a shark. When he finished the last case, before moving to the shelf displays of what-nots, he looked up at Finn and said, "It's a shame, don't you think?"

Finn's discomfort with the quiet had made him forget the man's previous statement. He asked, "What's a shame?"

"The reputation of this town. You have a nice store here. It's a shame this town is known for open crime. Certainly it affects your business." He continued to stare at Finn, no longer seeming interested in the store's contents.

Finn was in an uncomfortable spot again. As a business owner, Finn remained neutral on all subjects lest he offend a potential buyer. There was never any talk of politics, religion, money, or even sports. Finn spoke of only one topic, the weather. And even then, he had no preference for one season or another. It was only in the safety of his home where he spoke his mind.

"Any business is business," Finn replied as vaguely as possible. He knew the response hadn't matched the man's comment.

"If I were you, I would be furious about what's going on around here," the stranger said, sweeping his hand around him, indicating the outside. "A decent Christian man ought not to have to live in this debauchery." His voice had risen and clearly displayed his passion for the subject.

Stepping just one foot outside of his imposed entrepreneurial vault, Finn replied with little tone in his voice. "It can be difficult, yes."

"Difficult?" his customer asked in a shocked tone. "I'd say it was downright hell—excuse my French. I don't know how you all live here!"

His vault door now wide open, Finn's feelings rushed out of his mouth. "I have to admit I am enraged by the whole situation. I feel like an island in a sea of liquor and animals who love to swim in it. I have no choice but to live here with my business. I do what I can. I'm the lone Protestant among these beer-drinking Catholics. I've heard their priest even defies the law!" It felt good to speak his mind even if he still held back about his anonymous calls to law enforcement.

"I feel for you, pal. I know what it feels like to be the only one who cares. That's why I joined a group of fellas who share my feelings. It isn't right to break the laws. If we all did it, we would have anarchy on our hands. As a patriot, we must obey and support our government." This new compatriot was red in the face and fired up.

Finn felt the vault not only open, but he was brave enough to step through it. He had only spoken his true feelings to his wife. She agreed with him, but it wasn't the same feeling he got from being among other men who thought like he did. "I had never planned to stay here," he stated. "I've been around these people most of my life. Along with breaking the law, let's not forget they're un-American! Our boys spent years fighting and dying against the Germans. I know most of these people didn't fight against us, but they may have been spies. At the very least, you know they were pro-German! I don't understand why they were allowed to stay in this country when men were dying, fighting their Kaiser!" Finn's own face was now red, and he had unknowingly been banging his fist on his jewelry case to punctuate each thought, creating prints he would have to clean later.

The stranger's face was beaming with pleasure. He reached out his hand and introduced himself. "I'm Bill Andersen," he said. "Pleased to meet a man who sees things the right way. These Fishes are a menace to our country. And they're traitors!"

It took Finn a second to understand the fish moniker's meaning. Catholics ate fish on Fridays. He liked that term and would start using it himself. "Where you from, Bill? I don't recognize you."

"Brayburn," he said. "It's on the edge of Audubon County. You heard of it?"

Finn hadn't. He knew that area was Danish country rather than German. And they were Protestant. "You said something about fellas you meet with? What's that all about? Friends of yours?" Finn could feel excitement rising. He had never fit in with those around him. To have compatriots who were like-minded would be a relief. He could be himself, say what he wanted.

Bill replied, "Sure. We meet once a month. One of our members has a barn we use. There's about forty of us, I suppose. We drink coffee, talk politics, and plan some community events. We always welcome new members. Our next meeting is in March if the weather holds. You're welcome to come!"

Bill gave Finn the location details. They shook hands, and he exited the store. After he left, Finn realized his new associate hadn't purchased anything. Finn found that unusual considering men didn't browse, especially in jewelry stores. They came with a purpose and left as soon as possible.

Finn didn't say anything to his wife about his new friend, Bill. He wasn't sure why because he shared everything with her. Perhaps he wanted to enjoy this new acquaintance without her asking questions he didn't have the answers to: What does he do? What is his wife's name? Do they have children? Or maybe something was itching him a bit, and he didn't want to scratch and find out what it was.

The day of the meeting, Finn had difficulty keeping his mind on his business. Fortunately, March sales were little better than January or February, so time strung along. However, Finn could not keep himself busy enough to make it pass any more quickly. He checked the clock often, waiting for closing time.

Once home, Finn changed from his best suit to his second-best suit, leaving off the jacket for a less formal occasion.

Coming into the kitchen, his wife turned around from the stove, surprised her husband wasn't wearing his everyday clothing. "Are you going somewhere?" she asked in surprise.

"I've been invited to a men's meeting. I met a nice gentleman at the store, and he invited me. These men seem to be more like me. I don't know anything else about them, but I thought I would go this one time and see if I like it," he declared.

Before she could ask him questions, he gave her a quick peck on the cheek and left the house. In his excitement, Finn forgot to eat supper or bring a sandwich with him. And, because it was a men's meeting, he did not think there would be any treats.

Cars and trucks filled the farmyard, were parked on the side of the lane, and trailed down the edge of the gravel road. Counting the number of vehicles, Finn deduced nearly all forty members were already in the barn.

The large barn sat away from a small, white house, which was completely dark. A corncrib sat off from the barn, but other than the three buildings, the farm sat empty. Finn wondered if the place was an abandoned farm.

He glanced quickly at his pocket watch, worrying he was terribly late. He wasn't; he was twenty minutes early. Finn hated being late for anything. In his book, punctuality was actually tardiness. Arriving early, by at least twenty minutes, was being on time. Flustered by his confusion, he replayed the conversation in the jewelry store again. He thought he remembered the correct time. Finn prided himself in his fastidiousness regarding details. He double-timed it to the barn and found an entrance on the south side.

Finn opened the barn's side door, poking only his head into the building. Blocked by a large stack of hay, he couldn't see anything other than some old farming equipment, but he could hear men speaking. Finn wanted to go unnoticed, but the setup of the barn would make that impossible. Nevertheless, he took a breath, stepped through the door, and closed it without sound. Coming around the hay, Finn came to a large, open area set up with rows of haybales. Finn kept his eyes pointed at the barn floor and quietly found an empty bale and sat down. He looked around.

All except a few of the occupants were wearing white robes.

Finn may not have been knowledgeable of illegal activities happening right under his nose, but he was not so naïve he didn't recognize the Ku Klux Klan when he saw them. He realized he had been invited to a Klan meeting.

Instantly, fear settled through his body. He had heard of Klan happenings in the South on the radio. They were a violent group. They killed people.

Finn wanted to retrace his steps, walk back through the door, and drive home. He wanted nothing to do with killing. However, he didn't feel like he could leave as soon as he had come. These men might target him, and who knew what they may do.

As he sat waiting for an opportunity, one in which he could make his exit, Bill Andersen stood up and addressed the group. "Brothers, I would like to introduce my guest." Bill turned toward Finn, and so did every pair of eyes. "This is Finn Vries. He lives in Templeton."

When Bill said the word *Templeton*, Finn could hear the gasps. He felt both annoyed and ashamed simultaneously.

"I've invited Finn," Bill continued, "because he's on the front line. He lives among our enemies. We can support our new brother. Welcome Brother Finn." Men around him clapped him on the back. Others nodded their support.

With so much attention and support given to him, Finn could not sneak out the door. He had to stay, which is probably why he had been given the late time. Had he arrived before the meeting started, he might have left immediately, able to slip out without much attention. This way, he was somewhat locked into the meeting. Because he didn't appear to be in danger, given the welcome he had received, Finn decided to stay put, but as soon as he could escape, he would leave, never to return to one of these gatherings again.

Once Finn's greetings subsided, their leader walked up to the front and stood on a hayrack. Eyes turned to the front of the barn.

"Now that all our guests have arrived, we can begin our meeting. Brothers, welcome one and all. We believe in the upholding of the Constitution of these United States. We believe in law and order, and now there is an assault on that law and order. Those who oppose the Eighteenth Amendment oppose America. Those who break the law are anarchists who must be stopped!"

Loud applause and hooting paused the speaker. Once it stopped, he picked up again.

"The Audubon County Klavern stands for justice and law. The Audubon County Klavern stands for peace and order. And we will serve our country by helping our lawmen enforce the laws!"

The men stood on their feet and erupted into applause and cheers. Finn clapped along with them. He was surprised. Their view on Prohibition was his view.

"We hold our allegiance to the Stars and Stripes next to our allegiance to God alone. And those who don't are traitors to our country!"

Applause and boot stomping commenced with this last statement. Finn realized he was leaning forward, becoming more immersed in the speech. Nothing the speaker was saying was violent or untrue.

"Germans must be thrown out of this country! Their gluttonous ways, their beer-guzzling celebrations, their guttural language. We didn't beat the Germans just so we could bring their ways here!" Thunderous applause broke out again.

"And in the next county over, there are Germans who have no allegiance to our flag. They supported the wrong side in the war! They should have been sent back to their beer-swilling, Kaiser-loving country where they belong!"

The leader was referring to Carroll County. And those words had been Finn's words. The men turned and looked at him. He nodded his head vigorously to indicate his approval.

"We believe in decent morals. We believe that a church not founded on the principles of morality and justice is a mockery to God and man. And the Catholic church…'Fishes'…holds no morals. They laugh in the face of justice. Their priests drink liquor every Sunday during their service. They don't uphold the laws of this land!"

So far, Finn couldn't see anything dangerous about these men. They believed what he believed. They could see the right of things.

"Our duty, Brothers, lays before us. We must do everything we can to uncover the truth. To stamp out the unwanted. To stop these whiskey-making, fish-eating, Kaiser-loving radicals before they take over our country where anarchy will rule, and justice will lose!"

The men jumped to their feet again, and this time Finn joined them. He hooted and clapped his hands and stomped his feet. His body tingled with excitement, and he felt as if someone had released him from his chains.

After the meeting, the robed men gathered around their visitors, shaking their hands and introducing themselves. Finn realized they were not only from Audubon County but from counties across western and central Iowa.

Would he join them, they wanted to know? The cost was steep, ten dollars. Finn's clenched fist squeezed every penny tightly, so the dues were a potential barrier for him. He would have to think about it more before he could commit.

Finn remained silent about his new friends, even keeping Mary on the outside. He sat and thought about the meeting whenever he wasn't busy in the store. He laid awake at night and contemplated their beliefs. He could now see the Klan was not a violent group, like he had thought, but he was still hesitant to become one of them.

Perhaps only those in the South were violent? These men were from Iowa. And Iowa people were not violent. They would reach out a helping hand to anyone who needed it. Certainly these men would not perpetrate anything brutal, he thought.

And then there was the matter of the money.

Finn decided against joining. He devised several reasons for his decision: the cost of the membership, the distance to the meetings, the time away from his family.

Finn would have forgotten about his brush with joining the Klan, but an event a month later pushed him back in their direction.

A beautiful April afternoon, around 4:00 p.m., Finn was sweeping the sidewalk in front of his store. A gentle breeze blew down Main Street, and the sun shone on his back. From several blocks away, he could see a young boy coming down the street. Normally, young boys bounced, kicked sticks and rocks, jumped up to swat low-hanging tree limbs. However, this boy did none of these things. He swayed. He stumbled. He folded himself in half and wretched into the grass. Something was terribly wrong with him.

Finn put down his broom and rushed down the sidewalk.

The youngster collapsed before Finn could reach him. Finn squatted beside him, shaking his young body. He realized the problem very quickly. The adolescent was drunk. Finn quickly rolled the youth over on to his side when he proceeded to wretch again. A foul stream of undigested liquor streamed from his mouth.

Finn knew this child. It was Tim, the grocer's son. Finn picked up the light body, cradling him in his arms. The walk to the store was silent, the youth having passed out. As he traversed the path to the grocer's, Finn thought about Tim's predicament. He wondered where the minor had gotten the whiskey. Probably from his father's stash, Finn believed.

Alcohol poisoning was no light matter. Even if the boy had imbibed clean whiskey from Templeton, the amount of liquor in his system could kill him. This was exactly why the stuff was illegal. "It is for our own good," Finn said to the unconscious body.

After having deposited the young man in his father's store and receiving no more than a mumbled "thanks," Finn couldn't stop thinking about the incident.

He couldn't blame the boy. "Boys will be boys," he said to himself. "They will get into things they ought not to." As a child, he couldn't be held accountable for his actions. However, his father certainly could. The vision of the limp body, vomit around his mouth, lying in Finn's arms, pricked Finn's conscience. Then it pulled at him. Until it pulled him in the direction of southern Audubon County. Back to the Klan meeting.

Finn knew more needed to be done about the whiskey making. His anonymous phone calls to the federal agent had done nothing to make his town better. And now, an innocent child could have died because of the Wets.

It was time to do something different. It was time to open his tight fist and put down the money. Finn Vries would join the Klan.

CHAPTER 19

Steady rain dropped from the night sky, creating an orchestra of drums on Frank's car. A cover of clouds hid the full moon and stars, producing a veil of darkness. The summer evening in 1929 was perfect. Bad weather kept the Regulators from being overzealous, and the clouds covered the bootleggers' activities.

Frank remained in his vehicle with the engine running while the other men huddled in one of the other three vehicles and smoked cigarettes.

As usual, Frank didn't know any of these men. He recognized two of them because they had been on other jobs with him, but none had asked for a name. They seemed to know each other, which told him they were from the Templeton area. Frank, who lived in Dunlap, didn't join their evening smoke; he stayed secluded in his vehicle, alert for any activity around the area. If need be, he could throw his transportation in gear and be gone as quick as a jack rabbit.

The switch from large, heavy barrels to cases of twelve, quart-sized jars had provided the opportunity for different vehicles. Trucks were slow and heavy. If chased by the law, they couldn't outrun the lawmen's cars.

Frank always drove his own automobile, a used 1926 Nash Roadster. It had overhead valves and a five main bearing crankshaft. Frank had done some work on her himself. To carry a heavy load, he had installed extra suspension springs. He had also removed the backseat. Frank could haul twenty-two cases of whiskey if he loaded his front seat and boot along with his backseat. His Nash could fly at 80 m.p.h. even with a full load of whiskey.

His associates had also brought their own cars. The whiskey-running business demanded specialized vehicles, and each man wanted to drive something he himself had outfitted, giving him confidence of a get-a-way. He knew the engine under his car's hood and the way she handled as well as he knew his own woman's body. To pass time, the men frequently extolled the fastness of their cars, sometimes even meeting on a flat country highway to test the mettle of their machines against each other.

Frank appreciated Skeet's ingenuity with this new setup. The train, one of the boxcars carrying a load of coffins, would stop between Dedham and Coon Rapids. Officially, no stop existed between those two towns; however, this train would slow down after passing through Dedham until it had reached a complete stop. Frank and the other men would be waiting alongside the tracks, traveling with the train until they had met it where it rested.

Once stopped, the behemoth would remain stationary while two men climbed into the ordained boxcar. They would load the liquor into the coffins while two other men from below handed cases up to them. Strict instructions forbade them from spending longer than forty-five minutes to complete the transaction.

When the unloading was completed, one car would travel east until reaching the engine, giving the engineer the signal—flashing headlights—to carry on, while the other cars headed west toward home.

A single potential problem existed with the plan. The train's route upon leaving Dedham was close to Iowa Highway 161. A Regulator could be sitting on that road, his lights extinguished, and watch the train uncharacteristically slow down and then stop after it passed through Dedham. The tail of the train might be sitting just off the highway. If the train were closer to Coon Rapids as opposed to Dedham, the agent would not see it stop.

No plan was perfect, Frank thought. This was certainly better than running on the highways. After his winter brush with the law in Willey, Frank had become skittish about rumrunning. During that escapade, he had felt the Regulators nipping at his heels.

The men on tonight's crew had loaded five shipments in the past week without incident. Their success had transformed their diligence into nonchalance, which is why they were jammed inside their vehicles.

His compatriots had given Frank a hard time when he had declined their invitation to join them. He could see their cigarette red-hots from inside his Nash as they told stories and laughed with abandon. He was sure a flask was surreptitiously being passed from one man to the next. Skeet had a strict, 'no-drinking-on-the- job' policy. Booze fogged a man's brain and made him slow in his reactions. Drunk men were a liability on any job, and this job in particular needed employees who could think quickly and stay focused.

Frank sat with his hands on the steering wheel, his body as tight as strings on a fiddle. He peered through the dark, looking for distant lights from Highway 161.

Suddenly, Frank saw beams coming from that direction; his body tensed. Then, he relaxed; they were welcomed lights. Train lights. Frank put the Nash in gear and waited for the iron animal to whoosh by him.

The other men, too involved in their partying, hadn't noticed the train lights, but they did take note of Frank's car being put into gear and slowly rolling forward. They looked around and recognized the light. The men jumped out of their compatriot's car and loaded into their own vehicles.

The train coming from behind him like a steel bull, Frank felt the rumble of the beast. His car jounced with the power of the train, and the sound drowned out Frank's thoughts.

Once the train stopped, the men drove their vehicles through the weeds, lights extinguished, bumping along with the terrain of the ditch. The first time Frank had driven through the weeds, he worried over unseen obstacles that could puncture a tire or tear the underside of his car. Motorists weren't concerned about throwing unwanted items into Iowa's roadside ditches: worn-out tires, broken furniture. Frank had even seen an old bed with the mattress still on it.

Driving was different on this rain-soaked soil. The wet weeds slapped his car, and the soft ground made getting traction difficult. If he hadn't been on serious business, Frank would have enjoyed making muddy tracks by fishtailing his Nash.

The crew drove until they saw the marked train car. Someone at the other end of the route had put a chalk mark on the outside of the boxcar, making it look as if some hoodlum kids had been having a good time.

Pulling up alongside of the boxcar, they hopped out, leaving their engines idling. Each man had his own job. Two of them opened the train car door and climbed inside. The other two began unloading one of the vehicles. One of the runners grabbed the case and handed it off to the other, who then reached up and handed it up to the man in the boxcar. They had formed a 'bucket brigade' of sorts, except they were handing cases of whiskey instead of buckets of water.

Frank was always the number two ground man. He handed the whiskey up to his partner in the boxcar. By the time he had another case to hand up, the second boxcar man had securely stored the case inside of the coffin. Their movements were smooth and practiced.

The on-and-off rain made the job more difficult. Besides being soaked through, the men had difficulty handling the cases. They became slippery while being passed from trunk to train, making the handoff clumsy. Twice, one of the men in the boxcar dropped the crate. The first one was caught by the ground man, but the second one hit the squishy terrain, dumping bottles. The soft landing had kept them from breaking, but Frank and his partner had to scramble about, looking for errant hooch in the dark.

Two of the four cars unloaded, Frank stood holding the case, waiting for his partner to reach down for it, when he heard a sound. He looked around but saw no lights. "Shh," he commanded his partners. "I think I hear something."

The men froze, cases in midair. As if on cue, a lightning bolt raced across the sky, followed by the boom of thunder. "It's just the rain," one of the men in the boxcar returned.

A second bolt flashed, and in that flash they saw it. Coming toward them was a Ford Model A, unmistakably the preferred car driven by the federal agents.

Their surroundings went dark again, but they could now hear the vehicle. By the sound of the engine, it was running at full speed.

Each man stopped his movements, dropped whatever he had in his hands, and ran for his vehicle. Each man thought only of himself. No waiting for others. No concerns about the unloaded booze. This was the rule.

Once inside his car, Frank threw the stick shift into first gear and hit the gas. On his own, Frank had practiced switching gears as fast as his car could handle. First... second... third gear. His left foot stomped on the clutch while his right foot pressed the gas pedal with all his strength.

Frank's Nash, like a thoroughbred horse, responded to her rider. She hit forty in third gear. By fourth gear, she was galloping at sixty miles an hour, her engine working to capacity.

Frank directed his car east, running parallel with the train. When he passed the engine, he signaled the engineer to start the train. His vehicle's speed indicated the pursing lawmen, so the trainman put the full power of the locomotive into action.

He could see lights behind him. Some of them were his colleagues, and one pair was the federal agents.

Once he passed the front of the train, Frank needed to find a place where he could cross the tracks, getting him onto a road. If he tried to cross where he was, his tires wouldn't handle the rails, and they would pop, potentially rolling his car.

Frank had never driven in the ditch this far east. He was in unsafe territory. He pulled the lever to turn on his lights; there was no need to hide now. He just needed to get out of the ditch as soon as possible. The beams from the Feds' car were still behind him, but the other lights had dropped off.

Looking ahead, Frank saw his opportunity. The climb would be steep, but he was sure his Nash could handle it. Approximately two hundred feet in front of him, he saw a county road running north out of Coon Rapids. He needed to climb the ditch up to that road. If he could make it, he knew his car could outrun his predator.

Frank pushed the gas pedal to the floor, trying to get up enough speed to make the climb. He worried about the condition of the ground, the rain having created a muddy mess. He didn't know how many inches had come down, but it was a lot. His tires could sink into the soil just as he was at the climbing point, or they could spin out as he tried to climb the hill.

Frank didn't have a choice. He had to go for it. If he didn't, there was only one outcome. If he were going to get caught, he might as well do so while trying his best.

His Nash performed beautifully. She climbed the hill like a goat, bringing his machine onto the road. Frank said a quick prayer to Saint Jude.

Behind him, federal headlights were catching up. The rumrunners weren't the only ones who modified their cars. If they could make the hill, Frank was sunk. Once the Feds reached the same hill, they disappeared. Frank assumed their tires had either sunk into the wet mud or had spun out. Either way, he had evaded them for now.

Out on the road, Frank maintained his top speed. The Regulators would expect him to head north to Glidden and then west again to Carroll, but Frank turned east into Greene County, a county no more welcoming of illegal whiskey than Audubon, but Frank knew a guy.

Frank always knew a guy. He had learned that lesson from his uncle, who taught him the importance of relationships. "You never know when you're going to need something from someone," his uncle had espoused.

If Frank could make it to Rippey, he knew a farmer just north of the county road, a guy by the name of Roberts. He had bested Frank in a poker game a few years back. Even though the farmer had taken his money, Frank considered it an investment. He and Roberts had shared a few snorts of Frank's whiskey and shared stories of living in Iowa. By the time they had parted, Roberts shook his hand and told Frank to consider them friends. Frank knew Roberts had a barn and would be willing to hide a rumrunner for a few days.

CHAPTER 20

Father Joe stood at the lectern and looked out at his parishioners. He was giving his annual speech on "Good Neighbors." He found it necessary to remind his congregants of their Christian duty, especially when no holiday was on the horizon. Christmas and Easter, the high holy days, brought forth an abundance of charity; but the summer and fall could be lean times for those in need.

The fumes from the angel's share had wafted up from the basement and permeated the nave. The church, once perfumed by incense and women's toilet water, now smelled of whiskey. The rye grain scent was prominent, but there was also a surprising whiff of peppermint paired with smoke and oak.

Each time a door was opened, the draft pulled the aroma from below into the church. When parishioners entered, the whiskey fragrance hit them. No amount of incense could cover it, and the scent was unmistakable.

The first Sunday the aroma had filled the nave, Father Joe's flock whispered, their heads together as they sat in the pews. They looked around, trying to decide if a keg or an open bottle were nearby. Surely no one was disrespectful enough to drink in church, they thought.

After the service, as the priest stood in the back to greet his parishioners as they exited, some of them commented about the unusual smell: "Did Father know there was a smell?" "I could swear I smell whiskey," "Are you drinking in the sacristy, Father?"—the last being said with a wink and a smile. Father Joe didn't respond to any of their comments or questions; he looked perplexed like his sense of smell had gone on a permanent vacation. His reticence signaled his desire for secrecy.

Now, many Sundays later, no one remarked or paid attention to the whiskey odor. Joe assumed word had quietly spread about the barrels aging in the church's basement. He never heard one complaint.

His parishioners, dressed in their Sunday best, shifted in their seats. Small children wiggled with boredom and received stern warnings from their parents. He could see some of the men beginning to close their eyes for longer periods of time, telling him they were just about to doze off, their women ready to throw an elbow into their ribs if they did. The warm, late summer morning made the church stuffy, no air circulating on this windless day.

Finishing his homily, Father took one last look across the nave, his eyes sending signals to those who had not been neighborly as of late.

Joe noticed the families who were clearly struggling. Iowa's farm economy boomed during the war, but the 1920s had brought hard times, land values dropping along with corn prices.

The Schneider children were both puny and slumped in their pew, signaling a lack of proper nutrition. The Becker children's clothing was faded with many washings, and all of it looked too big on them. Widow Berg had been wearing the same hat for the past four years.

Family after family showed signs of poverty.

Joe's eyes landed on Cora Weber, widow to Jack, who had been killed four years past. Cora and her four children regularly sat on the left side of the church, halfway back.

Like the other ladies, Cora had on her Sunday best, an outfit even a priest recognized was worn often. Her hair was parted down the middle and pulled back into a tight bun. She had been attentive to Joe's sermon, never looking bored or spending time minding her children. Jack and Cora's children—fifteen, fourteen, twelve, and eight—sat ramrod straight. Their black, curly hair—their father's hair—looked a bit shaggy. They were clean and neatly pressed, but their clothing was also looking frayed and worn.

After Jack's death, the community had rallied around Cora. Piles of food—chipped beef, hams, new potatoes, string beans and beets in jars, pickles, and mountains of pies—had been delivered to Cora's house. Condolences and offers of help came from nearly every community and church member. Cora and her children had eaten on neighborly attentions for weeks.

Like any death, though, involvement eventually dwindles, people turning to the next crisis or needing to attend to their own concerns. By the second month, food deliveries cease along with offers of help. A widow must learn to survive on her own, they say.

Even Father Joe started to space out his visits until he had eventually stopped going by the house to check on her. As he now looked at her and the children, he realized he had been negligent in keeping an eye on her.

However, not all his congregants looked like poverty had taken residence in their houses. Albert and Mary Stange looked well fed and healthy. William Bennet looked well, and the faces of his many children were flush with health as they bounced around in their seats. Father noticed new clothing, and he had seen a new car in the church parking lot.

Clearly there were the 'Haves' and the 'Have Nots.' The 'Haves' had become flush with cash through the bootlegging business. Father did not condemn them for their prosperity, but he felt they should share more with their community members.

The 'Have Nots' were those members who had opted to refrain from breaking the law. They were making do the best they could. Father respected their decision.

Joe returned to his chair while the collection basket was passed down the rows, snaking around the church from one hand to the next. Church members were required to tithe, regardless of their financial situation. Tithing expectations were based on income, those with more giving more. When children became old enough to earn a little money, they were also encouraged to contribute part of it. The church considered tithing a part of being a good Catholic, wanting its members to get into the habit while they were young.

Cora and her two youngest children rose from their pew and went to retrieve the offertory. Cora carried the collection basket while her little ones brought the wine and bread. Standing in front of the sacristy, the family handed over the offertory. When Joe accepted the basket, he looked down in dismay. His homily had not had the effect he expected. The basket was heavy with small change, but the dollar bills were scarce.

As Father Joe finished mass, his mind remained on the collection basket. Church collections kept the church running, but they were also used to help parishioners in need. The needy outnumbered the not-so-needy.

When Skeet Miller had come to Father Joe requesting to age whiskey in the church basement, Joe had been willing to help. He knew whiskey money sustained the community. He had asked for nothing in return.

The whiskey business supported those involved with it but left out those who were not. Money flowed through the hands of the farmers who leased their land, the distillers who made the whiskey, the rumrunners who drove it to its customers, and businessmen who sold supplies to the distillers. If Joe asked any one of them directly for a financial contribution, he received it without complaint, but they did not voluntarily hand over money. They felt there was plenty of opportunity for anyone who wanted to make it themselves.

They failed to recognize the contribution of those who weren't involved in the business. Any one of Sacred Heart's members could contact the law and report the whiskey smell. Joe believed their restraint should be rewarded as much as any man who actively participated.

If the whiskey operators couldn't see their responsibility in helping their fellow man, then Joe would force them to. He would require a hefty sum from them to keep their barrels, and he would dole out the proceeds directly to those in need.

As his flock filed out of the church, Joe stood in the back, greeting each congregant, keeping an eye out for Cora Weber. When she came to him, he said, "Cora, would you mind staying for a bit, so I can talk to you?"

The last member having gone through the line, Father walked back into the nave and sat down next to Cora, who had returned to her usual pew.

"How are you and the children getting along? I've been meaning to stop by again," Joe said.

"We're doing as well as we can, Father. It's not been easy without Jack," Cora replied.

"I'm sure," he said. "How are you financially?" Joe decided Cora would be the first to receive some of the money he planned to procure from the bootleggers.

"I'm getting by," Cora said. "I have a part-time job at the café. After Jack's death, it was difficult to work outside of the house. The children needed minding. Now, my oldest is fifteen, and he works after school in the hardware store. My girl is fourteen, and she's able to take care of the others when I'm at work."

"If you need money, Cora, just ask. The church takes care of its parishioners."

"We don't take charity, Father. Jack always took care of his family, and I mean to do the same. We don't have a lot, but we get by. I appreciate the offer."

Back in the rectory, sitting in his favorite chair as Mrs. Smith prepared his supper, the priest thought about Cora Weber. If anyone had a right to take help from the church, it would be her.

However, Iowans were proud, and they believed accepting charity was a weakness. They took money only when they had worked for it. Joe knew Cora Weber would never accept a dime she hadn't earned by her hands or her brain. He would need to figure out another way to give it to her.

Manufacture of Illicit Spirits Has Not Stopped

Secretary Morgenthau Regards It as "Very Husky Industry

Washington (*P*) — Secretary Morgenthau told reporters today that manufacture of illicit liquor is still "a very husky industry. He said he planned to "hit and hit it hard"

The treasury head explained the department was "beginning to get interested in the illicit manufacture" of intoxicating liquors on May 10 the o'i prohibition unit will be transferred from the justice department to the bureau of industrial alcohol, under the treasury department

Morgenthau disclosed revenue agents have already started seizing stills and illegal spirits.

He said 73 stills were taken last week throughout the country, along with 84,000 gallons of spirits and 173,000 gallons of mash, valued at $17,000. "This illegal business appears to be as bad as it ever was," he said.

CHAPTER 21

Jimmy Krantz hated working in the hog house. The stench of pig shit permeated his skin and wove itself through the strands of his hair. When he swallowed, the smell went down his throat; he could taste excrement. All his clothing permanently smelled like pigs. The pails of water they were provided by the Stanges for personal use, pumped from the farm's well, were not nearly adequate in giving Jimmy an opportunity to clean up after he finished his work.

When he had agreed to become a setter, Jimmy never imagined spending hours in a hog shed. He had pictured himself in a barn, surrounded by the sweet scent of hay.

The hog house in the late June heat was a Dutch oven even in the middle of the night. The windows and doors were shut, sealing in the whiskey fumes; but it also confined the odor of pig droppings, creating a shit-yeast mixture. The air laid heavy on his skin and masked his face. Jimmy barely tolerated taking in the smallest of breaths.

The head setter and Jimmy's boss, Leo Stack, had explained the reason for cooking in the hog shed. The reek of hogs covered the smell when they were distilling. No other farm smell was as potent as pigs. To make the odor stronger, the men had left the pig droppings rather than clean the shed.

When Skeet had first hired Jimmy, he had assigned him the supply-run job. He and another employee sat in Skeet's trucks, the darkness surrounding them, waiting for the train. The sugar and yeast were deposited on the platform, and Skeet's men loaded it into the trucks before daylight broke. If Jimmy had reported to Alvin Truly, he would have no more interesting news than he had picked up a thousand pounds of sugar and a hundred pounds of yeast. Truly knew these were whiskey-making ingredients, but by themselves they were not illegal. Jimmy kept the information to himself, waiting to move up the employment ladder when he would be entrusted with illegal details.

After mastering his delivery job, Jimmy was promoted to setter, which gave him a small raise in pay. The setters made the mash and distilled the whiskey. They knew the locations of the stills. This is what he had been working toward, giving him the information needed, so he could finally be released from his indenture. He was also pleased he would be paid more for a more dangerous job.

Skeet had deposited Jimmy on Albert Stange's farm three months ago, on a stormy March afternoon. The temperature had dropped to thirty degrees, threatening to either rain or hail. Jimmy flipped up his coat collar and shoved his hands into his pockets. Stange showed him to his temporary bed, a mattress in the hayloft. Climbing the last rung on the ladder, Jimmy stepped onto the loft platform and saw two other men. They were his crew, men who would stay with him as they traveled from one farm to the next.

Rusty, Stange's dog, was the only friendly family member when Jimmy arrived. Albert and his wife Mary, along with their children, stayed within the confines of the house during the distilling process, not wanting to know any specific information. Jimmy occasionally bumped into Albert, but their conversations were short and limited to the weather.

Jimmy and the rest of the setters made the mash on two separate days, enough for a six-hundred-gallon run, and then returned later to distill it. Distilling generally took them one day, cooking from sundown to sunup. Once finished distilling and leaving another batch of mash behind, the crew moved on to a new location and took temporary residence in another hayloft. Skeet had other crews who also went from farm to farm. Each crew had a certain set of stills, never knowing what other farms belonged to the syndicate.

Jimmy's crew made the mash one month prior to their cook. They began by placing fifty-five gallons of tepid water, a half a block of Fleischmanns's baker's yeast, and a third of a bucket of rye grain into each fifty-five-gallon barrel. They sealed the container and left to finish the process at another farm. The men returned, pulled the lid from the barrel, and added the last ingredient: seventy-five pounds of sugar. The mash needed to sit another ten days before it was ready for distilling.

Jimmy had assumed the mash process was easy: just throw the ingredients in the barrel, put the lid on, and leave. However, he discovered there was more of a science to making the mash. The proportions of the ingredients were precise. Too much of one spoiled the mix. Occasionally, something went wrong with their concoction.

Usually, the setters would have distilled a mash made from their previous visit, but when Jimmy had opened the barrel, a vomit stench reached out of the brew and grabbed him by the throat. Jimmy immediately gagged and nearly threw up his supper. Something had been done incorrectly when they mixed it. The stench of the ruined mash hurried its way to the other setters. "Dammit, how the hell did we get a ruined batch of mash?" Leo Stack asked the group. Jimmy was relieved he had not made that batch because there would be a price to pay for ruined merchandise. Along with the cost of ingredients, their system was now thrown off, and money was being lost.

"Are they all that way?" Leo wanted to know.

Jimmy and the other setters proceeded to open the remaining barrels, gagging each time a lid was lifted.

"'Spose we got a bad batch of yeast?" Jimmy asked, hoping to pin the mistake on the product rather than the setters.

"Dunno," Leo replied. "Doesn't matter now. We got to make new mash."

Leo ordered the men to dump the ruined mash into the pig yard, the animals gobbling up the concoction, eating themselves into an alcoholic stupor.

To start again, the crew thoroughly cleaned each barrel, not wanting any of the ruined product to taint their new batch.

The first step in the process was to fill buckets of water from the farm pump and dump it into the many barrels. It necessitated room temperature, about 75 degrees. Summer was easy; the water was already warm when it came out of the well. Winter water had to be heated, inserting another step to the process.

The men then added the rye, mixed it, and waited for the water to take on the right temperature. It had to be around 70 degrees for the yeast to work. Any warmer, and the yeast would die. After they added the last ingredient and stirred the mixture, they put the lids on the barrels and left, hoping this new batch would be better. They would return to add the last ingredient, trusting this new batch would produce a fine whiskey.

Loading supplies, they traveled to their next location to distill the mash they had already made. For two days at a time, the setters worked a location.

Jimmy and his partners returned to Stange's farm on a Saturday to make the whiskey. Lifting the lid from the barrel, Jimmy put his head close to the mixture. A strong, yeasty aroma crawled up his nose, and then he listened. He heard nothing, which was good. The yeast had stopped hissing, meaning the sugar had converted to alcohol.

The men siphoned off the wash—the liquid from the fermented materials—and put it into a copper pot still. A fire was needed to bring the liquid to 173 degrees, the temperature at which liquid becomes vapor. The vapor rolled through the copper coils, which were submerged in an animal trough filled with water, turning the vapor back to liquid.

Jimmy sat at the end of the still, waiting for the clear liquid to come down the worm, and thought about the first time he saw whiskey being distilled. He marveled at the way a few household ingredients could become a concoction so powerful it could take away a man's worries and make him as happy as a racoon in a corn patch.

As soon as a trickle started, he reached for a cup, thinking he would have himself a little snort; however, his partner swatted the cup from his hand. "You don't drink the head, you idiot! That's poisonous. You'll go blind if you drink that stuff!"

"What do we do with it?" he asked.

"Throw it out. Once we get about two pints, we'll be into the heart, which is the good whiskey. *That* we keep. *That* you can taste."

When Jimmy was taught how to make whiskey in jail, no one had bothered to explain this to him. He had felt like a fool and worried about his back story as a whiskey maker. If he truly belonged to a whiskey-making family, he would have known about the heads and tails.

Once the batch had gone through the distillation process, Jimmy took the last of the liquid—the tails— and added it to another wash going through, starting the process again. The heart of the whiskey went into charred oak barrels, giving it a distinct flavor and the amber color. He had been skeptical when they poured the clear liquid into the charred containers, but his compatriots had assured him the burned wood would make the whiskey taste better.

Skeet wanted this specific batch to be a premium whiskey, nothing less than 115 proof. He had hinted that it was going to someone very special in Chicago. To check his work, Jimmy placed a clear bottle under the worm. When he was satisfied with the amount in his jar, he took the lid, screwed it on, and shook the bottle vigorously. Bubbles appeared and instantly dissipated, indicating the whiskey was high quality.

Because Skeet had been so adamant about the quality of this particular batch, Jimmy took a match and lit the liquid on fire. It lit quicker than a candle. If it were under 80 proof, it wouldn't have burned.

The setters would finish their work by Monday, the whiskey stored in oak barrels. Six months later, when they opened the barrel, the clear liquid would have transformed to the color of a penny. Although, not all cookers let their whiskey age that long. Needing quick cash, many of them sold it clear.

Storage of the aging whiskey was the bootleggers' biggest problem. The church basement could only hold so many barrels. Beyond that, distillers had to get creative: house basements, barn lofts, hog houses. Some of the distillers had built false floors in their out-buildings. Anywhere they could hide their product was utilized. Once aged, it went underground until it was sold.

At Stange's farm, the men had dug a trench in the front yard, placing the barrels in the ground until they were sold. To cover their work, they had taken the Stange children's playset and placed it over the top of the disturbed dirt. If Regulators came poking around, looking for the barrels, they would see a patch of mud in the midst of the lawn but assume the children's feet had been dragging along the ground as they sat in their swings.

Late Sunday night, the men, exhausted from hard labor and little sleep, heard a disturbance outside of the hog shed. It sounded like many feet. "Regulators!" one of the men whispered.

They immediately extinguished their lanterns and kicked dry manure over the fires. The hog shed hosted two exits, one at each end of the building. The Regulators would be standing at the doors with shotguns pointed, waiting for the men to run for safety. Jimmy kicked open the window in the back of the building, which had been nailed shut for security. Each man crawled through the window, landing with a thud on the ground, and crouched low to look for cover. A full moon shone brightly in the sky, lighting the way for the setters.

Jimmy, the first one through the window, peered through the night, trying to remember the escape path that had been scouted for this particular location. If necessary, he was willing to belly-crawl his way to freedom.

Fifty feet away from the shed, Jimmy rose to a half-standing position, preparing to run through the darkness. Having gotten away from the building, he could now see a bright light coming from the front side, toward the farmhouse. Had the Regulators used their car lights to catch them? Jimmy wondered.

By now, the lawmen should have made themselves known and started the chase, but they hadn't. If it wasn't the law, Jimmy questioned, who or what was it? Now certain there were no Regulators, Jimmy snuck around the side of the building and crawled his way closer toward the bright light.

In the farmyard, men dressed in white sheets were standing around two large, burning crosses. Each man held a shotgun, pointed toward the stars.

"We know you're in there!" one sheeted man yelled. "Show yourselves, you dirty Huns!" The rest of his compatriots cackled with amusement.

Jimmy had heard of the Klan, but he had never seen any. Tales of Klansmen riding horses and stringing up Black men had made their way north. The sight of this shrouded menace frightened him. He looked around at the trees, picturing himself swinging from one of them.

He remained on his belly, hidden by the weeds. Jimmy was certain the other setters were somewhere nearby and, like him, were afraid of the sheeted men.

Two shots ripped through the night air. One of the Klansmen fired at the hog house, the buckshot embedding into the wood. Jimmy didn't move. He was afraid they would shoot him if he ran. He decided to stay hunkered in his hiding spot, hoping they would eventually leave.

Stange's house remained dark and sealed up, the face of Albert Stange peering around the kitchen curtain.

Unwilling to go beyond the light of their crosses, the hooded men gathered into a group and entertained themselves. Occasionally, they called out to the cookers, taunting them with words like "kraut eaters," "swine," "homewreckers," and "traitors."

Jimmy's understanding of the Klan came from stories down South. He didn't know what they were doing in Iowa or why they were at a white man's farmhouse.

Before he could determine the answers, the Klansmen decided they had waited long enough for the setters to show themselves. "If you're too chicken to come out, then we'll just have to force you out!" one of them yelled.

They lit their torches and headed toward the shed. Jimmy saw fifteen or so lights coming his way and decided to find the escape path. He wasn't willing to stick around to see what they would do next, but he was pretty sure he knew what would happen.

His legs running at their full potential, fifty feet away from the building, Jimmy heard a whoosh behind him. Turning around, he saw the hog house go up in a blaze. It wouldn't be long before the fire reached the whiskey. Jimmy forced his legs to move faster, getting him as far away from the blast as possible.

A boom of thunder split the air, and the hog shed exploded. The black sky radiated light, and pieces of shed rained down around him. Jimmy wondered about his crewmates, but he had to think about himself first, so he headed toward a small creek, hoping no one had been hurt.

CHAPTER 22

"Brothers, we have achieved our first victory! Our klavern has distinguished itself with the destruction of a Kraut still. One down and many more to destroy!"

The group of Klansmen hooted, clapped, and stomped their feet—Finn Vries among them. He had been attending the monthly meetings faithfully. He had finally found his people.

Finn had not, however, been involved in the barn burning. Their leader had alluded to something big in the fight against illegal liquor, but no one had given specific details. And Finn had not been invited. He was in his store when word trickled down about Stange's hog shed burning. A jolt of lightening went through his body when the word *Klan* had been mentioned. Initially, Finn had been relieved they had left him out of their fiery activities, but later he felt indignant. He had clearly not gained trust with his brethren yet.

"Our work, Brothers, is far from finished. We will burn every still! We will send those Hun-Fishes back where they belong! We will purify our country! We will help our government in bringing back law and order!"

More stomping and hooting rang through the barn. Finn sweated in his robe, the air in the barn stuffy. In their meetings, they did not wear their hoods, which Finn appreciated.

"Next week, we are celebrating our country's birth, a country built by white Protestants. We will celebrate our ancestors and show our righteousness by marching in the Templeton Fourth of July Parade. Those Fishes will shake in their boots when they see our power. When we finish the parade, we will gather in the park and light our crosses. Who is with us?"

Panicked, Finn blanched at the thought of Templeton, thinking he would be seen, but a few minutes of concern finally settled into resolve. Because he believed in the Klan's cause, he would participate. He would march with his brethren, not stand along the side of the street.

The air vibrated with enthusiasm from the members, and the rafters shook from the stomping. Every Klansman was committed to showing the power of the Invisible Empire. Although they were proud to walk down the street wearing their robes and carrying a banner, they would be wearing their hoods to hide their identity. Finn hoped no one would identify him behind his covering.

When Sheriff Will Katz arrived at Albert Stange's farm, the hog house was already engulfed in flames. Nothing could be saved. He had alerted both the Carroll and Templeton fire departments, who could only keep Stange's house and barn from catching fire. Small towns had volunteer fire departments, which were slow in arriving.

Along with the blazing hog house, Sheriff Katz also saw two crosses, one of them no longer burning and the other one only burning on the left side. He had never dealt with the Klan, but he knew of them and shook his head, troubled they had moved into his territory.

As disturbed as Will was by the Klan's presence, he had to think about the town's up-coming celebration. The sheriff had parade duty every Fourth of July. The parade towns in Carroll County coordinated their schedules to be assured of the sheriff's presence. The town councils were jumpy after the Klan had made their existence known and were working their schedules to accommodate Will.

Templeton's parade was planned for noon, followed by a picnic in the park. The Fourth was the largest town event, bringing the townees along with the farmers from the surrounding areas.

Celebrants, decked out in their best attire, brought their tastiest picnic dishes. Sandwich meats of roast beef and cured ham; orchards of pies; varieties of cookies; strawberry, orange, lemon, and raspberry Jell-o; coleslaw; and potato salad—all were nestled in picnic baskets, waiting for the feast to begin.

Half an hour before the parade began, the community started to find their spots along the route. Women carried umbrellas to protect themselves from the July sun; men followed behind their women, swabbing their shining faces with red and blue handkerchiefs pulled from the back pockets of their overalls; children broke from their family unit, weaving through strangers, finding friends and creating animal packs. All eventually hunkered down to wait for the fire engine, signaling the beginning of the parade.

July in Iowa could be the most brutal month. The temperature had climbed to ninety-eight degrees, and the sun stared down at them with full intensity. Not even a whisper of breeze. American flags hung limp on their poles.

All heads were turned toward the beginning of the route with nothing in sight. A few notes of the band students, practicing their instruments before beginning to play their first song, floated down the parade path.

Sheriff Katz, sitting in his truck near the beginning of the route, suddenly sensed trouble. People were looking toward the end of the parade and pointing. Women were gathering their children and pulling them off the street, leading them to the park.

He drove his truck toward the end of the route, parked on a side street, and walked to the area of trouble. He ran into a wall of white. Thirty plus men in white robes were striding together toward the parade line. They intended to put themselves into the procession and march.

A group of horseback riders, who had taken the last spot in line, but were now in front of the Klansmen, had difficulty controlling their animals, spooked by the unrest among the crowd. The riders began yelling at the Klan members, who were yelling back. Will quickly jogged to the space between the Klansmen and the horseback riders.

Discordant participants from both sides had come to the burning point and were moving toward one another. Spectators on the sidewalk joined the yelling, insisting the Klan be thrown from the parade.

Will knew his own feelings, but he also knew the law. While he might not protect the Eighteenth Amendment, he would protect the First, and the Klan had the right to march like everyone else. Will would have to safeguard them. He hoped for a quick parade and people to settle down in the park for their lunch. The Klan would make their presence known and then go home.

Hearing the firetruck siren, Will began to march alongside the sheeted group. First he was in front of them, clearing the way; and then he was beside them, trying to keep Templeton men from attacking.

Out of respect for their local lawman, most of the onlookers confined themselves to yelling, careful to keep it clean as there were ladies and children present. Some, however, ran to their trucks and pulled apples and other food items from their picnic baskets to throw at the men in white, which only riled them.

Halfway through the route, at the most populous place, the leader of the klavern started to yell: "Americans only, no Huns! Americans only, no Huns! Americans only, no Huns!" His followers picked up his chant and joined him. As they yelled, they put their fists into the air and shook them in tempo with their words.

Their chanting stirred the crowd to a roaring fire with Will trying to hold them back. Will Katz was one-hundred-percent German and was as offended by their words as was every person in the parade and on the sidewalk. He just wanted to get to the end as quickly as possible, but the firetruck set the pace and didn't realize the near catastrophe happening behind it.

The parade marchers filed into the park, celebrants and participants mingling together, readying their feasts. The fire truck had passed the park and was headed back to the station. The front of the parade had little knowledge of the conflagration until the tail end reached the park. They, too, were then offended by the presence of the Klan.

Will was relieved when he could see the horseback riders dismounting and joining their families to partake in the picnic. He assumed the Klansmen would disassemble and return from whence they came. They had ruined the parade, but there were plenty of festivities yet to be enjoyed. Will decided he would hang about for another half hour or so and then head to Dedham for their two o'clock procession. He hoped the Klan did not intend to participate in every Carroll County parade.

As Will was heading for his truck, a ruckus broke out in the park. Now what? he thought. From across the street, he could see a large cross being erected by several members in the middle of the park. Other Klansmen were busy assembling an additional cross. They intended to light both on fire. Will could do something about the crosses.

He found the first volunteer fireman and told him to round up as many of the men as possible. They should head to the fire station and get the truck.

Will didn't wait for the fire truck. He shoved his way through the compacted crowd gathering around the Klan's activities until he broke through the mob.

His badge affixed to his shirt, Will yelled at the sheeted men, "You can't burn those crosses! It's a fire hazard in a public place!"

A large man who appeared to be their leader stepped up to Will and peered at him through the eye holes of his hood. "We got rights, and we know 'em. We got the right to free speech, and this is our speech." He stepped forward until he was chest to chest with Will.

The sheriff felt the coal of his temper flaming up, and he didn't move from his spot, staring at his opponent. "You apparently don't know the law of this town. We ban fires in public places, and this park is a public place. If you light those crosses, I'm going to arrest you for violation of the public burn ban."

Neither man moved even a hair. Eyes bored into eyes. Red face to sheeted face. Will would stand statue-like until the other backed down. His large chest, built up from years of blacksmithing, was twice the size of the Klansman's chest. Will's legs were tree trunks, rooted in his current spot. Any push or hit would bounce off his massive body.

Seconds passed with neither man giving in. The showdown was interrupted by the wail of the fire truck, the firemen driving it through the park, parting the crowd as they went. They didn't stop until they were parked in front of the crosses. Men jumped from the truck and started to unroll the hoses, ready to spray gallons of water from the truck's large tanks.

"You all get these crosses taken down. You don't have the proper paperwork for a public display," Will commanded.

Time seemed to stop as the Klansmen stood still, trying to determine their options. Finally, their leader stepped away from Will and directed the dismantling of the crosses.

Will breathed evenly, realizing he had been holding his breath. He had won this fight, but he doubted they would go away permanently.

The next morning, Finn Vries was in the back of his store, working on a broken watch when he heard the tinkle of his doorbell. In walked his stepbrother. He had not seen John Krupp for many months, and that was more than acceptable to him. "Mornin,' John. Looking for Betsy? Something special coming up? I've got some merchandise on sale I think she'd like." No matter how he felt about his stepbrother, Finn always affected a friendly tone.

"I didn't come to buy anything," John replied in a terse voice. "I came to tell you I know it was you."

"What was me?" Finn hated being lured in like a bass. John always started his conversations with vague accusations, making Finn uncomfortable.

"It's your shoes," John continued. "Nobody else wears those black and tan wing-tipped shoes." He pointed to Finn's feet.

Finn could feel the blood draining from his face, but he remained calm and pretended he was lost to the conversation. "What about my shoes?" he asked stupidly.

"You all are cowards wearing those masks, but I recognized your shoes. You marched with those ghosts yesterday. Go on, deny it!"

Finn didn't feel like kowtowing to his stepbrother. He had done plenty of that while they were growing up. "Yes, I marched yesterday. I am an official member of the Ku Klux Klan. We've had enough of this illegal whiskey making. It's ruining our community, our children, and our reputations. The law isn't willing to do anything, so it's up to honest citizens like me and my brethren to do it." Finn stood a little taller and stared into John's eyes. "As long as we're making accusations, I know what you're up to as well. You're one of them who's breaking the law. You've got a still of your own. Don't deny it."

Finn felt strong and righteous. For the first time in their relationship, he felt he had the upper hand. He was on the right side of the law, and his stepbrother was on the wrong side. Finn felt the power of John's fate in his hands.

"I know you been snitchin' to the law on me. When all's said and done, you won't have a pot to piss in. You've seen your last customer. Nobody is going to buy from a Kluxer snitch."

John didn't wait for Finn's reply. He wheeled around and walked out the door, slamming it behind him.

Finn stood in his store, the silence pushing in on him. Was John right? Finn had been so bold underneath his hood. He never imagined anyone knowing his identity. The ugly realization of the consequences slowly crept his way and encircled his body and then entered every cell.

Finn had made so many sacrifices for the store's success. Money donations, community participation, raffle ticket sales—so many unwanted activities in order to keep a thriving business. He had kept his opinions to himself, never wanting to offend a potential customer. Years of bottling up his beliefs to put food on the table and a roof over his family's head were now for nothing. He would have to close his store. His children would suffer at the hands of their schoolmates. He had been so stupid. And, for what? So he could feel better about himself?

Finn tried to build back his anger and sense of rightness. He and his brethren were supporting the law. They were in the right; the bootleggers were in the wrong. He would not be made to feel like he was the bad one.

Finn needed to make a choice: either stand up for the law and civility; or shrink back into his shell, keep his mouth shut, and maintain his way of financial living. If it had been only himself to think of, he would have chosen the former. Instead, Finn would quit the Klan and beg his stepbrother to keep the information to himself. He would become the best merchant and town member possible. If need be, he would show his support of the bootleggers and buy their whiskey.

His outward actions would display his false support, but his inward feelings would never change. The vault of his beliefs would lock again, never to be opened to anyone.

New Law to Raise Penalty Boosts Liquor Prices Here

Bootleg Alcohol Up $4 a Gallon Since Passage of Jones Bill.

BY SHIRLEY PRUGH.

The boost in liquor prices, which was felt in the east immediately following passage of the Jones bill, prescribing heavier penalties for liquor violations has reached Iowa, according to reliable reports from bootlegging circles.

Alcohol, said to be the chief intoxicant used by the average Iowa imbiber, has advanced in price approximately $1 a quart, or from $3 to $4 more for gallon lots. Smaller quantities are proportionally more expensive.

Some retail distributors still are peddling at the old prices, but in most cases, the liquid is said to be of inferior quality.

Many Complaints.

Numerous "squawks" from customers regarding the poor quality of bootleg alcohol have been received by liquor peddlers, who claim that although the price has increased in Chicago and other distributing points, the quality has been poorer.

One bootlegger in Des Moines quoted his advanced prices at $5 a quart and $15 a gallon. Former prices were $4 and $12 respectively.

Some Stuff Cheaper.

These quotations are Des Moines prices for "average good" stuff. Some is cheaper. Drug store alcohol, however, is reported to be higher. In the eastern part of the state and particularly in the river towns, it is even cheaper, as the hazards of transportation across Iowa are eliminated.

Glen Brunson, deputy prohibition administrator with headquarters in Des Moines, stated Monday that he was not aware of the advance, although he considered it likely that the price would go up if there was a raise in Chicago. This, he explained, was because Iowa depends upon the Chicago market for most of its alcohol.

Thinks Few Quit.

"They say some bootleggers are going out of business because of the Jones bill," Brunson said, "but I don't see why it should scare them. The five-year term is the maximum sentence and first offenders aren't likely to get that. I seriously doubt if many have quit business."

Brunson said he did not know how many bootleggers there are in Iowa, but added that he believed the ranks had been thinned.

"But there are still too many," he declared.

The prices of rye and corn liquor in the state also have advanced, according to latest reports.

Best Corn Liquor.

Brunson stated that "Templeton Rye," distilled on farms in Carroll county, enjoys the reputation of being the best stuff made in the corn state. Its biggest market is Chicago, it is said, where it enjoys a wide sale at a good price. It is sold in bottles under the trade name of "Templeton Rye," Brunson said.

A number of persons were arrested recently in connection with the "Templeton Rye" distilleries and paid fines in district courts.

Commenting on the local angle, police authorities in Des Moines pointed out that District Judge Herman Zeuch's declaration to hand out jail sentences to convicted bootleggers has had its effect on the increase in price as well as the assumption that some are quitting the racket.

CHAPTER 23

Alvin Truly felt like a rat catcher with a hole in his net. Any boot-legger he brought before the court was given a small fine, a gentle lecture, and released out into the world again, only to start making another still as soon as he returned home.

The law decreed anyone making or transporting illegal liquor be fined not less than $100 and not more than $1,000.00. They were to spend no fewer than thirty days in jail but no more than one year. The criminals could be given both the fine and the jailtime. Judges had discretion. Most of them doled out the minimum fine with no jail time. Even if they did exact the maximum penalty, the fee was far less than what the whiskey maker could earn with a few batches of liquor. Seldom did anyone spend any time in jail.

In sum, the penalties were too soft. Instead of a hammer, they were a rolled-up newspaper.

Alvin didn't have any control over the penalties. That was left in the hands of the lawmakers. Iowa Republican Senator Henry Dunn was Alvin Truly's only hope.

Henry Dunn stood nearly 6', 5" with a large belly and a square face. His dark hair was always slicked back, but a cowlick created an escaped curl, which sat on his forehead. His dark eyes bored a hole through anyone who disagreed with him but softened for any child.

Senator Dunn came from a large Protestant, farming family. They owned four hundred acres east of Boyden, a town in northwest Iowa. The northwest part of the state was recognized as being conservative and religious. They didn't abide drinking, gambling, or any other activity that didn't pertain to hard work or the Lord.

The Senator's family still farmed in that area and put in two hundred acres of corn, a hundred in beans, and a hundred in wheat each year. They attended church weekly and participated in anything church related. Henry's father carried a worn Bible with him on Sundays and was known for quizzing his children and grandchildren on certain passages.

Henry attended Northwestern College in Orange City and earned his degree in business. From there, he took the position of Osceola County Auditor but didn't like the monotony of the work, so he moved to Des Moines and earned his law degree from Drake University.

Missing his family and wanting to find a good woman from his part of the state, Henry moved to Remsen, settled down with the mayor's daughter, and opened his law practice. He was a good attorney; most of his community came to him to write their wills, settle land disputes, represent business owners, and apply his legal expertise to other small matters. Even though Henry was happy in his predictable life, he wanted more. He prided himself on his morals, common sense, and leadership. With those characteristics, Henry decided he would make a good politician, so he ran for the Iowa House of Representatives in 1914 and won by a landslide.

At that time, Iowa was in the heart of the Prohibition fight—legal, not legal, somewhat legal. By the middle of his term, he proudly claimed to be the deciding vote for Prohibition; however, that was not entirely true. He was one of many Representatives who voted in favor of it. Henry was already building his reputation, secretly planning to run for a federal position.

When Henry decided he was interested in a Senate seat, the federal government was also trying to pass Prohibition. In 1918 he ran on a Prohibition platform. Because Iowa had already decided Prohibition was the moral and ethical choice through their own state law, they chose Henry to represent them in Washington.

Senator Dunn had been the largest dog in his own yard, but now he was running with a vicious pack, and he was no longer the biggest; in fact, he was only a tiny mutt. He did not have the pedigree of many other Senators: he was not from a long line of politicians. However, Henry felt superior to them, believing only he had the morals and character befitting a Senator. Instead of using his reputation to throw his weight around Congress, Senator Dunn threw his physical body, pushing his tall frame and big belly through crowded halls. He made himself known among his political peers by his booming voice and impractical opinions.

Senator Dunn would have been embarrassed had he discovered the nicknames given him by politicians in both the Senate and the House: Big Britches, Boomer, the Big Bible, and Cornfed. They laughed at his naivete, his belief that Prohibition in Iowa had stopped all liquor and drinking, because he seemed to be the only one who did not know about the river of whiskey flowing across Iowa's ninety-nine counties, spilling into bordering states. Each time Henry introduced himself, he called himself the Prohibition Man from Iowa and did not seem to notice the eye rolls and snickers that accompanied his introduction.

In 1928, Senator Dunn moved his Iowa office from Storm Lake to Fort Dodge, bringing him closer to the federal courthouse. If he wasn't meeting with his constituents or working on a bill, he walked two blocks to visit the courtroom when he knew a bootlegger's trial was in session. What he saw displeased him.

Prohibition had been the U.S. law for nine years. Senator Dunn watched one bootlegger after another receive a fine, pay it, and walk out of the courtroom. A few of them served a few months in jail along with their fine. Nothing the Senator saw made him feel as if the great wheels of justice were working.

In November of 1929, Alvin Truly sat in the Fort Dodge courtroom, waiting to hear testimony for his most recent arrest. A pair of brothers from Webster City tried selling a pint of whiskey to one of his agents, who was undercover. While the pair argued a pint was hardly anything to get bothered over, the law stated anything over two ounces was enough for an arrest and conviction. Agent Truly wasn't hopeful they would receive anything more than the minimum fine. With each arrest, he was determined to extract as many dollars from their pockets as possible and keep them from distilling for the few months they sat behind bars.

Truly listened as his Revenue agent testified to buying the liquor. The agent had no more than walked into a poolhall before one of the brothers solicited him, offering him a pint for $10.

While listening to his agent tell the story, Truly heard a door behind him bang and felt a slight breeze as someone entered the courtroom. The newcomer sat on the other side of the courtroom, just behind Alvin's right shoulder. Curious, he glanced over and saw a large man with a square face. Alvin Truly had seen Senator Dunn only once, but he recognized him immediately. Alvin knew the trial would be a disappointment, but the opportunity to talk to the Senator was a present dropped into his lap.

Receiving the minimum, the brothers paid their paltry fine and walked away from the courthouse. Senator Dunn sat in his seat and waited for everyone to leave. Alvin Truly did the same until only the two of them remained in the empty room. Alvin got up from his seat and approached the politician.

"Senator, my name is Alvin Truly. I am the Federal Prohibition Agent for the Northern District. Do you have a few moments? I'd like to talk to you about what you just witnessed in this room today."

Senator Dunn invited Truly to his office. "It's just two blocks down the street," he said.

While they walked, the men discussed the matters of the day, the weather, and national sports. Both men were avid fans of the Chicago Cubs.

The Senator's office was small and bone bare, only a desk and three chairs filling the space. Nothing adorned his walls. His desk was free of paper.

"Pretty plain in here," Truly thoughtlessly remarked.

"I don't believe in frills," the Senator replied. "The people of Iowa pay me to represent them, not decorate my office. So, tell me about your job and what you believe needs to be done."

Alvin told the Senator his background and how he had been promoted from sheriff. He then described his typical day and finished with the brothers who were just released with a small fine. "You saw for yourself one of the problems," Truly stated. "The laws are too lenient. Most of these criminals are given a light fine, one they are happy to pay, so they can get back to their whiskey making. The big-time makers receive a small sentence to go along with that fine. They serve a few months and then go back to business as usual. The laws are not harsh enough to discourage whiskey distilling."

"Hmm. I've seen that for myself. I believe they should serve ten to fifteen years, based on the amount of whiskey. A man looking down the barrel of a fifteen-year shotgun is going to avoid the gun altogether. What are your thoughts?"

Alvin Truly could feel his body buzzing with excitement. Something serious was going to happen, and this man wanted his input. "Ten, at least. Two ounces to a gallon should be a ten-year minimum. The big makers, the ones who sell barrels to other distributers, should receive life. If you could help get the sentences toughened up, that would be great. And the fine should start at $5,000."

As Alvin spoke, the Senator nodded his head in agreement, scribbling notes on a small sheaf of papers he took from his jacket pocket. The agent felt hopeful "We also need more men," Alvin continued. "There are 134 agents covering Illinois, Iowa, and Wisconsin. That adds up to 273 counties, each one of my men covering two plus counties." Agent Truly had done the math many times. "If we could get enough funds to hire two agents for every county in those states, we could stay on top of the rumors and tips we receive from honest citizens." When he finished, Alvin looked hopefully to the senator.

"Federal Agent, let me tell you something about politics. Getting men to make the penalties harsher is just a matter of making them understand how little the current ones are working. That work can be done in a matter of months. But getting them to open the coffers and go on record for spending money is a much more difficult task. In this economy, the good people of Iowa want to hear how we are cutting spending. It could be the death of any politician, and they all know it."

Alvin felt his heart sink. Instead of focusing on what could be done, he thought only of the bootleggers who had yet to be discovered and arrested. Dozens of them would never see one hair on a Regulator's head.

Agent Truly thanked the senator for his time and received a promise of "I'll try."

Senator Dunn wasn't a man who told people what they wanted to hear for the sake of getting them out of his office. He said what he believed whether the news was wanted or not. He meant to carry through on his promise of "I'll try."

Back on Capitol Hill, Dunn talked to every Senator who would sit down with him. With specific examples of bootleggers being given a light fine or a few months in jail, his colleagues listened intently.

Senator Dunn no longer believed Iowa's Prohibition was a model about which he should brag. His conversation with Alvin Truly had awakened a great desire to put things right. He planned a way to truly eliminate the liquor-making business. The senator also saw an opportunity to pave the way to re-election.

Before Senator Dunn could put forth a bill exacting harsher penalties, two other legislators, a Senator from Washington and a Representative from New York, proposed the Jones-Stalker Act, also known as the Increased Penalties Act. The bill increased the maximum fine from $5,000 to $10,000. The maximum jail sentence went from one year to five. It did not address minimum penalties.

Dunn was furious. He had missed a sparkling opportunity to get his name in the newspapers as well as splashed around the Republican party. Additionally, the new bill did nothing to alleviate the problems he had seen sitting in the courtroom. It didn't force judges to give a severe minimum penalty. The bill still allowed them discretion in punishing the bootleggers. The bill passed on March 2, 1929, and was enacted immediately.

Trying to salvage some of his missed opportunity, Senator Dunn wrote another bill, requesting Congress to allocate an additional $240 million to hire additional Revenue agents. Like a cement-filled balloon, the bill sat in the dirt, the other members of Congress staying as far away from Senator Dunn as possible. The stock market had crashed only five months earlier, and America was hanging on by an economical cobweb. No politician wanted to ride the suicide train with Dunn.

The Dunn Bill was the last one the senator wrote. When he came up for re-election in November, his opponent used the bill against him, calling Dunn "The Spendthrift Senator," defeating him handily.

CHAPTER 24

Earl was already thirty minutes late, nothing I hadn't experienced before, but I was weary of his disrespect. The first few times, he had provided excuses so flimsy they could have been folded in half. The last few times he was tardy, he did not bother to say why. He just hopped into my truck and slammed the door, releasing a loud sigh.

During each meeting, he checked his pocket watch several times, letting me know he had better things to do with his time.

While I waited, I thought about the last five years. I had held more money in my hands than I had ever seen. My family was well provided for, and, at times, I was able to deposit money on Father Joe's steps for anyone in need. Unlike other bootleggers, I did not buy new cars and jewels or add on to my house. No one other than Earl knew I was making so much money. I recognized from the beginning it was safest to stay out of everyone's sights.

Instead of living in luxury, I took my profits and filled the floorboards of my parlor, stacks of hundred-dollar bundles, lined up like piles of folded sheets. I would be able to feed and clothe my children for the rest of their lives. We would never go without again.

My peace of financial mind juxtaposed against the trials of running a business. The operation was getting more difficult to manage. Enactment of the Jones Act in January made my men jumpy. Five years in prison, their families having to make-do without them, gave them serious thought as to whether the money was worth it. Some quit, but those who remained stuck together and demanded a higher wage. They were going to put away money for their loved ones in the event they went to prison.

The Klan had also become a major worry. I assumed they would show up somewhere again. Because of their activities, we buoyed our security. Even so, the destruction of Stange's property along with shots fired at my men had lost me some of my workforce. The remaining setters and farmers had demanded a man who would stand guard with a shotgun. The lookout would run if Regulators showed up, but he would shoot at anyone coming at him wearing a white sheet. To keep Albert Stange from dumping the operation, I promised to replace his hog house and give him a higher fee for each barrel.

A hike in wages, an extra man at each site, a new building for Stange—these took more money from under my floorboards. To offset costs, I had to bump the price of whiskey. Fifteen dollars a gallon went up to twenty-five. I wasn't worried about a drop in sales. No matter the cost, people wanted to have a good time, and they had shown they were willing to pay for it.

My biggest worry was Earl. In the last six months, he was harder to find when I needed a meeting. I knew he was dodging me. I also suspected he was running his own stills.

People in this town talk, and I heard some new farmers had joined the operation. I had no knowledge of anyone new being taken on, and if there were I would have been told. Perhaps this was only rumor or perhaps they had decided to start their own still, and people assumed they were with us. Or, perhaps there was a new boss starting his own syndicate, who wasn't Earl. All of this seemed possible, but unless I wanted to investigate it myself, I had no way of confirming anything I heard.

I was very certain Earl was skimming some of my profits. Each farm produced a given amount per week. It was pure and simple math. Lately, though, there was more 'ruined mash' and 'broken bottles.' Earl seemed to think I was dumb enough to believe his stories. The man had told many embellished tales to the fools in the saloons and now believed I was one of them. Perhaps I should look on the skimming as a positive sign. If he had started his own stills, he would not be stealing from me.

Whatever was true or false, my problem was how to handle him. If I squeezed Earl too hard or fired him, I would have to run the operation, which meant revealing myself as the boss. I had too much to lose to have the law chasing me. I couldn't spend a day in jail much less five years. If I let him continue his behavior, he would only push the line a little farther forward. I couldn't afford to ignore his conduct.

Picking my brain over my Earl problem, I was startled when he jumped into my truck. I had been so lost in my thoughts I hadn't heard his vehicle pull up behind mine. Once I looked in my rearview mirror, I saw why. Earl now drove a shiny, new, red F-29 Oldsmobile sedan, which drove like it was on clouds. This was his second new vehicle. Last year, he got himself a new Ford truck. Another problem was how to convince him to keep a low profile.

Without even a proper greeting, Earl said, "I don't really have time for all these meetings. What did you want?"

"I don't think one meeting a month is too many meetings," I countered. "I want to review the operation as I do every month. I've noticed a drop-off in production. Why is that?"

"You have to understand," Earl started in a condescending tone, "that every production place has its problems. You've got to take into

account human error. Those boys ruin about one batch of mash each month. They break bottles. Heck, I'm sure some of our product gets drunk or stolen and sold on the side."

"As far as being sold on the side, wouldn't you consider that a lack of control over your men? No one within the operation should be selling. And by my calculations, ruined mash and breakage is far more than it should be. I've kept track of production since I started this business, and the amount not making it to the distributors has gone up by thirty percent. If your men are that clumsy or bad at making mash, then you should find yourself different employees."

Suggesting he couldn't handle his own men or he was running the operation poorly would hopefully curtail some of his side selling. I could tell I had made him angry, but my own anger wouldn't let me back off. I continued, "Perhaps we should dissolve the employer-employee relationship. I can run the operation myself."

Earl blanched and looked at me, his eyes bugging from their sockets. "You? My men aren't going to follow you. You can't do this without me!"

He was absolutely correct, but I needed to put him back in his appropriate place. "And you think you can do this without me? You can keep the books, handle the money, keep the distributors happy? When we first put this together, you admitted you couldn't handle the bookkeeping end of the business."

Earl said nothing and stared at his hands. I could tell he was weighing my words and thinking about whether he could go out on his own. I knew he didn't want the headache of management. He enjoyed driving around, visiting each site, conversing with the farmers. In his heart, Earl Miller knew he would make a mess of the business.

"Let's just start over again," he said. "I'm out there putting my name in front of the Feds. If I get caught, I'm going away for five years. I think I deserve more."

He had a point. Alvin Truly wasn't trying to catch me. Earl's name as the kingpin had been on people's lips for several years. Truly would have loved to put the cuffs on Earl, but he didn't know a thing about me. Because I was making more than enough money, I decided he should be my partner instead of my employee. "Fifty-fifty," I said. "You can be an equal partner in the business. But, I want some changes made. No more ruined mash or broken bottles. I want whiskey output where it used to be for each farm. No more being late to meetings, and you will come with a more cooperative attitude. And, you really need to think about being more discreet in your living style."

Earl held out his hand. "All except the last part, we've got a deal," he said. "I don't tell you how to live your life, and you don't tell me how to live mine. Now, we do have some other business to discuss."

Earl listed off the usual problems: shortage of setters, farmers wanting more money for each barrel, and adding a supply truck to drop off materials to each farm. All were easily solved with more cash.

One problem was unexpected. John Krupp, who hadn't joined the business, wanted to use our train stop. The train traveled past his house, and it only made sense to him that he put his barrels on the train when we loaded our cases. "I want twenty percent from each barrel," I said. "We set up the train stop, so he's not getting it for free. If he doesn't want to pay, then he can find his own way to get his whiskey to wherever he sells it."

Finishing Earl's concerns, I brought up my main worry: our Des Moines distributor was asking for a larger share of the profits due to the Jones Act. We had been selling almost exclusively to this single distributor, who made enormous amounts of money when he sold to Chicago and Kansas City. When I began the operation, I didn't have contacts in those cities, which is why I went through the distributor. Now, I was at the point where I either needed to give him what he wanted or figure out a way to go around him.

"We should cut out Des Moines," Earl said. "They're taking thirty percent. If we ran the booze ourselves to Chicago and Kansas City, we could keep that percent, paying our setters and farmers more. It would pay for my half of the business while you would still take in more than what you're making now. It settles any money problems we would have."

He was right, and I knew it. "How are we going to transport it? The train goes to Des Moines. We'd have to switch trains in Des Moines to send it to Kansas City."

"We'll take it to the cities ourselves," Earl said. "We'll load barrels in stock trailers. I've already got a couple of drivers, and I'm sure I can come up with a few more. We'll either stagger the loads, one city at a time, or we'll send them all out the same night. Don't worry. I'll figure it out."

"If we can manage, I have another city we might add," I said. The Des Moines distributor had received an order from Omaha's liquor syndicate, and they wanted whiskey from Templeton. Des Moines reached out to me to request additional stock, which we were supposed to ship to Omaha ourselves.

Omaha's boss was Tom Dennison, also known as Pickhandle. Dennison's parents were Irish immigrants from Delhi, Iowa. He settled in Omaha in 1892 after a career as a prospector, saloon owner, gambler, and robber. He came from the West and settled in Omaha because it was "wide open" for his kind of business. His gambling operations were in Omaha's third ward, and he worked with temperance groups to shut down half of Omaha's saloons, obviously those who were his competition. He used his political power to get his own politicians elected to public offices and had his own mayor, 'Cowboy' James Dahlman, who was elected eight times. The Omaha police reported directly to Dennison.

Now seventy-one, Pickhandle did business from his home on Military Avenue. He wanted Templeton to start shipments to Omaha to supply his gambling operations.

"There will be repercussions from Des Moines when he finds out we've gone around him as well as added Omaha." I knew the apprehension in my voice was coming through.

"Don't worry about Des Moines. He'll find his booze from someone else. He doesn't have a choice. If we don't sell to him, then we don't sell to him. So be it. If he turns us in, he'll go down with us. Tell Omaha we're in."

Once again, Earl was right. Des Moines couldn't force us to sell our product to them and they were being watched by the Feds as much as we were, but I was sure there would be ramifications. I didn't know what they would be, but I felt we could handle them. By making Earl a partner, I had just solved the remainder of my worries. He was now more invested than he had been before.

CHAPTER 25

By 1930, three years after Jimmy signed on as Truly's snitch, he was promoted. No more sitting in pig shit. No more back-breaking work lifting barrels. Skeet wanted him to become a driver. Jimmy didn't know where or when; he just knew he needed to be ready to leave Stange's farm at ten o'clock in the evening.

Jimmy wouldn't have been promoted so soon after joining the organization, but some of the men had quit, afraid of being arrested and spending five years in jail.

When asked why he wasn't afraid of spending the prime of his life in jail, Jimmy replied he didn't have any family to worry over. In truth, he knew he would never be convicted because Alvin Truly would save him.

Skeet also owed it to him. Every man who had been running the Stange operation quit, except Jimmy. Skeet thought Jimmy stayed out of loyalty and wanted to reward him for sticking with the business. It also brought a deep trust. Jimmy was now considered a 'reliable man,' and with that came more knowledge of the syndicate's operations.

Jimmy's new duties required him to drive Skeet around, visiting the thirty operations in the organization. Jimmy had never known how many farms were involved because he had worked on the same five farms from the day he was hired. He was in awe of the size of Skeet's kingdom.

With his promotion also came a fat raise. Instead of a hayloft or basement, Jimmy now lived on the top floor of a family's small house. They had come upon tough times, and—unwilling to take a job in the whiskey business—the husband moved his seven children to the main floor of their house, renting out his bedrooms. Each evening, they spread out blankets and pillows in their parlor and kitchen. Jimmy felt guilty taking up two rooms, but he was not willing to share with any of the children.

After the evening's business, Skeet allowed Jimmy to drive his new Oldsmobile home. By twilight the next evening, Jimmy was to be parked in front of Skeet's house, waiting to drive him from farm to farm. No later than five in the morning, Jimmy dropped his boss back to his house and returned for his breakfast with the family.

Along with every Sunday, Jimmy was given one day a month to do as he pleased; however, he did not have use of the Oldsmobile. Skeet dropped Jimmy at his boarding house and picked him up for work the day after. Skeet never divulged his business on those monthly days; Jimmy assumed he visited a girl he kept secret for some reason.

After several months of spending nine hours a day in the car, Jimmy came to like his boss. Skeet was charming and funny. As they drove from one farm to the next, Skeet regaled Jimmy with his stories, ones he had told often in the saloon, but Jimmy was a new audience. Jimmy shared a few of his stories as well, and the two men bonded over illegal activities.

Jimmy had even asked Skeet's advice on girls he liked. Eventually,

Jimmy thought of Skeet as more than his boss. Jimmy hadn't seen his own father since he ran away, so he now treated Skeet as a surrogate.

When Jimmy had agreed to become a snitch, he didn't know any of the men involved in the business. It had been easy to consider only himself and his strong desire to stay out of jail, never thinking about the men he would send to prison in his stead. Jimmy's conscience was beginning to nag him.

He didn't believe whiskey making or selling was criminal, and as he became acquainted with the other setters and farmers, he discovered the reasons behind their actions. The farmers didn't want to lose their land, and many of the setters had no way of earning enough money to feed themselves or their families if they had one. With the increased penalties, Jimmy couldn't tolerate the thought of any man, especially Skeet, spending five years behind bars for making or selling something that had been legal for hundreds of years. If Federal Agent Truly got his cuffs on Skeet, he would do everything in his power to ensure the syndicate boss spent the maximum years in prison as well as pay the maximum fine.

Jimmy didn't want that crime on his life record, but he didn't know a way around it. If he told Skeet his deal with Truly, he might wind up in a roadside ditch, beaten bloody, with no money and nowhere to go. If he ignored Truly or fed him useless information, the agent would put him back in prison and make him serve a long sentence. The trick would be giving Truly what he wanted and making sure no one was caught. Impossible, thought Jimmy.

On a mild September evening, Skeet asked Jimmy if he wanted to make some extra money. Jimmy was always looking to earn more, especially since he hadn't been saving any of his cash. Instead, his pay went into his hands and out as soon as he could make it to one of the local businesses to buy a new pair of clothes, a pocket watch, several knives—some for hunting and others for his pocket.

When Jimmy pulled the Oldsmobile onto Stange's farm, Skeet was there with a large truck. It wasn't a pickup truck; it was an animal trailer. Jimmy noticed several men standing around the vehicle; some he recognized, and others he didn't.

"Men," Skeet started, "we've got a big job ahead of us. We're going to dig up the aged barrels and load them onto the trucks, starting with this farm and then moving on to a few more. Once each truck is loaded with whiskey, we'll load the animals. When a truck is ready, the driver and his partner will head out. I've got the destination on a piece of paper I'll hand the driver."

Jimmy could see his system immediately. Each farm had hidden barrels and animals heading to the stockyard. Each pair of men would be given their own truck and address for the drop-off. Just like the setters, the drivers didn't know anyone else's destination, only their own. If they were caught, they didn't have much information to share.

Jimmy and the other men grabbed shovels from a pile lying on the ground and began to dig. Jimmy had been one of the men who had buried the Stange barrels after they had aged.

With the first cask out of the ground, Skeet pried off the top and sunk an empty pint Mason jar into the amber liquid. He brought it out and tasted it, smacking his lips after it went down his throat. "Good stuff," he pronounced. He then passed the remaining liquid around to the rest of the men. When it was Jimmy's turn, he smelled it, enjoying the notes of alcohol and oak. When he took a sip, the liquid slid down his throat with a bit of a punch on the back end.

While the other men continued digging, Jimmy sidled up to Skeet. "No more bottles, boss?" he asked.

"Takes too long. The other side will bottle the booze. More profit this way." Skeet wasn't in the mood to converse.

"Just one more question." Jimmy knew when he could push Skeet and when he couldn't. The long hours in the car had given him a sense about his boss. "Why the animals? We could fit more barrels if the truck was empty. And why are we loading them after we load the whiskey?"

Skeet grinned, pleased with his own cleverness. "No Regulator wants to go into a trailer full of smelly animals. Chickens and hogs are the worst. They'd have to wade around in shit, which would get their fancy shoes dirty. Besides, this is a new way to transport. It will take them awhile to catch on—if ever. Why the animals last? Do you want to try to load those kegs while the hogs are in there? This way, the animals will work themselves around the barrels."

Jimmy admired Skeet's talent. He could outthink anybody Jimmy had ever met. The man had an unnatural capacity for being sly.

"You're headed out first, son. Think you can drive one of these?" Skeet asked.

"You bet. I can drive anything with wheels. Where to?"

"I'm putting you with Frank. He's a good man. Been with me for a long time. He'll take care of you if anything happens. Follow whatever Frank tells you. He's been in some scrapes and has a good head on him."

Skeet handed Jimmy a piece of paper. On it, in Skeet's own handwriting, was written an address in Kansas City. It would be more than a four-hour drive with a trailer loaded full of booze and hogs. Jimmy realized Skeet had just handed him a piece of evidence.

With the animals loaded, the men stood around the truck, waiting for the final 'go ahead.' From inside the trailer, they heard the hogs grunting in the dark, working at the barrels. The animals would continuously belabor the containers, probing them with their snouts and pushing on them with their heads.

"I hate hogs," Jimmy announced. "They're stupid and smelly."

Frank corrected him. "They're actually very clean and smarter than dogs. They're also very curious. Until they get them barrels figured out, they'll keep at 'em. Didn't you grow up on a farm?"

"Hell no! I hate animals, especially pigs. But I do like bacon," Jimmy said with a grin.

Frank was not impressed by Jimmy's humor or his lack of farm knowledge. How could someone who had grown up in Iowa be so ignorant about farm matters? he wondered. Frank had never lived on a farm, but he had a general knowledge and loved all animals. He hoped to own a few acres with some horses and cows someday. Jimmy's comments were the materials Frank used to build a fence of animosity between himself and his partner. After this trip, he hoped he would never have to work with the man again.

Given the 'go ahead,' Frank immediately jumped into the driver's seat, leaving Jimmy with no other option than the passenger. "I thought I was supposed to drive," Jimmy said, looking across at Frank.

Staring straight ahead, Frank replied, "I don't mean to be offensive, but I don't know you. And I'm not putting my freedom in your hands. I've been behind the wheel of a truck most of my life, so I'm going to drive." He started the vehicle and put it in gear.

The men would travel east on county roads and then take the newly paved Jefferson Highway south to Kansas City.

Feeling rancor from the driver's side, Jimmy tried to make amends with Frank. "What kind of music do you listen to? Myself, I like country. I could listen to Jimmie Rodgers all day long. I bet I can yodel as good as him. Wanna hear?" Jimmy started to clear his throat.

"No. And I don't want to hear you sing either." Frank scowled into the windshield.

Trying a new topic, Jimmy asked, "Where you from? You're Irish, right? What are you doin' workin' for these Germans? Don't the Irish make whiskey?"

"I'm from None of Your Damn Business," Frank retorted. "I got a question for you since you seem to like questions so much. How did you get into whiskey making?"

Discomfort immediately crawled up Jimmy's back. Frank had chosen the one topic Jimmy wished to avoid, but he wanted to please Frank and become friendly with him. "My grandfather. He taught me."

"Is he still alive? Still cooking? Where does he do his business?" Frank sprayed questions at Jimmy shotgun-like.

While in jail, Jimmy had concocted a background around his whiskey-making knowledge, but it had not been told often, and now—in his nervousness—he was unsure of the details. Instead of keeping the information more general, Jimmy affected Skeet's storytelling style and began weaving a new background. "He lives in Lake View, a little cabin along Black Hawk Lake. It's convenient, you know? The water and all. He taught me how to make whiskey when I was just eight years old. We would cook whiskey all night, and he always let me taste it. In fact, I had a better palate than he did. I could tell just from a teaspoon of the mash if the whiskey was going to be good or really good. He passed his secrets down to me."

Frank's suspicion antennae had dialed in station 'Bullshit.' Perhaps the grandfather part was true, but the last? Who lets an eight-year-old child cook whiskey in the middle of the night? "Why aren't you cookin' for yourself?" Frank wanted to know. "Seein's how you're such an expert on it all."

Jimmy's stomach dropped a little. He hadn't expected the question. Instead of backing up and admitting he didn't know as much as he claimed, which would lose him credibility with Frank, he decided to wade in a little deeper. "He offered me a fifty-fifty partnership, but I wanted to get out of Lake View."

"Oh, why was that?" Frank continued to pummel him with questions, wanting to see how far he would go.

Relieved he was back on ground made of truth, Jimmy replied, "Got in trouble. A little car theft." Jimmy proceeded to tell the story of the neighbor's stolen car and his fleeing from the law. "I was released into Carroll County," he said, finishing his fugitive tale.

Frank was silent and thought, Jimmy was caught in Harlan, which is Shelby County, and released in Carroll County? Something wasn't right. Jimmy wouldn't have done time for car theft in a county jail. He would have been taken to Fort Madison in Lee County, the southern tip of Iowa, which is also where he would have been released. He was either lying about his time in jail or he was telling the truth. Either way, he was not to be trusted.

Frank decided to pretend he believed Jimmy's story, but he mentally took notes on the details. When they returned from Kansas City, Frank vowed he would have a private conversation with Skeet and compare stories. He was sure his boss had vetted the setter, but how well did they really know him?

This caravan of trucks rolled into Council Bluffs with reinforcements from Sioux City for farm holiday. Sioux City men were in the crowd which surround house when 61 men were held in jail.

BAND TOGETHER IN LOCAL BODIES

Statewide Action Is Contemplated.

By J. S. Russell.
(Register Farm Editor.)

Emphasis on the farm and chattel mortgage foreclosure problem in Iowa has shifted from national and state legislative channels to individual local communities.

...ized farmers in a number ...ies have announced their ... to resist foreclosure and ...sion. A more recent de... ...t, however, is the at... ... work out plans whereby ... in financial distress may ...o continue farming.

COMING FARM AUCTIONS

TUESDAY, JAN. 19.
Farm sale 4 miles south of Lisbon by George Nost.

THURSDAY, JAN. 21.
Farm sale 5½ miles east of Springville by Neal Larson.
Farm sale 5 miles northwest of Alburnett by Gust Carlson.

CHAPTER 26

Hard times were not our fault. It wasn't because we were lazy or loose with our money. We didn't overplant because we were greedy. And I resented anyone who blamed us for our situation.

Just like Prohibition, Iowa's experience with hard times started well before the rest of the country. During the 20s, the stock market and the East Coast took off like hot air balloons, but the farming economy and the Midwest dove like submarines.

Iowa farmers enjoyed a boom during the war. The federal government needed additional food to feed the troops as well as ship grain to a war-torn Europe, so our farmers stepped up and rose to the call of need. As a benefit, commodity prices soared. Farmers took out federal loans to buy more land and equipment. Better machinery made large-scale farming easier, allowing farmers to plant more crops. Anyone passing through Iowa saw acres of corn, beans, wheat, and rye—every inch of Iowa soil bearing harvest. Large feed lots sprang up with hogs or cattle. Large farming operations thrived while the small-time farms died.

After the war, and especially when Europe recovered enough to start feeding its own people, there was no longer a need for so much food production. Prices dropped, farm loans couldn't be paid, and farmers started to lose their farms.

Our own Republican congressman, Gilbert Haugan, introduced a farm relief bill in conjunction with Charles McNary from Oregon in 1924. The legislation gave the federal government the authority to buy surplus agriculture at pre-war rates, hoping to regulate prices again. The first two attempts to pass the bill failed due to Southern congressmen who would not vote for it. After some negotiating, the bill finally passed the House and the Senate. We gave a collective sigh of relief until President Calvin Coolidge vetoed it. He opposed price fixing and thought the farmers should be able to engineer their own way out of the farm crisis.

What was he thinking? He was the son of a storekeeper, not a farmer. He grew up in the Northeast, not the Midwest. He twice vetoed farm-relief bills.

When 1932 rolled around, corn was selling for 8 cents a bushel; pork, 3 cents a pound; beef, 5 cents a pound; and eggs, 10 cents a dozen.

Trying to save themselves, three thousand Iowa farmers, led by Milo Reno, held a convention in Des Moines and planned a farm strike for July 4. Their slogan—"Stay At Home, Buy Nothing, Sell Nothing"—led to a milk strike in the Sioux City area. No strike or Farm Holiday solved the agricultural crisis. If anything, they only led to hostile division among the farmers.

We lost our voice in the White House in November when Iowa's only president, Herbert Hoover, who had been dubbed "The Great Humanitarian," was defeated by Franklin Delano Roosevelt by over seven million votes in the 1932 election. As proud as we were to have one of our own sitting behind the Presidential desk, Hoover did nothing to help the Iowa farmers at the federal level, believing individual states should step up to provide the charity.

Roosevelt was not an avid proponent of Prohibition. After more than ten years of the "noble experiment," few believed it had achieved its purpose. If anything, the opposite had happened. The federal government was losing tax revenue from liquor sales while spending millions to enforce. Many restaurants, no longer able to sell liquor, had closed their doors. Thousands of Americans were dying each year from drinking tainted liquor. An even greater consequence was, in my opinion, that the law was making criminals out of us. To survive this horrible economic hardship, many of us have had no other option than to break the law.

By the spring of 1932, notices of farm auctions covered pages of local newspapers. Some farmers tried honoring their loans by selling everything they had; others allowed the bank to repossess their property. I watched as farms around me were auctioned off for pennies. Land that had been in families since the sod was first broken by their ancestors was gone, bought cheaply by another family. It cost farmers more money to produce and harvest their crops than they were paid for it.

Economic times were dire across the United States.

Iowa farmers were desperate, and those who had been too afraid of breaking the law now wanted in. Earl's name was passed to them by their neighbors, who were buying new farm equipment and paying their bank mortgages. Afraid of foreclosure, the men came begging at his door: save them, save their farm, save their children. They would take less money for the use of their farms if he would include them. They promised to be discreet. Their desperation showed in their eyes and sounded in their voices.

One man begged Earl on his knees, the bony whiteness showing though his thin overalls. After that night, Earl no longer lived in his house. He moved around like an alley cat, never staying in one location too long. He didn't want to peer into another pair of anguished eyes.

Sitting in my truck the following Thursday, Earl relayed each request, describing the state of each suffering man. His own eyes stared into mine, wanting to hear we would take them all. For all his brash talk, Earl Miller had a heart that would reach out to any creature in need.

He enjoyed being the kingpin, the big boss, until it was time to carry forth a difficult decision. Now, he wanted to recede, to give me back his portion of the business. "Please," he said. "I can't." He would keep the money, but I would make the final decision. We would not collectively decide who to take in and who to leave out; he would make me do it. His conscience would remain guiltless, allowing him to sleep at night.

I did not sleep. I paced the parlor at night like a caged tiger, my family tucked safely in the bedrooms above my head. Without my illegal income, I would have had no house for them. I imagined my own desperation, my loss of control. I too would have been on my knees if I thought it meant saving my only means of support. I had not been on the other side for so long that I had forgotten the feeling of vulnerability, dependence, and helplessness. I held the power to save them.

But I could build the empire no bigger without losing control or being caught. Each new farmer or setter or runner was another person who knew the business. Another person who might be in the hands of the Feds already. Another soul on my list of responsibilities.

Some of our farms had been raided, and Earl and I were fortunate; no one talked. We paid the lawyer and the fines, as we promised we would, but each arrest kept me pacing the floor at night, wondering if Earl's name would be given in exchange for freedom.

We had been lucky, but everyone knows luck is limited. Eventually, you run out of it, and you are left with a mess.

Therefore, I held at thirty farms and the men needed to run the operations. Outside of the syndicate, other farmers and anyone who could hide a still made their own whiskey and sold to whoever would buy it. Some were cautious, and others were too desperate to ask enough questions.

Barrells, Mason jars, pint jars—anything that would hold liquid was filled with illegal hooch. Carroll County residents joked about dogs not being able to bury bones without running into liquor. The church basement was filled to capacity, barrels were buried on every farm that made it, bottles of the stuff were hidden inside corn cribs. The Regulators crawled over our county like fleas on the back of a dog, their long rods probing into anywhere they thought whiskey might be hidden. Sometimes they were right, and other times they were wrong. The worst sound of Prohibition was the crack of breaking glass as their probes went through dried ears of corn and into a bottle.

Some days I breathed easy, knowing they were on the trail of another bootlegger in some other part of Iowa. Other days, I knew they were scouring our county because of some new intel.

Sheriff Katz had telephoned the pool hall every time the Feds were headed into our county. Someone in our syndicate had reported the light, seen on the outside of the hall. Because we couldn't get the word out fast enough, the sheriff had even agreed to drive through the county hatless, indicating the law was close behind.

Alvin Truly knew our syndicate existed, asking questions of anyone who was caught. Everyone's lips were as tight as the lids on the jars we used. It didn't matter if they were part of our organization or not. They could have offered up Earl's name to get themselves out of trouble, but there seemed to be some kind of code among bootleggers. We were decent, hardworking Iowans; and who was the federal government to tell us how we could make our living, especially in such dire economic times? A band of pride wound around us and drew us close to one another when it involved outfoxing the Regulators.

However, it was wearing on me. My stomach ached and my teeth were starting to loosen. I didn't know how long we would continue our enterprise. Before Earl told me he wanted no part in the decision making, I had hoped to sell him my part of the business. I wanted out. I wanted to live a stress-free and peaceful life. I had enough money to last us ten years if I was careful. I was counting on the Depression coming to an end. Then, perhaps, I could open my own store. My business would be legal, and my mind would be worry-free.

For the foreseeable future, however, I would need to hang on a bit longer. I felt an obligation to those in my employ, but only as far as the Depression would take us.

You can't fight the Devil with cream puffs

BILLY SUNDAY is called sensational. He is. He doesn't believe in fighting the devil with cream puffs. He gets audiences—and converts. TRUE STORY has been called sensational. It is. This magazine believes in fighting the devil with his own weapons—it gets readers and results.

Hundreds of thousands of people jam the biggest auditoriums in the United States to hear Billy Sunday. He doesn't believe the road to heaven is paved with soft words.

Yes, TRUE STORY is sensational—the Master Himself was sensational—when He turned to those who were about to stone a fallen woman, and said, "He that is without sin among you let him first cast a stone,"—when He advised the rich young man to sell all he possessed and give the proceeds to the poor—when He scourged the money changers and drove them from the Temple.

Perhaps you decry sensationalism and because TRUE STORY is sensational, you think "something ought to be done about it."

Then you have never read TRUE STORY with an unprejudiced mind.

If you read TRUE STORY with the thought of getting something uplifting out of it, something you can pass along to others, who perhaps need the lessons it teaches more than you—then you cannot be disappointed.

TRUE STORY is life's mirror. It will not change—unless truth changes. It will be tomorrow what it is today—the most frank, sincere and helpful magazine in America.

We have not known a single instance of any human being, young or old, that has been harmed by reading TRUE STORY. On the contrary thousands have told us that TRUE STORY has guided them through mazes of evil forces and evil influences, into the light of moral sanity and reason.

A ministerial board passes on every story submitted to this magazine. TRUE STORY is the only magazine that ever adopted this policy to protect the moral and spiritual welfare of its readers.

Indeed, TRUE STORY is such a great moral force that many ministers recommend it to the young people of their congregation and it goes into millions of homes, and helps solve the problems of religious workers where the searchlight of truth is needed.

If to fight the devil with real weapons is sensational, then TRUE STORY is sensational—just as Billy Sunday is sensational.

TRUE STORY is truly the Billy Sunday among magazines.

Read These Heart-Stirring Stories in True Story for June

"His Wife's Past"—The dream of Celeste's life was to engage in an exciting romance. And her dream came true when she met and married the fascinating adventurer, Andre de Rohan. The result of that foolish marriage was an ever-growing load of sorrow and misery. A true-life story of unusual interest.

"I Came Home in Disgrace"—Lured to New York by glowing tales of success, Mary expected to have an easy time finding work. There were plenty of positions to be had but—well Mary's own story which tells what she found out and what she finally did and why. A story every girl who longs to go to New York should read.

"The Fool That I Was"—Alice thought beautiful clothes, and a superior manner were marks of good breeding. She determined to make a "lady" of herself, cost what it might. But she failed to foresee the price she would have to pay. A startling story of intrigue, adventure and excitement frankly told.

Other Thrilling Stories in the June Issue Include:

"When Jealousy is Good"
"Her Father's Secret"
"Was She to Blame?"
"My Unwed Husband"
"A Woman's Heart"
"His Double Life"
"Love's Turmoil"
"A Jest of Fate"

BILLY SUNDAY

The world's most famous evangelist in one of his characteristic poses.

A MACFADDEN PUBLICATION
25 CENTS

JUNE

Use This Coupon If You Cannot Get True Story at Your Newsstand

TRUE STORY MAGAZINE
64th St. & B'way
New York City
I want to take advantage of your Special Offer. I enclose $1.69, for which please enter my name on your mailing list

CHAPTER 27

Excitement and intrigue wove through the farmlands and towns of Carroll County. A large tent had been erected between Templeton and Carroll. It was not a circus tent.

Speculation wound around church parking lots on Sunday mornings, up and down the aisles of grocery and dry good stores during the weekdays. Women and men alike bantered it across fences. Who was assembling the tent and why?

Unknown men affixed flyers to store windows and church bulletin boards.

Evangelist Billy Heaven

• Sunday, September 23, 1932

•Sermon at 10:00 A.M.   •Healings from 11:00-1:00 P.M.

•Tuesday-Wednesday, September 25-26

•Sermon at 6:00 P.M.   •Healings from 7:00-9:00 P.M.

God's-will Donation Appreciated

Along with the information, the flyer espoused miracle testimony from real people.

"I have been a drinker for more than twenty years, and Preacher Billy Heaven cured me. I haven't had one drop since then."
    –Stern Wedwood, Moberly, Missouri

"I'm walking again after I broke my back."
    –Mike Gaines, Schuyler, Nebraska

Jimmy Krantz stood looking at the poster from behind several other heads in front of the grocery store in Templeton. Billy Heaven was obviously trying to ride the coat tails of a formerly popular evangelist, Billy Sunday.

William Ashley Sunday was Iowa born and had spent some of his childhood in the Iowa's Soldiers' Orphans' Home. His prowess as a baseball player led him first to play for Iowa teams. Discovered while he was playing in Marshalltown, Billy found his way to the majors and spent the next eight years in the outfields of professional baseball fields. As a beginning preacher, Billy Sunday came back to his Iowa roots and started in Iowa's counties, quickly branching out to neighboring state, Illinois. When his popularity grew too large for the small churches and town halls, he purchased a tent, traveling across the United States, spreading his message.

Soft whispers filtered through the crowd as the townspeople looked at the preacher's poster, most of them reminding one another of Father Joe's stern warning about attending such an event. On the street in daylight, Catholics wouldn't be caught dead at a tent revival. Their religion came from one place only: inside a Catholic church. However, in their own homes, some of Sacred Heart's congregants planned to attend the service "just for a few minutes." The unknown of another religion, especially one that healed the infirmed, piqued their curiosity beyond their control.

Jimmy held no reticence in attending; he was raised Methodist although he hadn't stepped foot inside any church since he was six-teen. Jimmy didn't relish a sermon and would have liked to come just for the healing, but he didn't want to draw attention to himself by arriving late. Therefore, he planned his day accordingly. Bootleg-ging took Sundays off: setters, rumrunners, and farmers all sitting in the pews of their local churches. Jimmy was free to spend his time as he wished, and he wished to see what was involved in a faith-heal-ing happening.

Normally, Jimmy slept in on the Lord's Day, not even opening an eye before 9:00 a.m. Thinking the evangelist service would draw a large crowd and wanting to get a seat toward the outside back in the event he decided to leave early, Jimmy hauled himself out of his warm bed, arriving at the tent-church by eight. Very few attendees were sitting on the benches, brought in by the preacher's crew. Eight in the morning was mass time for Templeton, Carroll, Willey, and Dedham. The majority population of Carroll County were sitting in churches, their priests reminding them to forgo the temptation of false ministries.

The atmosphere in the tent was dim, lit only from the outside through its entrances. In front stood a platform, eight feet wide and six feet deep, raising the speaker a few feet off the ground, just enough so those in the back could see him while he preached.

A wide aisle went up the center of the tent, rows of wooden benches on either side of it. At least a hundred people could be seated inside the tent, Jimmy thought.

As soon as the Catholic church doors released them at nine, some of the faithful decided to take a drive in the country, "just to look at the fields," they said. Parking on the south side of the tent, wanting to hide their cars from their neighbors, a few at a time crept through the tent opening and slid onto a bench. Once seated, they cautiously looked around, surprised to see people they knew, the men nodding at one another in understanding. Obviously, it had been the wives' desire to see the doings; they were only obliging their women.

By quarter to ten, the canvas-church was more than half filled. Most audience members were from Carroll or Audubon Counties, but there were also strangers in the crowd. Perhaps they had driven a distance to be healed, thought Jimmy.

Exactly on the hour, an out-of-tune guitar started playing, "Precious Lord, Take My Hand." With the first chord, a sea of eyes swept to the player. As Catholics, they were trained to stand when the priest entered the altar, brought in by a choir or organ. Confusion crossed their faces, and they looked at one another, silently asking if they were to stand with a Protestant preacher. Taking their cues from the non-Catholics attending, they glued themselves to their benches, but the unfamiliarity of the service kept them jittery.

The preacher entered the tent from the rear and started walking up the aisle toward the front, singing loudly with his left hand raised, clutching a Bible, and his right hand its lifted counterpart. He had slicked his blonde hair back from his large forehead, and his small frame sported a blue suit, white shirt, and red tie. The suit hung on him like a flour sack.

When Jimmy turned to see the minister as he walked by, he felt a shock up his back. He knew the preacher. Billy Heaven was Jimmy's prior cell neighbor.

Five years had passed since he had last seen Lyle. He questioned whether the former criminal had grown a new skin. Had he become a man of God? Jimmy was now more interested in the sermon to be delivered and wouldn't be leaving early even if his pants caught fire. He settled into his collar and pulled his hat lower, wanting to keep his identity secret. If his ex-friend was running some kind of scam, he didn't want to scare him off.

Once settled on the dais, Preacher Heaven began his sermon.

"Are you saved?" he asked in a booming voice as he held his Bible high in the air. "Or are you in the grips of the Devil?"

The Catholics didn't know if they were supposed to answer or if this question were rhetorical. They had never experienced questions being asked during a service. They only knew their memorized responses, the same for every mass they attended in every Catholic church across America. Before they decided to respond, Billy Heaven continued.

"The Lord is asking you to stand up... stand up to sin." On cue, the guitar started playing "Old Rugged Cross," and a pair of singers joined the instrument, one female and one male, their voices joining together like vines wrapped around a pole. Jimmy assumed the singers and guitar player were part of the tent-church.

The congregation stood up and sang to the hymn, one that is known to Protestants and Catholics alike. Jimmy could see the Catholics becoming more at ease, their ability to partake in the music the sole reason for it.

After the song ended, Preacher Heaven, who had been belting out the religious tune, his voice above the two singers, came to the front of the dais, his Bible held above his head again. "This is the Word of God," he said, holding the Bible out to his congregants. The black book was worn as if it had been paged through every hour of the day. "Those who don't follow the Word," he warned, "will find themselves in the fiery pits of hell and shall never see the sweet face of our Lord Jesus Christ! Can I hear an 'Amen'?"

"Amen!" shouted the crowd with a few sprinkles of "Jesus save us."

"I want to talk to you today about a very important matter, one that is nearest to my heart," Preacher Heaven continued, placing his right hand over his heart. "Love thy neighbor. These are Jesus' own words in the Bible, and in these desperate times, I ask you, have you loved your neighbor? Have you reached out and helped him, not caring whether he was Catholic, Jew, or Protestant?"

Jimmy looked down at his shoes, trying to keep himself from laughing aloud. There wasn't a Jew for miles around, and who was Lyle Lang to talk about loving his neighbor? Jimmy recalled their jailhouse conversations and Lyle bragging about stealing from anyone who was trusting enough to get near him.

"I was a sinner like you," the preacher continued. "I turned my back on those in need because I was too selfish to care about my fellow man." Once Preacher Heaven started talking about his own faults, the congregation sat a little taller, wanting a good look at the sinner in front of them.

Jimmy thought, here is where he'll tell about all of his misdeeds if he's changed his ways. Here is where I'll know if he's become a different man.

"Let me tell you good folks about this sinner," he continued, slapping his chest to emphasize he was talking about himself. "I've spent time in jail!"

With the word *jail*, the audience collectively gasped.

"When I was a young man, only eighteen-years-old, I wrote checks on other people's accounts and took the merchandise for myself. I even stole from the man who took pity on me and gave me a job!"

Jimmy couldn't believe what he was hearing; Lyle Lang was telling Jimmy's crime. As he thought back to their story swapping, there wasn't one offense Lyle could have confessed that didn't reveal how low his morals really were. Jimmy pictured Lyle standing on that dais, one town after another, conveying Jimmy's own shameful actions. Instead of ducking into his coat collar, Jimmy was now sitting tall, looking straight at Lyle, hoping he could catch his eye, daring him to continue his fabrication.

"The Lord looked down on me and took pity on my miserable soul. Yes, he did. I was arrested and put into jail. And there I found God. I was given this Bible," he said while holding it above his head, "and I started to read it." At that point, the minister looked up and raised both of his hands above his head, as if beseeching the Almighty. "God spoke to me, a lone sinner. And He said, 'Love thy neighbor.' And I knew what he meant. No more check writing. No more hurting my fellow man. And from that day forward, I was born anew!"

The word *anew* prompted the guitar player to start again, and Pastor Heaven began singing "Onward Christian Soldier." The audience jumped to their feet and joined him. Jimmy reluctantly stood and mouthed the words to his favorite country song, "Weary Prodigal Son" by the Carter Family.

Once the hymn finished and the church goers had resumed their seats, Pastor Heaven continued his sermon. He spoke on the importance of helping your fellow man and being a good Christian. He used a combination of inspiration and guilt to enforce his message. He referred to the cars parked behind the tent, shining clean in the morning sun, as evidence of their ability to financially support their neighbors. Heads dropped in embarrassment when he pointed through the canvas tent in reference to their automotive possessions.

Jimmy was surprised he did not rant on the evils of drink and the illegal activities perpetrated in Carroll County. Every tent evangelist spent half his sermon warning of the wickedness of alcohol, the famous Billy Sunday among them. However, a con man like Lyle knew better than to insult the hand that would potentially feed his wallet.

By nearly eleven in the morning, the September sun had warmed the air and crept into the tent. The heavy canvas blanketed the audience, keeping out any breeze. Forty-five minutes into the sermon, heads had begun to nod. Preacher Heaven knew his limit and finished his service with several religious songs: "Go Tell It on the Mountain," "Amazing Grace," and "What a Friend We Have in Jesus." While the congregation was singing, several men left their benches and passed along a wicker basket. Men dug coins out of their pockets, sorting through, looking for quarters. They had just done the same action in their own churches but felt guilty for not giving a little something for a religious service. It wouldn't have been polite to fill their hearts with God and leave God's basket bare.

Jimmy watched the basket as it passed from one hand to another. When it came into his possession, Jimmy put his hand deep into the basket; opened his palm, releasing only air; and scooped up a few quarters as he drew his hand back. He considered it payment. If Lyle were going to use Jimmy's sins, then he could pay a little something for them.

At precisely eleven o'clock, Preacher Heaven rose from his chair, having sat during the collection of money, and asked, "Is there anyone here who needs healing? Come to the front."

Congregants sat tall, straining their necks to raise their heads above the crowd, to see who would rise and walk to the front of the tent. A young man on crutches, dragging his right foot, made his way to the front. Murmurs rippled through the tent, neighbor asking neighbor if the man was known to anyone.

Silence descended on the crowd as Billy Heaven spoke to the man, loud enough for everyone to hear, "Tell us your name and ailment, my friend."

"Name's Timothy. My foot ain't been right since I was a child. I was born with a club foot. Can you help me?"

The evangelist indicated the man sit on a chair, brought out by one of his helpers, and laid his hands on Timothy's head. The crowd collectively held their breath while the preacher prayed. Even Jimmy was entranced, wondering what would happen next.

"Get up!" Preacher Heaven said. "Get up and throw those crutches aside!"

Timothy rose on one leg and gingerly placed his afflicted foot on the ground. He took one tentative step, then another, until he was walking normally. He turned around to face the crowd and said, "I'm healed! The preacher healed me!"

The assembly erupted into clapping and cheering. A voice from the middle of the room yelled out, "I need healing!"

A middle-aged woman wearing dark glasses was escorted to the front by another woman. Her cane and glasses announced she was blind. Once in front of Billy, the same scenario was enacted again. Billy laid his hands on the woman's head, prayed, and told her to remove her glasses. She gleefully claimed she could see again.

The throng of Christians was now on its feet, cheering and clapping. A wooden chair, two small wheels on the back and two larger wheels on the sides, carried a young child who was being pushed to the front of the tent. The young boy was known to the community. William Becker had been born with spina bifida. His parents had been told by every doctor within traveling distance there was no cure for their son. Desperate for any hope, they had brought him to the service and now were pushing his slumped body, strapped to the chair, down the aisle in search of a miracle.

Jimmy, rather than watching the parents and boy, trained his eyes on Lyle. The preacher's face tightened and lost color. His hands remained by his side, clenched. Jimmy recognized the tells. Lyle Lang was terrified.

The preacher stepped down from the platform and waited while the parents navigated the bumpy terrain, the father pushing the awkward chair. "Let the little children come to me," the preacher quoted from Luke 8:16.

Jimmy's eyes and ears remained trained on the convict. The first two miracles were certainly fakes, he thought. He wondered if his former friend was really going to attempt to heal this child. Certainly, he didn't believe in himself, did he? When he didn't succeed, what would happen to him? Would the crowd tear him apart?

When the boy was within only a few feet from the evangelist, Lyle Lang dropped to the ground and started to convulse. The crowd moved forward but were warned back by the two men who had taken the collection. "He's overcome by the Lord!" one of them yelled. "Give us room!" Each man took one end of the minister and carried him out of the tent. William and his parents were left in front, looking confused. The audience stood, staring at the tent's opening to the outside, wondering if the preacher would return.

One of the healer's men returned and stood on the platform, his hands raised to quiet the crowd. "Sorry, folks. The service is over. Preacher Heaven has exhausted himself this morning. He asked that you pray for his recovery." Without waiting for an acknowledgement, the helper left the tent again.

For a minute or two, the crowd stood in their places, looking at the opening where they last saw Billy Heaven. Then, they gathered their belongings and exited the tent. The last people through the opening were young William and his parents. Jimmy decided to remain in his seat and see if Lyle or his helpers would return. He was not leaving until he confronted the convict regarding his plagiarized 'confession.'

Jimmy sat, cleaning his nails and winding his watch, for almost an hour. The two helpers eventually came back through the opening and saw Jimmy sitting on the bench. "I'm sorry, sir, but Reverend Heaven isn't well. Were you at the service?"

"Tell Lyle Lang I want to see him. Tell him an old friend of his from the Shelby County Jail wants a word."

The men's faces changed from polite to irritated. Without acknowledging his command, they left the tent. A few minutes later,

Lyle Lang himself walked through the opening. He was still wearing his preacher suit, but he had left his Bible behind. "Jimmy, I see God's love has brought you to me."

"Don't," Jimmy said. "Don't give me that preacher stuff. I know who you are, and I know the story of your redemption. It's all bullshit! That's my crime, and you know it. So drop the act."

Lyle grinned, knowing he had been caught. "What brings you to my tent? Looking for God?"

"I didn't know it was you. But I'm sure you aren't full of the Lord. You haven't changed a bit. You just found a new way to cheat people. Those people you healed, they weren't sick, were they? That's just a scam." Jimmy's voice gave away his indignation.

"You caught me. If it hadn't been for that gimpy kid, I would have brought in a haul on the last collection. I hate it when real sick people show up. And you? How's the rat business? I haven't forgotten the game you're playing. Thought you would have been long gone by now."

Jimmy didn't want to talk about his situation. He, too, thought he would have moved on. No matter how much information he had passed to Agent Truly, he hadn't been allowed to leave. It was never enough. It wasn't good enough. He hadn't given concrete evidence on the kingpin. The reasons for his still being indebted to Truly were never-ending.

"I need a favor," Lyle said. "I have two more shows, and I need some information on this place. I can't have another gimp kid show up. I'd like you to watch everyone who comes to the show and report to my men who might have come for healing. I need to know what's wrong with them. Some ailments I can make them believe they're healed for a few days. Power of suggestion and all. Others, like the one today, I want no part of. I'll pay you ten dollars a night."

"Thanks, but no," Jimmy said. "I don't need the money, and I've got no time. I'm driving the boss these days, and he likes me to be available, especially at night. Sorry." Jimmy could have done the favor, but he didn't want to help Lyle. He found Lyle's actions loathsome, and it made his stomach twist. He thought it best they just part ways, and he hoped the ex-convict would pack his tent and move to another part of the state. He hated to see people swindled, especially those he knew.

"Does your boss know you're a snitch? What would he think about you relaying every move he makes to a federal agent? I think you've got time to help an old friend." Lyle wasn't giving him an option.

Jimmy felt trapped. In addition to a lawman, now he was also under the thumb of a criminal. He couldn't afford to have Skeet find out he was gathering information on him, but he also couldn't stomach helping a thief rob his community. "Sure. I'll be at the next meeting."

Jimmy laid in bed late Sunday morning, thinking about his new predicament. Instead of extricating himself from one thumb, he was now under two. Although he had agreed to help Lyle Lang, he had done so only to give himself more time, but he was quickly running out of it. The next service was Tuesday. Jimmy concluded he needed help, but he wasn't sure whom he could ask.

He considered telling Sheriff Katz about Lyle's past; the sheriff sometimes met with Skeet, Jimmy sitting in the car while Skeet sat in the sheriff's truck. If Jimmy told the lawman, he would have to admit his own crimes, which would be a different version than what he told his boss. He was sure the sheriff would, at some point, pass along Jimmy's story while he and the kingpin were conferring.

He contemplated telling Alvin Truly, but he seriously doubted the federal agent cared about bootleggers being scammed. He seemed to have one goal, and a dishonest preacher was not part of it. Besides,

Jimmy hated any conversation with Truly. It always ended in threats of his going to prison.

He deliberated telling Skeet, who had enough sway with most of the county and could convince them to forgo attending any more tent revivals. However, the same reason about his dishonest past would need to be revealed. Skeet would not put his reputation out there without knowing all the details.

Jimmy finally landed on telling the most powerful person in Carroll County—Father Joe Klein. He was the most senior priest, having influence over the other priests in the county. If he demanded his congregation stay away from the tent, they would obey. If he told them the preacher was a fake, they would believe him. And Jimmy could tell the priest anonymously.

Confessions transpired on Saturdays at 4:00 p.m. The confession box was not like the chapel, open at all hours. However, if a member of the church needed confession, he could leave a note on Father's door, asking for a certain time and day. If the note disappeared, it meant Father would be sitting in the box waiting for the sinner. If the note were still posted on the door, an available time and day would be written below the original.

Late Sunday afternoon, the sun setting by 5:00 p.m., Jimmy came from the shadows and snuck up to the priest's door. He knocked loudly and ran into the nearby bushes. On the note, he asked for a 10:00 p.m. confession, not knowing the priest went to bed by 9:00. Father himself opened the door, a dinner napkin attached to his shirt. Seeing the note, he tore it from the nail and read it. Jimmy could hear the priest, "For the love of Jesus, we just had mass this morning. What could have happened since then to need an emergency confession? Murder?" Jimmy hoped he would be forgiven for his poor manners once Father Joe knew the circumstance.

Thirty minutes before their meeting time, Jimmy crept to the side entrance of Sacred Heart and entered the building. He was certain no one had seen him, the residents of Templeton preparing for their evening repose. Jimmy had never been inside a Catholic church and wasn't sure where to find the confession box. He started at the front of the building, checking out the sanctuary and sacristy. Nothing looked like big boxes with doors on them. He made it down the side aisle, but there were only church pews across the nave of the church. In the rear of the church, he saw a door; when he opened it, he found chairs and kneelers. A storage room, he realized. Finally, he found what he thought were the confessionals. There were three doors: the middle one had a seat covered by a purple cushion, the two outside ones had kneelers and no seats. Jimmy supposed the middle one was for the priest. He reasoned if the father were there for several hours, he would need a comfortable place to sit. He couldn't kneel that entire time. Jimmy opened the door on the left, stepped in, and closed it. Jimmy stood there, unsure of his next move. He had heard Catholics did a lot of kneeling, but he wasn't Catholic and didn't think it appropriate for him to do so. He couldn't comfortably sit on the padded part of the kneeler, so he decided to stand.

At precisely 10:00 p.m., the little door in front of the kneeler slid open. "*In nomine Patris et Filii et Spiritus Sancti.*" Father Joe sat quietly and waited for the other side to say their part.

"Uhh. Father? I just need to tell you something, and then I'm done."

The confessional box hid the identity of the confessor, but Father Joe knew the voice of every Sacred Heart member. He did not recognize this voice, and the man's lack of confession protocol gave him away as a non-Catholic. The priest was sure he had heard and seen it all, but this was something quite unusual. "Go ahead. What do you need to tell me?" Joe sat forward in his seat and put his ear close to the divider.

"That tent preacher is a fake. He's taking people's money. He pretends to heal, but he's just a common criminal." Jimmy felt the burden lifting from his shoulders. Perhaps confession wasn't such a bad idea, he thought.

"How do you know? I believe you, but how do you know he's a fake?"

Jimmy was disappointed. He had chosen the priest to avoid having to tell his past. He thought he could tell the information and leave. He hadn't expected a return question. "I was in jail with him. And, he admitted to me he was conning people. He just wants their money."

"I assumed as much. What is it you expect me to do?"

"Tell your people!" Jimmy said a little too loudly. "Warn them!"

"The Lord gave us free choice. I've already warned them about false ministers, but I cannot keep them from attending." His voice sounded weary and disappointed.

"Sorry I bothered you, Father. I guess there's nothing either one of us can do." Jimmy was devastated.

At home in bed, unable to sleep, Jimmy thought about his next move. He couldn't shut the tent down, he couldn't make Lyle move along, and he couldn't keep people from attending. These were all out of his control. He could only decide what he would do, and he was not going to help Lyle fake-heal more people. He would lay low until the tent came down and moved along to another town. Jimmy had no other option than to take a chance on Lyle's following through on his threat.

Before it happened, if it happened, Jimmy would plan what he would say. It would be one convict's word against another, and Jimmy hoped he had built enough of a relationship with Skeet to save himself.

CHAPTER 28

Frank Hogan never created problems, and he had never asked for a private meeting before. Skeet immediately felt the seriousness of the request and offered to meet him halfway between Templeton and Dunlap, where Frank resided.

Frank had requested to meet him alone, meaning Skeet would need to drive himself. When he pulled up to St. Peter's Community Hall in Defiance, Iowa, Frank was already parked out front, smoking a cigarette, his flat cap pulled low over his eyes. He was wearing a pair of work pants and shirt, nothing special for a Sunday.

Skeet had chosen the community hall because the parish was not finished with the construction, and it would be void of workers on a Sunday afternoon. As he surveyed the progress of the building, he could see it was going to be a fine addition to the town. The bricks had been salvaged from Council Bluffs when the city council had voted to tear out their brick streets, replacing them with modern concrete. Seeing an opportunity to save some of the building costs, Father Emil Schumann had purchased them for a few dollars and a lot of prayer.

Both men exited their vehicles. Skeet noticed Frank had driven his 'day car,' as he liked to call it. Frank preferred to keep business away from his daily life. For the business, Frank drove his refitted 1926 Nash, but for his own personal use, he drove a dark blue 1928 Chrysler 75: hydraulic brakes, 75 horsepower, and a six-cylinder engine. When it was new, the car had turned heads and made men wish they owned one. Now four years old, the car had seen better days. Its original owner had put it in the ditch, scratching the paint down the driver's side and denting the front fender. Frank bought it cheap and never fixed the damage. When asked why, he replied, "You should never draw attention to yourself." He rarely washed the car, and when he drove it down the street, it didn't draw even a single glance.

In comparison, Skeet's own car was washed twice a week because the dirt roads he traveled from farm to farm kept a layer of dust on his vehicle. Like his car, his clothes were also immaculate. While he didn't spend nearly as much money or look as dapper as the Chicago kingpin, Skeet now dressed more like him than he had before he had taken on such a distinguished role. Before Earl Miller had become the kingpin, a pair of washed-out overalls was his daily uniform; now, he wore Sunday slacks and a button-down shirt. His work boots had been traded for a pair of wingtip shoes. Each time he returned to the backseat of his car, he took a cloth—especially for this purpose—and wiped the dust from his wingtips.

"Thanks for making the trip, Skeet. I appreciate you comin' out on a Sunday," Frank said, offering his hand to his employer.

"Not at all. I know we didn't come to look around Defiance, so what's the news?" Skeet took out his pipe and tobacco pouch, starting the process of a smoke.

"I don't know if I'm all wet on this, but I got some suspicions about Jimmy Krantz. Told me he was cookin' with his grandpa at age eight. And then he told me he was arrested for car theft in Shelby

County but released in Carroll County. It doesn't add up. He would have been sent to prison for car theft, not a county jail. What did he tell you?"

"Said he learned to cook from his grandpa's hired man. Hired man or grandpa—that don't make a difference. But I see your point on the jail piece."

"Either he's tellin' the truth and he did serve his time in Shelby or Carroll County—and if that's so, then he knows someone with some pull, someone who could keep him out of prison—or he didn't serve at all and has been lying about his background. I don't know any man who lies about serving a prison sentence if he's into illegal jobs. Gives him some credibility." Frank sat and stared at Skeet, waiting for him to make the next move. Frank had done what he came to do, and now it was out of his hands. He wasn't responsible for the men in the operation.

"So, you think he's a snitch? Maybe a Fed?" Skeet's life started to flash back, focusing on his time with Jimmy: farm locations; setters; routes to Kansas City, Omaha, Chicago. All the information Jimmy had about the operation. It made Skeet sick. Their conversations started to roll back like a newsreel, and Skeet remembered giving him advice on girls and doling out his wisdom on life. His stomach told him Jimmy was a snitch, but his heart wouldn't believe it. He was now hoping Frank would give him direction.

"Why else would he have a reason to lie to us? He doesn't seem like a Fed, though. His personality is more like a criminal. Brash, big talker, show off..." Frank realized he was describing his boss and shut his mouth, hoping Skeet was too absorbed in the problem at hand to notice the comparison.

"Whatdya think ought to be done?" Skeet was afraid of the answer. If they were in any one of the cities they sold to, especially Chicago, there would only be one answer, kill him. Al Capone, a violent man who had probably killed without compunction, would slit the throat of any snitch or any man even suspected of being a snitch. Skeet had read the newspaper articles about Capone's violent actions. He and his Chicago counterpart were not alike in this regard. Skeet was no killer. He was just a man who liked to make whiskey and prided himself on outsmarting the law. He had never even hit a man. If things got heated in a saloon, Skeet could always joke his way out of a fight. "Maybe I ought to fire him?"

"No. If he's in with the law and he's suddenly let go, they'll move in right away. And that doesn't give us any time to take care of things. And if he isn't with them, then we've fired a good man." Frank sighed in frustration. He was not the boss. He didn't want to be involved, but he was, just by the sheer fact Jimmy knew he ran liquor for the syndicate. If the boy started naming names, Frank Hogan's would be among them. "I don't like to accuse a man before I got proof. If he's just creating stories to impress me, that's stupid but not a crime. I say we keep a close eye on him. And, you've got to find a different job for him. He's been driving you around, so now he knows the location of every distilling farm. You'll need to do something with the stock barrels and aging barrels. Dig new trenches and find some new hiding places. If all they get is a still, some mash, and what's coming out of the still, there's not enough there to carry a huge penalty. Damn it, Skeet. This is going to take a lot of manpower."

Skeet was embarrassed Frank was the one thinking logically, but he appreciated the help. "I'll put him back on supply pick up. He can deliver to our first set of farms. He'll have access to only five of them if something does go down. I'll also put a couple of guys on him. They can watch him after work hours to see if he meets anyone."

A plan in place, the two men shook hands and parted ways. On the drive home, Skeet thought through every conversation with Jimmy. He liked the kid. Jimmy reminded him of himself at that age, which is why he had chosen him as his personal driver. Skeet liked to think he was grooming the young man. The betrayal, if it were a betrayal, made him sick. He had only done right by this kid, and this was how he was being repaid?

Skeet then thought about his boss, the real kingpin. He didn't want to admit how badly he had screwed up—that is, if Jimmy were a snitch. If he weren't, there was no need to say anything. This would all blow over, and the whiskey business would be back to normal. Skeet decided to keep the information to himself. He would confess his error only if something big happened.

When he returned to Templeton, he swung by Jimmy's boarding house. The fall day was warm, and Jimmy had taken advantage and was sitting on the front porch where he could hear the baseball game, which was playing on the radio in the parlor. The Yankees and Chicago Cubs were playing the last of four games, the Yankees ahead by three. Each game had been a blowout, the first game a six-run difference, so the final game wasn't much of a nailbiter.

Skeet stepped up onto the porch and sat down in a wicker chair next to Jimmy. "Hiya, kid. Mind if we talk a little business while you listen?"

"Not at all. Not much of a game, anyway. I'm surprised to see you on a Sunday. I figured you'd pick me up tomorrow evening. What gives?"

"I need to switch your job again. I've had some problems with my pick-up man. He's delivering supplies to the wrong farm, getting lost on the back roads at night. He's not getting the job done, and I need a reliable man. I can't afford to switch any of my setters, and I don't have time to find a new guy—which wouldn't do me any good because he wouldn't know where to go either. So, my only option is to move the man who can absolutely complete the job as well as not create a hole in the system. I can drive myself around. Always did before. I just liked the look of being driven. I'll loan you one of my old trucks for the job. You can drive it here after you're done. Same pay." The lie rolled off Skeet's tongue as smoothly as skating on ice. He had spent most of his drive back to Templeton thinking up the fib and practicing it aloud.

"Sure, Skeet. Whatever you need." Jimmy's toes curled in concern. This was the first Jimmy had heard about any delivery problems, and it had only been a week since Lyle Lang had folded his tent and moved on. Jimmy didn't believe in coincidences. It appeared Lyle had shot his mouth off before he left town, knowing it would eventually reach the right man.

With only a "thanks much," Skeet backed his car out of the driveway and headed to wherever he was resting his head for the night.

Jimmy remained on the porch, too deep in thought to hear the Yankees finish off the Cubs, 13-6, winning the 1932 World Series. He tried to remember whether anyone had mentioned a bad employee. The story was completely possible. He himself had struggled to find the farms when he first started that job. If Lyle hadn't threatened him, would he now be nervous over a job change? Probably not. Men were moved around frequently.

Jimmy's overactive imagination, fueled by his pulp fiction magazines, created grim visions of what would be done to him if he were discovered. He pictured being shot in the back of the head, or beaten to death while tied down, or dragged behind a vehicle until his arms fell off. Skeet didn't seem like the type who could kill someone, but nobody truly knew a man and what he was capable of if cornered.

Jimmy ran scenarios through his head. He could go on the lam. How far could he walk by morning? How much money did he have in his pocket? The answers were not very far and not very much. He chastised himself for not putting away his earnings. If he were to leave, he would need to hop a train and head whichever way the train was going, but he would have little money once he got there.

He could hide out and see what happened in the next few weeks. If he hitched to Carroll, the biggest town in the county, he could rent a new room under a false name. But, again, the money problem. Jimmy berated himself for not ensuring he had the means to flee. This scenario was the worst one. He would most likely be recognized by someone who would report back to Skeet. Not much happened that his boss didn't know about.

The most sensible scenario was to do nothing. Jimmy wasn't certain Skeet knew about his relationship with Alvin Truly. Lyle Lang had big plans, and he couldn't afford payback if he revealed Jimmy's reason for being in Carroll County. Most likely, he had threatened Jimmy only to try and squeeze something from him.

Jimmy would walk the straight and narrow for the next month or so. He would show Skeet he was a committed employee and allay any fears Skeet may have of him. If Jimmy got even a whiff of something askew, he would hop the next train going through Templeton and deal with the lack of funds later.

After he made his decision, Jimmy felt good about his plan while still being a little skittish about his position in the syndicate. His next problem to solve was Alvin Truly. Jimmy had given Truly crumbs to keep him happy. He relayed the location of a few farms in the organization, ones that had one still with a small production. Jimmy knew the setters and the farmers, if caught, would get a small fine, which Skeet would pay. Even if they spent a month or two in jail, no long-term damage was done.

Unfortunately, Alvin Truly was never satisfied with a farm here and a farm there. He wanted the kingpin, and Jimmy would remain imprisoned by the deal he had signed. If he wanted his freedom, Jimmy Krantz would have to decide between himself and Skeet, and his past suggested he would choose himself.

CHAPTER 29

Advent, beginning the fourth Sunday before Christmas, began the holiday season. December of 1932 brought a light layer of snow, the needed ingredient to evoke Yuletide feelings.

People trekked to wooded areas, looking for a perfectly shaped tree. Boxes of decorations were brought down from the attic and sorted through. Holiday adornments, both inside and out, required days to get them perfectly hung. Pounds of butter and sugar were mixed into a variety of Christmas baked goods, traditional German recipes being a favorite.

Religious members took time out of their days to ensure their churches were perfectly prepared. Sacred Heart's choir began practicing the songs for the midnight and Christmas masses. Volunteer ladies cleaned the church until it shone, hauled out the nativity set to be placed at the front of the sacristy, and hung the altar linens, which needed ironing. Father Joe's advent stoles were also unpacked and ironed.

Volunteers and business owners spent days adorning the town's center. Wreaths decorated with red bows hung from each lamp post.

Firemen, climbing tall ladders, affixed the center's crisscrossed garlands to streetlamps. Businesses decorated their windows and displayed the season's merchandise. Christmas time was both busy and
exciting.

The town's annual tree celebration, where residents gathered
around a large pine tree to set up the nativity set—minus the baby
Jesus—and sing holiday music before they retreated to the community
building for warm drinks and baked goods, was scheduled for December 15. The Sacred Heart Ladies Guild was responsible for cleaning
and mending the nativity pieces. As was custom, the baby Jesus would
only make His appearance on December 25, the Christ child's birthday.

Jimmy Krantz's bedroom window gave him a view of the town's
center. These days, he spent most of his free evenings with the family,
listening to Jack Benny's new program along with *Buck Rogers in
the 25th Century*. By nine each night, Jimmy headed to his own
rooms and hunkered down to read for a bit. He was rereading his
issues of *Detective Story Magazine*, a twice monthly pulp-fiction
series. As soon as he had secured a stable job, he never missed an
issue, but with his recent devotion to saving money, he no longer
purchased the new editions.

After his jarring conversation with Skeet, Jimmy ceased all
unnecessary spending, hoping to build a little stash of cash in the
event he needed to run. His hours had been cut back significantly.
He was no longer running product or filling in for any of the setters.
He was strictly picking up supplies and delivering them to a small
set of farms. As Skeet had promised, the wage for each run was the
same as before, but he sensed he could be cut at any time. He was
also staying in nights when he wasn't working, trying to display an
uninteresting life to anyone who might be watching him.

Jimmy didn't participate in the December evening festivities,
preferring to watch the nativity setting and holiday singing from his

window. As expected, the bulk of the town came to participate in the season's first event.

Jimmy had never felt completely accepted by the community. Iowa towns were always wary of newcomers, and it took years of community participation before no longer being referred to as the 'new person.' He didn't have children in the school to introduce him to the other parents, and he wasn't a member of Sacred Heart. His only interactions had been with those employees of the syndicate and Skeet. He wasn't the type of person the men would bring home for their daughters, nor was he a good dinner guest for the wives.

Being separate from the town, and now pushed out of his position, Jimmy felt completely alone, a wolf run off from the pack. Before he came to Templeton, he had never felt connected to a group of people. He was not close to his own family in Lake View, and his indiscretions had isolated him even more. When he was hired by Skeet, he had begun to feel part of something. He had bonded with his group of setters, and when Skeet took him on as his driver, Jimmy considered himself a pack member. Skeet gave him advice and treated him as someone special. With his reputation now tipped out of balance, he was once again disconnected, running the prairie alone. If Skeet had been told about Jimmy's undercover activities— even if he didn't find the information credible—there would never again be that trust.

Jimmy's heart hated to snitch on Skeet and the rest of the organization, but there was no reason to protect them.

After the festivities, the town died down, people returning to their homes. A light snow, which would delight the children when they awakened the following morning, was falling; it was the first snow of the winter season. Not much was expected in accumulation, the flakes being small and light. The wind had also gone to bed, leaving the night as still as a spooked deer. No clouds covered the moon, leaving a bright light to see into the town's square.

Jimmy had stayed up late, having gotten deep into one of his mystery stories. Even though he had read it before, it had been so long he had forgotten the plot and remained riveted with each page he turned. Now, geared up from the adrenaline coursing through his frightened body coupled with his constant worry of being confronted by Skeet the following workday, Jimmy could not sleep. It was nearly 2:00 a.m.

Instead of diving into another detective mystery, Jimmy stood at his window, looking onto Main Street. He often stood at the window and named the businesses that sold to, took money from, or were part owners in the organization. Only a few of them did not fit into one of those categories.

As he was about to turn away from the scene, deciding to head for his bed in hopes he could bring on sleep, Jimmy saw a lone truck driving slowly down the street. "Why would anyone be out at this time of night?" Jimmy asked himself. No businesses were open, and the festivities had long ago been vacated for the evening. The truck stopped under the crossed garlands and killed the motor. Jimmy had seen the truck before but couldn't remember its owner. He was interested in what would happen next and decided to remain at his post rather than take to his bed.

The door of the truck opened, and a figure in bundled clothing and cap exited, holding a large object close to their chest. Walking around the side of the truck and stopping at the rear end, the stranger opened the tailgate of the vehicle, set the object into the bed, and proceeded to scramble into the back. Being shorter in stature, the unfamiliar figure struggled to climb onto the gate and into the back of the vehicle. Once accomplished, the form proceeded to climb onto the cab of the truck, using a feed bucket to help shorten the step, while carrying the object. Jimmy watched the stranger stand up on the cab, tuck the object between their legs, and pull a wire from somewhere inside the bundled winter gear. A small hook had been formed at the end of the wire, and Jimmy was puzzled as to where the hook would go. "Are they going to hang a wire from the crossed garlands?" he asked himself. Once the hook was placed at the crossed point, Jimmy watched as the decorations were pulled low until they reached the height of the person's chest. The wire disposed, the unknown character brought forth the large object and affixed it to the crossed garlands. Jimmy couldn't see any writing on it, but the object's form was recognizable; it was a whiskey jug.

Finished with the task, the small-framed form reversed their steps until they were back in the cab of the truck, started it again, and drove down the street until Jimmy could no longer see the taillights of the vehicle.

Jimmy stood at the window a few minutes longer, wanting to see if the mystery person would return, while staring at the cutout of the jug. The only other time the jug had appeared was before Jimmy had arrived in Templeton, the story of its mysterious appearance and disappearance having been told and retold by those in the bootlegging business. The identity of the prankster had never been determined, but the consensus seemed to point to Skeet.

Perhaps Skeet had been the original joker, which would very much be just like him, but Jimmy was certain this was not Skeet tonight. He owned various vehicles, but this truck was not his. As well, the form was not his. Skeet was taller and had the physique of a football player who played defense. Tonight's stranger was a small man, both short and skinny. Jimmy's mind ran though his index of employees in the organization. He could think of one or two who were about the height of this Puck, but both men were also quite wide. One was so rotund he couldn't possibly have climbed onto the truck.

Jimmy undressed and slipped under the covers. His mind was clicking with information. He systematically went through each farm, thinking about the farmer as well as the setters. No one's form fit the one he had seen on the street. And then there was the truck. He had seen that truck within the last few months. But where? Again, he was systematic in his thinking. No farmer nor setter drove that vehicle.

An idea finally sparked. Frank Hogan. He was fairly short, perhaps about the right height. He was a skinny fellow. With the layers of outer gear, it was hard to tell the approximate weight. It was possible it could be Frank's frame. Additionally, Jimmy wasn't aware of every vehicle Frank drove. He had seen his '26 Nash, but that was his rumrunner car. He certainly could afford additional vehicles.

Yes, Jimmy thought, it's probably Frank. Jimmy liked putting together puzzles. The family below him always had one set up, and Jimmy enjoyed sitting at the table and adding pieces to the growing picture. However, often his pieces didn't quite fit. When he returned to the puzzle, he could see a family member had removed some of his work and replaced it with the correct pieces. This puzzle was the same. It looked like Frank Hogan was the correct piece, but he didn't quite fit.

Frank lived in Dunlap, forty-eight miles away. Why would he drive all that way to put up an effigy of a whiskey jug? Why would he care? Frank gave the impression he was only concerned about himself. He did his job well but then always returned immediately to Dunlap. He did not attend any events in Templeton. He was not even a full-time employee of the business. Whoever strung up that jug cared about the enterprise.

Jimmy struggled to attain his nightly slumber, putting in and taking out puzzle pieces. As dawn's rays broke through the night sky, Jimmy jolted from his bed. "I know who it is!" he said to no one. "I saw her outside of the grocery store!"

$50,000 IN LIQUOR, 22 PERSONS TAKEN IN BIG BOOZE RAID

Federal Officers Sieze Score of Stills in Southern Part of Carroll County.

DIDN'T GET THEM ALL

Claim Many "Plants" Were Carried Away in Vicinity of Templeton And Dedham.

Liquor valued at $50,000 and stills worth many thousands were taken at Dedham and Templeton, in the south part of Carroll county, Tuesday by federal and state officers in what is declared by Des Moines newspapers to have been the largest raid ever made in the Central West. The officers arrested 21 men and one woman against whom charges of manufacture and sale of intoxicating liquor will be filed.

More than 2,500 gallons of mash, 21 barrels of beer and 78 gallons of "moonshine" were confiscated. V. C. Schwaller, justice of the peace, and Rupert Kasperbauer, township constable, were among the victims.

Carry Sawed-Off Shotguns

In the vicinity of Dedham and Templeton a veritable nest of distillers and sellers of liquor was found. The officers who made the raid assert that sentiment was so strong against the officers in places that a show of sawed-off shotguns had to be made by the raiders.

Some of the stills, notably that found at the home of Max Kastle, were the most approved make. Kastle had a nice cooling arrangement that the officers said must have cost hundreds of dollars. He told the ifficers he was getting $2.50 a pint for his hootch.

The persons detained and the evidence which the officers say they found are:

CHAPTER 30

Skeet sprinted across the fields, slipping and falling as he made his way. Suddenly, his left foot sunk in deep, wet snow; and when he pulled it out, his shoe came away and remained in the icy pile. With no time to dig around in the dark to find his missing footwear, Skeet, lightning fast, decided to leave it behind and continued his race with one shoe and one sodden sock. His surroundings were thick black, and he could hear voices in the dark, some he recognized and others he didn't. Skeet felt his way along in the darkness, falling between bursts of movement.

Skeet had the advantage of knowing the terrain; they did not. The hump of cornrow made running difficult, so he stayed between the rows, still stumbling over mounds of last autumn's picked stalks. The rows would lead him to his destination. His chest was on fire, and he swore to himself he would lose some weight. Finally, he could feel the farmland turn into uncut weeds. He was heading toward a patch of trees adjacent a small creek, which ran between two large fields. He hoped he could lose his trackers in the wooded area.

Unable to run any longer, Skeet crashed through the trees and made his way to the creek. He scuttled down the bank, now devoid of snow because of its west exposure, to the water and lay flat against the earth, covering himself with last autumn's few dead leaves, hoping to avoid a spotlight. They would eventually look in that area, so he laid close to the icy February water. Skeet blended his body into the nature and hoped to pass for a large broken limb. He waited.

Skeet, with his new protégé, had been making his weekly rounds, visiting the distilling farms—twenty-two a week—delivering supplies, picking up cases, and making payments. He had cash in hand. Several hundred dollars. He met with the owners of the property as well as his workforce. The owners liked the reassurance that everything was going well along with the pile of money on their palms. Skeet stayed at each farm for approximately an hour. He didn't begin his work until sundown, which, at this time of year, was around 5 p.m. He always finished somewhere between three and four in the morning. Nothing seemed out of the ordinary.

Skeet's seventh stop, his last stop, the Kuhl farm, had taken him a bit longer. There had been some problems with one of the stills, so he rolled up his sleeves to work out the hitch. He knew the workings of a still better than he knew any woman's body. At the tender age of ten, Skeet could build a still by himself. He made his first batch of mash at twelve and completed the whole process from start to finish by fourteen. The pride in his father's eyes practically lit up the barn.

Distrusting his half-asleep driver, Skeet had directed his man to hop into the passenger side. With the mended still flowing whiskey like an unimpeded stream, Skeet stepped back into his truck, but he and his protégé didn't get more than five miles down the road before Skeet realized he had forgotten his tools. Those tools had been handed down generation to generation and had built or fixed more stills than he could imagine. Tired from his long night of work, Skeet briefly considered continuing home and retrieving his property the following day, but his father had taught him it was always better to get a job done right away. He made a three-point turn and headed back.

Still a quarter of a mile from the farm, Skeet had seen lights in the barn yard, a storm of flashlights and lanterns, shining one way and another. Lights were not unusual on a farm in the middle of the night, especially one distilling whiskey, but the number of them and the directions they were pointing seemed odd. Skeet slowed his vehicle to a crawl as he thought about the scene in front of him. Suddenly, the truth revealed itself: Regulators. He needed to get far away from the farm…and fast.

Skeet had slammed on the brakes and killed his lights. He put the truck in reverse, backing up a quarter of a mile, and then pointed his truck into the ditch, having found a field without barbed wire protecting it. Regulators most likely had seen his vehicle's lights and were jumping into their cars. They would follow the roads, looking for his vehicle.

Muddy from melted snow, farmland had not been his best choice. Skeet didn't get far when the tires had sunk into the muck. Forward. Reverse. Forward. Nothing was working. He was sinking farther into the dirt. No choice but to run.

Both men had jumped from the truck and sprinted, bent over as low as they could. The Feds had seen the truck coming up the road and were looking for them, their vehicle lights shining down the dirt path. Skeet broke off from his protégé. Anytime the law was involved, it was every man for himself. Skeet was heading for the small creek.

The other men, his workers, were also on their own. He was sure each man had dropped what he had and they had taken off in all directions, scattering like pool balls after the break. Some of them would probably escape; others would be caught.

Richard Kuhl, the owner of the farm, had not been home. He had taken his wife to a barn dance in Templeton to raise money for a family whose farm was going up for auction. He had told Skeet he planned to stay in town overnight to get their shopping done before returning home. The agents would return for Richard, but nothing much would happen to him. The Feds were only interested in the ones making the liquor. And they were especially interested in arresting the kingpin, the one who owned those thirty liquor operations.

As he had run across the field, from behind him, Skeet could hear the Regulators' vehicles coming fast down the dirt road. Instead of taking the field, they had parked their cars and started chasing on foot. Dozens of lights shone across the landscape, and Skeet could hear them yelling to each other. He considered taking refuge where he was, but no cover was available. The Feds would sit on that area until morning, waiting to use natural light to hunt for him again. His best strategy was his original one, hide in the wooded area along the creek.

Lying like a dead catfish on the side of the bank, Skeet now listened to the voices coming closer to him. He hunkered down into the leaves as much as possible. Shouts from the Feds echoed through the area. Skeet imagined a chain of them, sweeping across the field, coming closer to his location. Around him, in closer proximity, sounds of crunching leaves and snapping limbs exploded in the air. His workers, he thought. They had probably taken the same path and run for the wooded area, hoping to hide as he had done.

Eventually, there was only nature's silence: the far-off wail of a coyote contrasted with the sharp screech of an owl. No more men's voices.

Had the Feds gone in a different direction? he wondered, hoping he had escaped them. Realizing he had been holding his breath, he began breathing again, taking only shallow breaths. Each heartbeat throbbed in his ears. Suddenly, he heard a voice from above him. "Get up! I can see you laying there!" A light shone directly into his eyes. Skeet was caught.

Climbing out of the gully, not even a hand to help him, Skeet reached the field and put up his hands. The form continued to direct the light into Skeet's eyes, leaving him blind. Rough hands grabbed him by the arms, and the click of tight cuffs broke the silence. Into the dark, the voice shouted, "Looky here. I got the Kingpin. The Bootleggin' Boss himself. You're going to jail along with every man you led me to tonight. By the way, I should introduce myself. Name's Alvin Truly, Federal Agent of the Northern District. And, sir, you're going to prison."

Skeet said not one word in reply, but he thought many of them about Truly—and none of them good.

In the dark, the dawn of truth started to penetrate Skeet's brain. Truly and his men had been following him. For how long, he did not know, but certainly it had been throughout the evening. How had he not seen someone tailing him? Skeet wondered.

He had been sloppy. In the beginning, Skeet had varied his routine, never taking the same route. He went through fields and ditches instead of using the roads. He had been as nervous as a new mother. But the years had gone by with few arrests, and he had never even been close to the law. And all that caution took him extra hours. Then, he started taking the roads only when he was in a hurry. Nothing bad happened, so he added 'being tired' to his list. Then it was 'not in the mood.' Weeks, months, and then years went by with no repercussions. Lately, he hadn't even looked in his rearview mirror. "It's my own damn fault," he chastised himself. He had also gotten his men arrested. Business was going to suffer.

Truly escorted Skeet to his vehicle. He would spend the night in jail, somewhere. Within a few days, he would be driven to Fort Dodge and secluded in federal lockup. Skeet was curious how much his bond would be, but he wasn't worried. He was certain his boss would have things in hand. He didn't know how many other men had been captured, but he guessed he would be finding out very soon.

Twenty-one men and one woman were spread out in four jail cells in Denison, Crawford County's seat. Alvin Truly didn't want the men anywhere near Carroll County in case sympathizers tried to help them escape. The accommodations were tight.

Skeet was not with his men. Truly wanted him in a secure location, so he brought him to Audubon County's jail. The federal agent still had former colleagues working in the sheriff's office and was confident they could keep Skeet's location and any information locked down. Truly had been guaranteed by the man who had replaced him when he took his federal agent's badge. If Skeet had no contact with any of his men, perhaps they might be more willing to inform on him, Truly thought.

Sitting in Denison's jailhouse, the detained men began sharing information regarding their own arrests. Once Truly had the locations of the stills, he had put together a major sting. The Feds jumped on every farm at the same time. Some of the locations had been empty. Some had only the product with no makers. Seven of the landowners were not home. They arrested who they could and would most likely go back for the landowners to make arrests.

Alvin Truly had been after the kingpin since the beginning of the operation. He had arrested a fair number of bootleggers—some with the operation, some not—but he would not be satisfied until he had gotten what he wanted. He was a bloodhound after the fox. Truly tore up Carroll County looking for the one man whom he thought would serve hard time for breaking the law. The possibility of the kingpin slipping through the fence drove Truly day and night.

With the most-wanted bootlegger locked up in jail, Truly's Christmas wish had been delivered. He could rest easy knowing he had just curtailed the largest illegal liquor trade in Iowa.

News of the raids ran through Templeton, Dedham, Willey, and Carroll like water through a broken dam. Names of farmers and setters were passed around, some accurate and some not. "Was it John Krupp? I heard Albert Stange." Details of the raid—"they shot their guns at them," "wasn't but a pint or so they found"—were relayed over and over, all of it pure fabrication. Speculation about prison sentences and fines bounced from one local to the next. "It'll be five years, for sure," "With that new law, you know…." Accurate information was scarce; anyone escaping the night's raid hid until the turmoil died down. As small towns do, gossip ran strong for a few days; what they didn't know they filled in with their imagination. All of it would eventually die down when the next big event came along.

Newsmen from the *Carroll Daily Herald*, the *Sioux City Journal*, the *Des Moines Tribune*, and *The Des Moines Register* descended like buzzards on the area, hoping for intel and interviews. They visited Templeton businesses, picking at the merchants and shoppers. They accosted citizens on the streets, asking how they felt about the raid. They wouldn't rest until they had picked clean all the meat of information. Locals from Carroll County banded together and provided protection for their own. Their wagging tongues were stilled if a newsman were in sight.

Father Joe had gotten calls in the middle of the night from wives whose husbands had not returned home. The women did not worry about automobile accidents or illness; broken schedules meant arrest. They all needed support and possibly a ride to Fort Dodge when the trial was held. Joe promised each of his congregants he would do what he could.

Sheriff Will Katz was the only citizen who knew the details of the arrests. Alvin Truly had been waiting in his vehicle outside of the sheriff's office the morning after the raid, almost giddy as he relayed the details of the night's excursion. When Will confronted him about not making known when he planned to enter Carroll County, Truly shrugged his shoulders and said, "Must have slipped my mind." Will wore his official face when out in public and continued his daily duties, letting the law run its course. Inwardly, he was furious he had not been able to warn the men and worried for their outcomes.

Finn Vries may have been the only happy Templeton citizen when he heard the news. Around 10:00 a.m., a customer walked through the door. Finn perked up, hoping for an early sale. "Did you hear the news?" his customer asked.

"No. I came straight to the store this morning."

"The Feds raided a bunch of farms last night. I heard it was twenty or so. Rounded up a whole bunch of cookers and farmers!"

"Do you know any of the names?" Finn asked. "Was John Krupp one of them?"

His customer named several men, but Finn's stepbrother was not mentioned. Finn kept a serious demeanor, expressing his concern over the men and their families. He didn't dare take on a condescending tone or allow his feelings to cross his face. Once the gossiper left his store, Finn went into the back, made himself a cup of tea, sat down at his desk, and let out a loud whoop. Ten years had passed since his first telephone call to Sheriff Katz's office. Many calls and letters later, the Wets had finally gotten their due.

Frank Hogan heard nothing from his home in Dunlap. He had not been available to run booze to their out-of-state clients, so he hadn't seen Skeet since they met in Defiance. Frank had been working on expanding his poker-game business. He liked being his own boss, and he kept all the profits from his work. He heard about the big bust the evening after the raid. He was in Buck Grove running a game when one of the players said, "Hey, you all hear about that big raid in Carroll County? Heard they busted over ten farms. Hell, they even arrested a woman!" No matter how many questions Frank asked, the man had no additional information. Frank feared Skeet had finally been caught. Instead of running to the fire, Frank Hogan smartly ran away from it. He had known for years something like this would eventually happen. He was happy he hadn't been there when it went down. Assuming the business would now break apart, Frank vowed to be done with rumrunning.

Skeet's associates sat in Denison for two days. Alvin Truly sent for one man at a time and interviewed him personally. Truly wanted just one of them to flip on Skeet. Even though he had the man in custody and Jimmy Krantz to testify against him in court, Alvin wasn't going to feel confident until he had at least one of the setters or farmers name Skeet as the kingpin bootlegger of Carroll County, but he was not going to get what he wanted. Each man was willing to own his part in the syndicate; however, he was unwilling to name anyone else or admit to Skeet Miller being part of the business. The federal agent threatened them with long prison sentences and large fines. He constructed a future in which they would not walk their daughters down the aisle or bounce their first grandbaby on their knee. He predicted they would be old men, so bent over from the damp of their cell, they would hardly be able to walk out of prison.

When threats didn't work, he changed his tactic and offered rewards for smaller pieces of information: steak meals, more yard time, a visit from their wives. "How many men set with you? How many other men do you know in the business?" Again, he received no information. Because he thought the rewards were not enticing enough, he promised shorter sentences and smaller fines. Their lips remained sealed. They would not squeal on another man, especially their boss.

Skeet sat in the Audubon County Jail, replaying his arrest and conversation with the federal agent. Alvin Truly, up front in the passenger seat, twisted around so that he peered into the back seat. The federal agent couldn't help bragging to Skeet how much he had on him. Truly named off the farms they had raided, the number of men arrested, the gallons of whiskey confiscated. Because Truly himself had only focused on the location of the kingpin, he didn't actually know the number of men or gallons confiscated, but he wanted to taunt Skeet and frighten him.

Skeet didn't sleep that night in jail. He wasn't worried for the men who worked for the organization. An attorney would meet with them once they were in Fort Dodge. They would either have a quick trial and pay a fine, or they would just plead guilty and pay the fine. No one was serving time, except for perhaps himself.

He doubted he could slip out of this mess. His conversation with Frank Hogan came to mind again. Skeet was certain his former driver had been responsible for the night's raid. He hadn't seen Jimmy for several days, but that didn't mean anything. Jimmy had his own list of responsibilities and had proved he could complete them without supervision. However, Jimmy would have known Skeet's location at the time of the raid. He knew the schedule and route Skeet took each week. If anyone could have given the Feds specific information and Skeet's exact location at a certain time, it would be Jimmy.

Interest ran through Fort Dodge's residents; a flurry of activity was happening at the federal courthouse. Twenty-one men and one woman had been brought to their town the previous day, and they would now stand before a judge for the first time.

A wake of buzzards followed the criminals, planning to sit in the courthouse and report on all details pertaining to the raid. The day of the arraignment, the courtroom was packed with them. They all looked like they had been dressed by the same tailor: white shirt, dark vest, pants with suspenders, and a fedora. Some had glasses;

others did not. They all had their long sleeves rolled up to their elbows and wrote furiously in small notebooks.

Families, along with Father Joe, sat behind the accused on the right side while the federal agents sat behind the prosecuting attorneys on the left, Alvin Truly directly behind the lead attorney. The remaining courtroom seats were filled in by interested Fort Dodge citizens. They hoped for a spectacle, one that would bring some sparks of interest to their usual Tuesday.

A single lawyer sat on the side of the accused. He was dressed in a plain dark suit, white shirt, and wing-tipped shoes. His dark hair was combed back from his forehead, and his steel-rimmed glasses sat on his short nose. His name was Patrick Keane, and he had been hired by an unknown voice on the telephone. Patrick had a small law firm in Fort Dodge, but he had a fair amount of practice with cases involving the Volstead Act.

A large envelope of cash had been rushed to Fort Dodge. Most of it would be used to pay fines; his service fee was included in the many hundred-dollar bills. If more were needed, it would be delivered post haste, he had been promised. His directions from the unknown voice had been simple: "Do whatever it takes to get them free."

When the chain of lawbreakers came single file through the courtroom, all eyes turned toward them. The newsmen started scribbling, writing down first impressions and descriptions of the bootleggers; the federal agents watched with satisfaction, their handiwork on display for the newsmen; and families of the prisoners watched intently for signs of rough treatment by the lawmen.

Patrick sat at the defendants' table, his clients next to him and behind him. "All rise," announced the bailiff. "The Honorable Thomas Kavanaugh presiding." Like a flock of birds lifting for flight, the bulk of the courtroom stood on cue with stragglers struggling to stand from their seated position.

Judge Kavanaugh shuffled to his seat, settled himself into his chair, and sifted through the papers in front of him. Eventually, he settled his glasses and looked up at the convicted. "Looks like we got quite a few this morning, that right?" He looked in the direction of the lead prosecution. "Any of these men…and woman…pleading guilty?"

The defense attorney stood up and said, "Yes, your Honor. Twenty-one of them are pleading guilty."

The judge showed surprise, his eyebrows arching. "Let's do those first. Send them forward." He rested his elbows on his bench and laced his fingers together.

One by one, the convicted stood up and placed themselves next to the defense attorney. The judge read the charges, the bootlegger admitted guilt, and the sentence was proclaimed. Some were given a hundred dollar fine; some were given two or three hundred.

The one woman, Anna Hoelker, had been arrested along with her husband. The Hoelkers owned a small farm just outside of Dedham. They had gone into the bootlegging business together, trying to maximize their earnings by making the product themselves. Anna was released without a fine; however, the judge didn't let her go without giving her a lecture about a "woman's place" and "motherly duty."

Skeet, the remaining man, came to the front and stood next to the defense attorney. He still wore his work clothing and shoes. He had done his best to clean up his garments and finger-comb his hair and wash his face. He wished he had been able to put on his church clothes; he wanted to be as respectable as possible in front of this federal judge.

His crimes were read aloud. "Sir, you are charged with ten counts of unlawful manufacture of illegal spirits, twenty counts of unlawful sale of illegal spirits, and five counts of unlawful transportation of illegal spirits. How do you plead?"

Skeet looked the judge in his eyes and spoke loudly, "Not guilty,

Your Honor." Behind him, he could hear reactions from the spectators. Benches squeaked as they leaned toward their neighbor, whispers rippled through the crowd, and a few newsmen stood up and
hurried toward the exit.

The prosecuting attorney piped up, "Your Honor, we request no
bail. These are serious charges."

Patrick Keane countered, "Your Honor, this man is tied to his
community. He has no previous convictions."

The judge slammed his gavel down and said, "Bail is one thousand dollars." The remaining newsmen exited, and Skeet's lawyer
leaned down and whispered in his ear.

Waiting for his bail to be posted, Skeet sat in jail once more. He
was alone. When he had arrived in Fort Dodge, he had been segregated
from the group, but he could hear the other men talking back and forth
between the cells. He knew Alvin Truly had been interrogating them,
but he didn't know if any of them had told the agent anything. He
would have no access to his crew until he went back to Templeton.

Without anyone to perform for, Skeet released all his worry. As
he pictured his future in prison, he ran his hands through his hair.
While his logic had warned him this could be his eventual consequence, his devil-may-care attitude had swatted away his logical concerns. For twelve years, no harm had come to him; not even a whisper
of danger had wafted his way. The longer he had run the operation,
the less he worried about consequences. Skeet now chastised himself
for his sloppiness. Five years in prison would change him, would
break him down.

CHAPTER 31

Fines and bail money had taken a major chunk out of my little nest beneath the floorboards of my parlor. I told myself when I began this organization it would be the cost of doing business, but seeing the gaping space where the bundles had been made me uncomfortable.

The fines had cost me $2,100 plus Skeet's bail. I would recoup Skeet's money, but we didn't know if he would later receive a fine. Given the number of charges, he alone could cost me another $2,100—or worse, $5,000. I could complain when I was alone, but I would never say a word to Skeet. I had made promises, and now I would be required to keep them.

When I started this business, I had an end goal in mind. I needed a way to support myself and my children. I needed respectable work I could do on my own. I didn't have the skills or physical ability to farm. I wanted to open a little enterprise, and I felt my years as this organization's leader had proven I had business savvy. My plan of quitting when the hard times had passed was now in question. I would probably need to stay in a little longer to build back my nest.

I had close to thirty thousand still hidden in my parlor. It sounded like a lot of money, but if I had to support my family with no income, it wouldn't last long. If I wanted to buy an existing store or open a new one, I wasn't sure what kind of money that would take.

I could have had a larger nest egg, but I had been generous with my ill-gotten loot. When I recognized a family was suffering, I put a few hundred dollars on their front porch. Father Joe opened an envelope each Sunday with a hundred-dollar bill tucked inside. When the firehouse needed a new roof, I dropped several hundred-dollar bills into the collection box. Any man, woman, child, or civic entity in need of money received at least a hundred dollars. In these hard times, the need was great, and it was often. I told myself my generosity was the penance I paid for breaking the law.

Skeet and I had agreed to meet at a new location a few days after his release. With his notoriety, he would be noticed and watched. We picked east of Templeton.

I arrived early and sat in my truck. Staring out across the fields, I thought back on the last few years and imagined what my life would have looked like now if circumstances hadn't pushed me to this point. I try to avoid such thinking because it doesn't change anything. I needed to keep my thoughts in the now, in reality. I had a major problem sitting in front of me, and I was as much responsible for Skeet's freedom as he was.

Skeet pulled up behind me, exited his car, and crawled in beside me. He didn't look good. His skin was ashy, and his eyes puffy. He no longer had that cocky look about him. "How are you doing?" I asked as soon as he slammed the door.

"I'm not going to lie; I'm scared," he admitted. "I'm going to prison." Skeet looked me straight in the face, his eyes as wide as an owl's. "I need to confess something to you. I made a huge mistake, and I've been keeping it, trying to work it out for myself. There's been a mole in our operation."

Skeet proceeded to lay out the hiring and promoting of Jimmy Krantz. He took full responsibility for allowing Jimmy too much access to too many parts of the syndicate. "I got lazy," he admitted.

As he laid out each piece of the story, my stomach churned like I was riding a roller coaster. Skeet's arrest was not a simple matter of paying a fine or thirty days in jail. I could now understand his gray face. He was right; he was probably going to spend time behind bars. The impending fine was almost negligible compared to his being locked away.

I couldn't lay all the fault on Skeet. I should have kept on him about rotating men and varying his schedule and routes. After a few years in business, I hadn't involved myself enough. As long as I was stashing cash under my floorboards, I was happy to remain ignorant. However, as my grandma used to say, "There's no use crying over spilt milk; what's done is done." Now, we needed a plan to get out of it.

"I'm sorry," Skeet said. "This is all on me. If you don't want to help out with the fines, I got money put away."

"I appreciate that, Skeet. But I made a commitment to you and to the men. I'll hold up my end of the bargain. Any of the other men flip on you?"

"Not a one," Skeet said with pride. "They admitted to their part in the business but wouldn't say a word about anybody else. I heard Truly offered 'em all kinds of things—food, visitors, even shorter sentences—if they'd roll on me. But they stuck to their guns and kept their mouths shut."

How long until your trial?" I asked.

"Three months...maybe longer. There's all kinds of lawyering going on." Skeet didn't want to talk about the trial. I supposed it reminded him of his potential loss of freedom "What are we planning to do about the rest of the locations? Shut them down or keep 'em runnin'?" he asked.

Skeet's voice sounded anxious and worried. I could tell he was hoping I would suggest we shut them down. Since the night of the raid, not a single drop of whiskey had trickled from our stills. What we had was buried, and the setters had scattered, presumably having gone home. Some of the farmers had vacated their property, planting season months away. Even if we did get the stills cooking again, Alvin Truly wouldn't be far behind. Jimmy Krantz had only given him the information pertaining to Skeet's capture that night. It seemed he hadn't given Truly every location. We needed the cash, but I didn't want to risk it.

"We should shut down the rest of the locations," I said. "Maybe we can sell the stills to others outside of our operation. They're worth good money."

"What should we do with the remaining whiskey?"

"I was never brought up to waste," I said. "We're going to sell it. I'll reach out to our Des Moines guy. It's the closest location. I know he's not happy with us, but product is product. And he needs as much of it as he can get. Unless he's the kind of man who would cut off his nose to spite his face, he'll put aside his hurt pride and buy our product. How do you think we should ship it?"

"Truck. If Jimmy told Truly about our method for shipping to Kansas City, Chicago, and Omaha, he'll have men on those roads. We can take back roads to Des Moines. If we haul the liquor in the same trucks we've been using but put in fewer animals, we can probably get all the product to Des Moines with a few trips."

"How much is there?" I wanted to know, waiting to do quick calculations in my head.

Skeet sat and thought for a bit. I could see his fingers moving as he started adding product. "Maybe five hundred or so barrels? A little more or less."

"How many can one truck haul?"

"Sixteen if we don't use the animal haulers."

"Let's stack them. I know we have never hauled that way because they can be seen through the sides of the truck, but I think we're better with fewer trips. If we do that, how many trips?"

"Five trucks at thirty-two barrels...Should be no more than three trips even if we're under a hundred."

"Do we still have anyone willing to drive for us? I'm sure we're about as desirable as an infectious disease." Just because we had product didn't mean we could get it there.

"We'll have to pay them double, but I can find a few willing men. Give me a few days, and I'll get it done. The least I can do is take care of this for you."

"On a different note, I heard Roosevelt is moving toward repealing Prohibition," I said hopefully. *"If he does, you can't be convicted. It'll no longer be a crime."*

"I heard that, too. Even if he does, he'll probably wait until January to revoke it. My trial will finish by then. I'll be in prison." Skeet didn't want to be hopeful.

"It'd be something, wouldn't it? On one hand, it would keep you out of prison. On the other hand, a lot of folks around here will be out of jobs. The Depression will finally find its way into Carroll County." When I said it, I pictured the destitution it would bring.

Skeet held out his hand.

Not since the first meeting had we shaken on our partnership. I was sure he was saying goodbye because, if he went to prison, it would be the last time we would see each other.

Without even a 'fare well' or 'so long,' Skeet opened my truck door and exited. I watched him walk away via my side mirror.

FORMER COIN RUM RUNNER STAR WITNESS

(Continued from Page One)

court yesterday afternoon, Dean, one of the 29 defendants on trial for conspiracy against the national prohibition act, testified for three hours against his former employers, Nick J. Coin and Ed Lathrop, and implicated Jack Wall, Mike Talarico, Florence Ozias, Coin's stenographer and bookkeeper at the Tri-City Malt and Extract Co., Mr. and Mrs. Jack Coin, Mrs. Jewel Coin, wife of Bill, another of Coin's sons, Ralph Knight, Muscatine, Emory L. Keith, Davenport, and Dominic Leonetti, Des Moines.

Employed by Coin and Lathrop during 1929 and then discharged by Coin, Dean told of delivering liquor to almost a dozen places in Davenport; of making calls almost as regularly as a milkman; of tipping "joints" off to raids, and of making trips to a still near Muscatine.

Star Witness

Jack Dean (above) made sensational disclosures regarding activities of a Tri-city liquor ring when he took the stand at Peoria after turning state's evidence.

moved it by truck. Lathrop was

CHAPTER 32

The accused stood as the judge entered. He wore a look of confidence along with his favorite mustard-colored suit. He turned slightly around to look at his people behind him, a grin crossing his face as he sent out a quick wink. He looked over at the jury and smiled. He had been charged with three felonies and two misdemeanors. He was sure he would beat those charges and 'make tracks,' returning to his loving family. Al Capone, leader of the Chicago syndicate, stood trial for tax evasion in a Chicago federal courthouse on October 5, 1931.

Over four hundred miles away, on the same day, another criminal stood in front of federal judge in Fort Dodge, Iowa. His face was pale and his eyes worried. Many of his fellow townspeople stood behind him, having been subpoenaed to testify against him.

Skeet's trial began at 9:00 a.m. precisely. Judge Kavanaugh had readied himself for a long, hot day, the Indian summer bringing about the unusually warm temperatures. Court attendees, interested in watching one of the biggest trials Iowa had ever seen, brought along paper fans, waving them in front of their faces.

Worried Skeet would beat his charges, the federal office brought their number one hitter to the prosecution's table. Bob Woodrow was a seasoned attorney, having earned his degree from Drake Law School. He had been Polk County's attorney for ten years and had recently made the switch to the federal office. He missed living in Des Moines, but his goal of becoming a federal judge had pushed him to get some experience at the federal level. He hoped to be back in Des Moines within a few years, having been assigned to one of the state's benches. Woodrow was hungry for the win, banking on it to catapult him to his judgeship.

The prosecuting attorney started the trial with his opening statement, one that took him four minutes. He read from the Volstead Act and tied Skeet to each part of it: how he violated the making and selling of liquor. He ended his speech by promising he would prove to the jury how "this mob boss" had involved the entire community in helping him create this "nest of crime."

Skeet's attorney countered by promising to prove the evidence was only circumstantial with no concrete evidence to prove Skeet was involved in the making or selling of illegal liquor. Patrick Keane's speech was under two minutes.

The jury settled and the lawyers ready to start the game, Bob Woodward called his first witness, Michael Thielen, president of Carroll County Bank. "Mr. Thielen, is Earl Miller a client of the Carroll County Bank?"

"He is."

"How often did Mr. Miller deposit money into the bank?"

"Every week or so, though most of my clients deposit money into the bank pretty regularly. Keeps people from stealing it out of their house!" The bank president gave a chuckle with his response and was pleased to hear quiet laughter from his fellow citizens sitting in the courtroom.

"Does he deposit large amounts of cash?"

"Large amounts, Mr. Woodrow, is a relative term. I have many clients who deposit less and many clients who deposit more. Mr. Miller deposits about the right amount."

Getting nowhere with his witness, the prosecuting attorney decided to go for the throat. "And how does Mr. Miller earn his money that you so readily deposited into his account?" Woodrow asked in an aggressive voice.

"The law does not require me to ascertain the method in which my clients earn their money. I'm just happy they have the money to deposit. If they didn't, we would be required to shut our doors along with many other banks when they went under. I appreciate Mr. Miller's business and hope he continues to bank with us." The courtroom broke into a collective applause, requiring Judge Kavanaugh to bang his gavel and bark at them about courtroom etiquette.

"You are not at a movie theater," Kavanaugh reminded them.

Realizing Michael Thielen was not a helpful witness, Woodrow turned him over to Skeet's lawyer. "Mr. Thielen, using your knowledge of average amounts held in clients' accounts, does Earl Miller have a lot of money in his account comparatively?"

"Less than some, but more than others," he responded.

"So, would you characterize the amount as average?" Patrick Klein pursued.

"I would say so," the banker answered.

Skeet, like most bootleggers, did not keep the bulk of his money in the bank, for this very reason. A large amount of cash brought about questions as to what occupation would generate the revenue. Like many people after the crash, banks were no longer a trusted entity. The defense attorney released the banker from the chair.

The prosecuting attorney moved on to his next witnesses. "Richard Wagner," shouted the bailiff.

Richard Wagner had owned the bakery on First Street for many years. It was his father's business before his and would be his son's when he decided to retire. Without the cash infused from the bootleggers, his father's legacy would have gone under.

"Mr. Wagner, you own the Templeton Bakery. Is Mr. Miller a baker to your knowledge?"

"Don't know," he replied and added no further information.

"He buys a great deal of yeast from you, is that correct?"

"A good amount, I'd say."

"How much is a 'good amount'?"

"Forty bricks a week, I think."

"And since he doesn't own a bakeshop himself, what did you think he was doing with all of the yeast he purchased?"

"Making bread for the needy?" A cacophony of laughter came from the audience.

Angry he was being made to look the butt end of a joke, the prosecutor dismissed his witness and called up Ron Fischer, who owned the grocery store. Ron's testimony went the same way as that of Rich Wagner. He, too, thought Skeet was making bread for the needy.

Louis Jager, the coffin maker, was the next to be called. He did not dress in his Sunday best for his day in court. Jager had warned Skeet he would not lie for him, but Jager hated the federal government and was incensed he had been dragged to Fort Dodge to testify. He didn't have feelings for Skeet one way or another, but his stance on the federal government interfering with a man's right to drink alcohol was well known in the county.

After establishing Louis' profession and Skeet's purchase of copper, the prosecutor started the same line of questioning. "What did you assume Skeet was doing with the copper he was buying?"

"I figured he was putting it on his house and barn," the witness replied.

"Why would a man put that much copper on his house?" the lawyer wanted to know.

"Make it look pretty? What do I know what a man wants to do with his purchase? The government's got no right in knowing what a man does. If he wants to copper his roof and the inside of his house, why do they care?" Jager's tone gave away his attitude about cooperating with the prosecuting attorney.

After Jager stepped down from the stand, the judge spoke up. "Mr. Woodrow, does the prosecution plan to bring up the entire town of Templeton to testify? How many more business owners are being called?"

"Just one more, Your Honor."

The tone in the judge's voice relayed boredom and irritation. Even with the windows open, the courtroom had become an oven. In his robe, Judge Kavanaugh sweated from every pore, and the liquid ran down his back and from under his arms. He used a handkerchief to wipe away the trickles running from his hair. The circus of Templeton performers was wearing thin, especially since they gave no concrete evidence of wrongdoing.

Skeet's defense attorney had asked only one question of each witness: "Is Earl Miller an upstanding citizen?" Mr. Keane was in a difficult position as the defending attorney. He knew of Skeet's illegal activities. He could not, as an officer of the court, ask questions knowing the witnesses would perjure themselves. The question he did ask involved a word with many meanings depending on the person who was asked. *Upstanding* could mean a good community member, one who looked out for his fellow man and wanted the best for his town. In that sense, the accused was very upstanding. Each of Skeet's community members answered with a resounding "yes," feeling that they had told the truth.

Raymond Kohler stepped forward as the next witness. He owned the Oldsmobile dealership in Carroll and had sold cars to many of the county's bootleggers. Sometimes he traded in whiskey, sometimes in cash, and sometimes a combination of the two. Unlike the other business owners, Ray was terrified of getting on the stand. By taking whiskey as trade, he himself had broken the law, and he certainly knew Skeet was selling it.

His hands shaking, Ray put his hand on the Bible and swore to tell the truth, but he had no intention of keeping that promise. After announcing his name and occupation, he admitted to selling cars to Skeet.

"How often did Mr. Miller buy a new car?" the prosecution wanted to know.

"Usually once a year," Ray admitted.

"And how did he pay for each car?" Bob Woodrow looked directly into Ray's eyes, daring him to lie.

"He paid cash," Ray said.

"He always paid cash for his purchase?" Per Jimmy Krantz's information, Woodrow knew the dealer traded for whiskey.

"Always," Ray lied.

"He never traded whiskey for cars?" The lawyer drilled the question into Ray.

"Never. Always cash." Ray lied again, this time with more confidence.

"You do know you perjure yourself when you lie."

"I'm not lying," the car dealer insisted. "He paid cash."

Unable to shake him from his lie, the attorney continued. "Where did he get the money for his cars?"

"The bank, I suppose. My clients all get the money from the bank. Either they have it in savings or they take out a loan." The audience chuckled again, but Ray was trying to answer the question without lying.

"Is Mr. Miller a whiskey maker?" The prosecutor hoped to rattle him with the bold question.

The truth was written on Ray's face, but he looked Bob Woodward in the eyes and lied as boldly as humanly possible. "Not to my knowledge, no."

Kohler's testimony completed, the judge rapped his gavel and called a recess for the day. Because the heat had reached ninety degrees with not even a puff of air, Judge Kavanaugh postponed the trial for two days, hoping the heatwave would break and bring fall weather.

Back in Chicago, the prosecution fought hard to pin twenty-three counts of tax evasion on Capone. Their first witness, a tax collector, testified Capone hadn't paid taxes from 1923 through 1929. The federal attorneys also brought evidence of Capone's owning gambling halls, one of them disguised as the Hawthorne Smoke Shop, from which he made substantial profits. A raid on the shop produced gambling machines. Two witnesses from the raid testified to Capone's ownership of the shop as well as the profits made from it, which added to approximately $550,000 for two years. The most damning evidence, given three days into the trial, was from the accused's own lawyer, who had written a letter to the IRS, offering to settle his client's tax liability. The final witnesses testified to Capone's lavish lifestyle, followed by the last witness, who was the cashier of a different gambling house in 1927.

The prosecution at rest, the defense took the floor. In a single day, they presented two witnesses who testified to Capone's gambling addiction. The defense lawyers did their best to persuade the jury the defendant could have lost as much as $627,000 in six years of betting. Even if the jurors could swallow the lies, gambling losses can only be deducted from gambling gains, leaving the original crimes of tax evasion intact.

Skeet's trial picked up again on October 8, the weather finally shucking off its summer garments. The prosecution continued, calling up the federal agents who had raided the farm.

Scott Holsten was a native Nebraskan, having grown up in Omaha. He had served in local law enforcement in his home state but switched to the federal level to make more money, relocating to Iowa's northern district. He had no opinions on Prohibition but followed the law as closely as his grandmother had followed her favorite recipes. In his mind, there was no grey when it came to law enforcement.

On the stand, Agent Holsten relayed their arrival at the farm, capture of men, and seizure of whiskey and mash. He gave the details in an objective and professional manner. The prosecuting attorney allowed him to give the particulars without interruption or many follow-up questions. For the first time, defense attorney Keane rose for questioning.

"Did you see Mr. Miller at the farm during the raid?"

"No."

"Did you observe Mr. Miller with any whiskey or mash?"

"No, I did not."

After Agent Holsten vacated the stand, Bob Woodrow called Erik Saunders, another Prohibition agent. This second agent conveyed the same facts. When asked the same questions by Patrick Keane, he responded with the same answers.

The last federal agent called was, of course, Agent Alvin Truly. He strode to the front of the room; his 6'2," 185 pound frame accentuating his importance. In the silence of the courtroom, his boots announced his authority with each thud on the wooden floor. His uniform looked crisp and freshly pressed. His hat was clean, and after he sat on the chair, he hung it on his knee.

After swearing to 'tell the truth,' Truly was prompted by the attorney to give his background as a lawman: five years as sheriff and eight years as federal agent. He detailed the number of bootleg-ging arrests in Carroll County to establish the scope of illegal activity in a small area. Finally, he came to the night of Skeet's arrest, describing with exaggerated adjectives the chase and capture of the assailant. Under Woodrow's questioning, Agent Truly appeared to be the only person keeping the entire northern district from complete anarchy. As Truly sat on the stand, his chest puffed out with impor-tance; he looked like a prairie chicken preparing to mate.

Keane stood behind the podium and started his cross examina-tion. "Agent Truly, you testified Mr. Miller was close to the farm when you noticed his vehicle and began the chase. Exactly how far away was he? Three feet, twelve feet?"

"Maybe a quarter of a mile?" Truly guessed.

"So, he wasn't on the farm's property?"

"No."

"When you made the arrest, did he have any illegal liquor or mash in his possession or in his car?"

"No, but he was out there to check on the whiskey making."

"How do you know his purpose? Did he tell you this?"

"No, but nobody is out in the middle of the night unless it's got to do with whiskey making. They make it in the middle of the night," replied Truly defensively.

"You said 'nobody is out in the middle of the night,' but you were out in the middle of the night. Were you making whiskey?" Keane quipped, and the courtroom rippled with low laughter. The Judge scowled with the intentional antics.

"Of course, I wasn't! I was hunting down whiskey makers!"

"Couldn't he have been out for an evening drive or going to a sick friend's house or checking on cattle who may have gotten out?"

"He could have, but he wasn't. He was out there to pay his employees and check on the site."

"You have no solid proof of his intent. Is that correct?" asked the defense attorney.

"I was told by an inside man," Truly replied.

Keane didn't follow up on the response because he knew the inside man would be the last witness. "We'll come back to your inside man later. Let's go back to your evidence. You chased a car and then a man on foot because of what you thought he was doing. Am I correct?"

"He was running. I chased him because he was trying to evade the law. Only guilty men run," Truly said with conviction.

"If we use your theory of anyone running to be guilty, then we better arrest Babe Ruth. He runs all the time." The courtroom erupted into full laughter.

Judge Kavanaugh didn't appreciate the sarcasm of the statement and scowled down at Keane. "Watch your tone, Mr. Keane. This isn't a comedy show."

Patrick Keane had strategized for weeks in preparation for Truly's testimony. He continued his questioning, showing the jury the federal agent had no solid evidence. Once completed, he allowed Truly to leave the witness box. Yet, Truly wasn't the most damming witness.

The prosecution had saved its most incriminating witness for last—Jimmy Krantz.

Wearing pressed clothing, Jimmy Krantz walked through the courtroom and took the witness stand. His hair, still damp from a quick wash, was tamed and cut short. He fidgeted with his hair, smoothing it down, and tugged at his tie, indicating he was not used to wearing one.

Bob Woodrow rose from his seat and went behind the podium; he shuffled his papers and organized his notes. He didn't look at his witness immediately, preferring to concentrate on his papers. With each second ticking by, Jimmy became more nervous.

"Mr. Krantz," boomed Woodrow's voice, causing Jimmy to jump, "what was your job in the whiskey organization?"

"Set—" Jimmy started to answer but then needed to clear his throat. He started again, "Setter and then driver."

"For our jury members—who don't make whiskey—can you explain those jobs?"

"When I was a setter, I made the mash...the ingredients were put into a barrel to make the whiskey, and I watched the cooking and switched out the containers the whiskey went into. After that, I was Skeet's—Mr. Miller's—driver."

"When you were a setter, did Mr. Miller visit your cook site?"

Skeet had visited once a week, as he did every cook site. Jimmy had received pay from him and had seen him pay the other setters as well as the farmer. He had directed the loading of whiskey. Jimmy, from his position in the courtroom, looked directly at Skeet. The answers, which would have to be given in front of Skeet, had been his worry from the moment he gave Truly what he wanted.

The information was enough to catch and convict Skeet. Since that moment, he had vacillated between finishing his contract and testifying in court or running. Suspicious Jimmy would take off, Truly had assigned one of his men to escort him to the courthouse and stay with him until he took the stand.

Jimmy had been tethered to Truly for six years, and it was six years too long, he thought. Anger over his treatment by the federal agent had been building inside him, and the distrust—though rightly earned—brought Jimmy to a new level of anger. Skeet had only been kind to him, and this SOB had done nothing but berate and threaten him.

Sitting on the stand, Jimmy knew the answer he would give to the prosecutor. "No, I never saw Mr. Miller at any of the locations I worked." Jimmy glanced at Alvin Truly whose eyes were now boring into him.

Shocked by the unexpected answer, Woodrow reiterated, "You're saying he didn't come and pay you along with the other setters?"

"No, he didn't. I did not see him." Jimmy looked straight into the attorney's eyes, daring him to call him a 'liar.'

Flustered by the unexpected answer, Woodrow tried another angle. "When you were driving Mr. Miller around, did he have you stop at farms?"

"He did," Jimmy replied honestly.

"And what did you see him do at the farms?"

"He visited the farmers," Jimmy briefly answered.

"Yes, but what did he do with the farmers? What were his conversations?"

"I wouldn't know. My job was to stay in the car and wait for him. I never saw him do anything but talk to them."

"What did you assume he was talking to them about?" The prosecuting attorney was now angry with Jimmy's lies and evasions.

Skeet's defense attorney jumped up and called, "Objection, Your Honor. The witness can only testify to what he actually heard and saw."

"Sustained," ruled the judge.

"What other driving did you do besides drive Mr. Miller around?"

"None. I just drove Skeet."

Deciding he was not getting any helpful evidence from Jimmy, the prosecuting attorney released Jimmy to the defense. When Woodward got to his seat, he turned around and looked at Alvin Truly. The federal agent leaned forward and whispered into the attorney's ear, his hands waving wildly, displaying his anger.

Attorney Keane had pages of questions and notes ready for his cross examination of Jimmy. Skeet had conveyed all Jimmy had seen, heard, and done involving the business. However, the attorney now thought his best move was to forgo his examination. Nothing Jimmy had said helped to convict Skeet. Any more words out of his mouth had the possibility of opening a new avenue of inquiry for the other side. "I have no questions, Your Honor."

Jimmy quitted the witness chair, strode down the aisle, and exited through the doors. Alvin Truly had not made plans for Jimmy following his testimony, so he had not assigned an agent to follow the witness.

Having called their last witness, the prosecution rested, leaving the defense to begin their work. When Judge Kavanaugh directed Patrick Keane to call his first witness, Skeet's lawyer decided to make a bold move, one he had never made before. "No witnesses, Your Honor." The gasp from the spectators sucked the air from the room. The judge pounded his gavel.

"You are not calling any witnesses?" The judge wanted to be sure he had heard correctly.

"That's correct, Your Honor. The defense rests as well."

The defense attorney had originally planned to bring forward several character witnesses, who were now sitting in the courtroom, ready to testify; but he had used the prosecution's witnesses to establish Skeet's character. Additional people would only prolong the trial and irritate the judge. He had already expressed his vexation when Woodrow put a string of businessmen on the stand. If Skeet were convicted, Keane wanted the judge to have positive feelings about his client when sentencing him.

Judge Kavanaugh had estimated two additional days for the defense's witnesses. Planning to conclude early and allow the defense to start the following day, the judge had informed his wife he would be returning from court early that day. Seeing an opportunity to conclude and turn it over to the jury for deliberation, Kavanaugh settled into his chair and called for closing arguments.

The prosecution went first, standing in front of the jury, his hands punctuating his points. Bob Woodrow began by relaying the testimonies of the federal agents. He reinforced their good character and years of experience catching bootleggers. Without solid evidence, the lawyer tried to persuade the jurors the federal agents would know a bootlegger by his actions, and Earl Miller had all the markings of a bootlegger. He concluded by stressing the importance of Prohibition and its effect on the moral character of Americans. Without much of a logical argument, Woodrow tried to manipulate the jurors' sense of patriotism. He didn't know their personal feelings about Prohibition even though each had proclaimed to be a proponent of abstinence during the voire dire. Some of them could have lied and been on Skeet's side the entire trial.

Patrick Keane rose and addressed the jury. "Ladies and gentlemen, let me review the facts of the case. Earl Miller was arrested, but no evidence was found on him. No evidence was found at his home. He was not even at the location where they found the illegal whiskey; he was merely out for an evening drive and was at the wrong place at the wrong time. It is true he stopped and turned around, but the sight of men with guns would make anyone turn around. Agent Truly asserted he ran because he was guilty. Earl Miller ran because he was being chased; he was afraid. You heard a known associate tell you he has never seen Mr. Miller participating in illegal activities. The prosecution's case has faulty logic. Mr. Miller is being accused of being a bootlegger because he is behaving like one. That isn't hard evidence proving his guilt. That is speculation, which you cannot use to convict a man. Perhaps you yourself believe this man is a bootlegger, but believing and knowing based on hard proof are not the same thing. The law requires hard proof. You must find Earl Miller not guilty."

Judge Kavanaugh instructed the jury, then released them to deliberate. At five o'clock, they still had come to no decision. They left for the day and returned again the following one. After three additional days, they finally notified the bailiff they had a verdict.

Jury members voted according to their beliefs; the Wets finding Skeet innocent and the Drys finding him guilty. It took long hours of haggling to bring one person to the other side.

Six days after Skeet's jury came to a decision, Capone's jury read his verdict—guilty. They had deliberated not a month or even a week; they came to their decision in eight hours. Six days later, the judge sentenced him to eleven years, the longest term ever for tax evasion. Capone was led away in cuffs and yelled out, "I'm not through fighting yet!"

Twelve jurors in the Fort Dodge courtroom filed back into the courtroom. The bailiff took the verdict and carried it to the judge, who read it and had it returned to the lead juror. Skeet and his attorney rose.

"Have you reached a verdict?" the judge asked.

"We have."

"And what say you?"

"Not guilty."

Skeet's knees grew weak with relief. A collective sigh released behind him. When the verdict sunk in, the audience erupted into cheers. Skeet turned around and gave them a thumb's up.

Skeet had escaped, and he wasn't planning to put himself into such a precarious situation again. While sitting in jail, he had promised himself if he kept his freedom, he would find a different profession. No more organization and no more whiskey making.

'Templeton Rye' Doomed; Plan to Distill Legally

Templeton, Ia., Dec. 9.—(U.P.) —Manufacture and flow of "Templeton rye," prohibition's illicit slaker of agricultural throats, apparently is doomed to die with prohibition's repeal.

Throughout the dry years, manufacture of the now famous contraband product of Temple's evirons went merrily on. The bootleg, jugged throughout Iowa and adjacent states, attained considerable popularity and not a little revenue for some of Carroll county's hard-pressed farmers.

Resourceful farm distillers adapted to a mass production basis a secret "ageing" process borne out of the Kentucky and Tennessee hills.

The process, according to those who make this rye whisky, imparts to day-old product a "genuine bourbon" flavor and mellownes detracting not a particle from a "kick" calculated to shame a Missouri mule.

With prohibition's death knell, the more energetic farmers planned to manufacture the whisky as a legal product if Iowa's liquor laws are repealed.

CHAPTER 33

Upon hearing the news of Skeet's verdict, I inhaled deeply. I hadn't realized until then I had been holding my breath in anticipation, cowardly hunkering inside my house, more worried about my own freedom than his. Guilt for my need to hide from my crimes instead of taking my rightful place alongside Skeet had been trapped in my body, and upon hearing the outcome, it gushed out and ran rivers down the street. This near catastrophe had obliterated my confidence, and I wanted nothing more to do with illegal whiskey making. Whatever money I had accumulated would have to be enough.

Skeet came back into town like a Greek hero, the glow of outsmarting the federal government emanating from him. He would go down in our town's history as a legend, the Hercules of bootleg. Generations of Templetonians would tell the story of how the kingpin had defied authority and skirted punishment.

Two months after the trial, Utah voted for a repeal of Prohibition, the 36th state to do so. Just like that, we were back to the way we were before the Volstead Act... almost.

Ironically, legalizing alcohol made buying it more difficult. Each state was given authority over liquor laws, and Iowa set forth to regulate it. Legislators left the power to towns and cities, who could decide, with a vote, whether liquor licenses would be given. The city councils would issue authorization to those entities whom they deemed responsible.

Again, needing a way to support my family, I applied for a license, intending to start a saloon. I had proved to myself I had a head for business. And I had certainly learned much about the booze industry.

When Iowa laid down the regulations for drinking establishments, conditions were included: nothing could obstruct the view inside of the bar—painted windows, screen, or blinds (I suppose they wanted to see inside to make sure nothing illegal was happening); no gambling or gaming (including billiards) could take place; and no food could be sold or given away on the premises. No females or persons under 21 could be employed.

The last regulation was one I needed to bend—just a little. Persons under 21 was not my problem. The female ban needed some creativity. When I stood in front of city council, in defense of my application for a license, I did some of my own arguing. The law said females could not be "employed." I would not be an employee; I would be the owner of the establishment.

Upon conclusion of my argument, the councilmen excused themselves to discuss the application. I was counting on the continuation of defying the law to do what they felt was just. I was a widow of Prohibition. My husband Jack Weber had been gunned down by Alvin Truly, a representative of the government. Surly I was owed some compensation, even if it only came from my own town.

Within a few days, I was granted a liquor license, my faith in the goodness and rightness of my fellow man still intact. I bought the building, which used to house the Kuhl Saloon, and began renovations.

I installed a beautiful new oak bar with matching shelves and a large mirror behind it. A shiny, brass footrail framed the bottom of the bar, and for my clients' comfort, I ordered eight padded stools mounted to the floor. Brass spittoons sat like squat toads around the bar, ready to receive tobacco juice. New tables and chairs dotted the room. I decorated the walls with pictures of the old depot and locomotives to honor the history of our town as well as remind myself how I made the money to own such a fine establishment. I named my business **Cora's Saloon***, but the townspeople shortened it to* **Cora's***, and in their usual supportive fashion, spent their money and their time in my bar.*

Skeet was one of my best patrons, visiting the saloon several times a week. As one of the town's most famous sons, his approval of my establishment brought in other patrons. Movie-star like, he sat at a table, a crowd around him, and retold stories of his bootlegging days, the favorite being his capture by Alvin Truly. No matter how many times he told his tales, his audience always wanted more. True to his word, Skeet never let my name slip from his lips.

Many of my other employees turned up to rekindle with Skeet— some of them were setters; others, farmers. Bits of conversation drifted behind the bar, and eventually I was caught up on each man's new life. Most of them had decided to travel the straight road, Skeet's near imprisonment turning them away from the bootlegging business. While I had known them, they had never known who I was in the business.

Occasionally, our best rumrunner, Frank Hogan, walked through my doors and took a front-row seat at Skeet's table. After listening to a few tales, the other men scattered, knowing Skeet and Frank liked some time to themselves. Frank no longer dealt in illegal liquor, but he was still making money from illicit activities. Snippets of back-room gambling stories drifted within my hearing. I never really knew Frank, trusting Skeet when he said Frank was a "good kid." Something sad had attached itself to his eyes, and it never seemed to leave him. After a time, he quit visiting, and I lost track of him.

No one had seen hide nor hair of the snitch, Jimmy Krantz. When he walked out of the courtroom, he disappeared. We all supposed he had hopped a train, trying to get far away from Alvin Truly after he had double crossed him. We never knew why he had become a snitch, but we supposed he had troubles of his own and had gotten into a tight spot, his only way out being a deal with the Devil. Skeet didn't seem to hold a grudge; after all, Jimmy had refused to testify against him. I personally believed Skeet had taken quite a shine to that boy and forgave him for his double crossing.

Sheriff Katz occasionally visited my establishment, pretending he was checking on the legality of the business, but I think he just missed talking to Skeet. Fortunately for the sheriff, the Klan never made another attempt to step inside Carroll County again. They could no longer decry our defying federal law, and the harsh feelings against Germans seemed to fade the further we got away from the war. The sheriff went back to dealing with petty theft and mediating small rifts among county citizens.

My saloon did enough business to keep my children and me from starving. Most of my clients wanted beer, but I kept a respectable stable of hard liquor for those who preferred it. The liquor bottles lined up on my shelves like show ponies, gleaming in the reflection of the mirror: Smirnoff Vodka, brandy, Burke's rum, gin, bourbon, and Glenlivit Black and White whiskey. The same bottle of Glenlivit sat untouched for years, no customer asking for a shot.

Although I swore I would walk a straight line, I must admit I wavered just a tiny bit. A jug of rye whiskey, made by the light of the moon, sat beneath my counter. Every man who walked into my business knew he could order it by saying, "I'll take the house special."

One late morning, Skeet walked into my saloon and sat at a table. The business didn't open until 1:00 p.m., but I always arrived early, keeping my books up-to-date, ordering supplies, and completing some general cleaning. I was surprised to see my old partner so early in the day. I wasn't sure what had brought him because he asked only for coffee.

Something about the tone of his request made me stop my duties and join him. "I'm glad things are working out for you, Cora," he said, looking around the bar.

"Thank you, Earl. I couldn't have done it without you. I never did tell you how much I appreciated everything you did, and by everything, I mean keeping my name silent. You saved my family."

"I never told you—or anyone for that matter—but I owed your husband Jack. I got myself into a bind some years before Jack's death, and he got me out of it."

Skeet's evasiveness intrigued me. Good manners told me to drop my inquisitiveness, but given what we had done together, I felt more like family instead of an acquaintance.

"I'd like to hear the story if you're willing to tell it."

Skeet didn't respond immediately. He sat looking at his hands, folded into a prayerful position on the table. "Back around 1915, I played quite a bit of poker; truthfully, I can admit I had a gambling problem. One night I got myself into a heap of trouble. I had some good hands at the beginning but then ran a streak of no winners. Like a lot of gamblers, I tried to win back my money by continuing to play, betting higher amounts the more I got myself into a hole. Jack was at that game. I'm sure you didn't know he liked to sit a hand or two now and again, but he always walked away when he lost his limit. Anyway, Jack tried to get me to quit, but I wasn't about to leave the table with so much money lost. By the end of the night, I owed the house three hundred. I didn't have it.

"The game was run by Maniac Mike Hogan, Frank's uncle. Mike

came by his nickname honestly. You never knew what that guy would do. And his games were backed by a Des Moines guy who was connected to the Chicago mob. Frank was running some of the games and learning the business from Mike, and that's how we met. When I couldn't pay my debt, Mike threatened to break my fingers, one for every hundred I owed him. Jack stepped in and paid one of the three hundred, guaranteeing the rest by the next day. Because I was a degenerate gambler, I didn't have the credibility to walk away with debt, but Jack's reputation as an honest man who always kept his word was enough to keep my fingers.

"I repaid Jack the money, but I never found a good enough way to repay him for his friendship. When he started into whiskey, I was the one who taught him the process and helped him build his still. After he was killed, I felt responsible. I was sick with guilt when he died. And then you came along. Helping Jack's widow was a way I could repay him. After we were in business for a few years, I forgot about my debt. I quit thinking of you as his widow, especially when making money became my new obsession. I wasn't a gentleman. I'm sorry for that. When I was arrested, I sat in that jail and had time to examine my life. I remembered my commitment to you, which is why I would have spent years in jail without ever giving anyone your name."

"Earl, next to my husband, you are the best man I know."

Skeet grinned, reached across the table and squeezed my hand. He quickly finished the rest of his coffee and placed his hat on his head. "See you around, Cora."

Instead of finishing my morning chores, I sat at that table and thought about his story. "Liar," I said to myself. My husband hated cards; he wouldn't even play an innocent game of Old Maid with his children. I appreciated Skeet's desire to make his actions seem as if they were owed to me. I'll never know his true motivations, and I guess I'll have to leave it at that.

Looking around my saloon, I was proud of my accomplishment. My establishment with its train theme was both rugged enough for my male customers while being nostalgic for me. There was only one item not train-related in the room. My eye landed on a large object hanging from the ceiling—a cutout jug with white lettering. It may have started as Jack's legacy, but it was mine now.

AUTHOR'S NOTE

I grew up in Crawford County, the western, adjacent county to Carroll. As early as my teens, I knew of its bootlegging history in a general sense. I think most people in that area know a few of the stories and feel a sense of—dare I call it pride?—in what the people of that area did during the agricultural downturn during the Twenties as well as the Depression. With each generation, more of the story slips away.

None of the characters in the story are based on real people. Some of them take on bits and pieces from people I know. As they read the story, I hope they will enjoy seeing themselves in the novel. None of the plotline comes from that time, either. It was completely a work of my imagination. The background—how, when, where, and for what reason—comes from research and represents what actually happened in the bootlegging business.

My research started by visiting Templeton Rye Distillery in Templeton, Iowa. I met Keith Kerkhoff, who gave me a tour and began our journey of Keith's sharing stories of his bootlegging family. Keith is the grandson of Alphonse Kerkhoff.

I also reached out to Heath Schneider, who is grandson to Lorine Sextro. Heath's grandmother was one of a few women who illegally distilled. Heath helped me with some of the technical issues and relayed some of his family stories. He also invited me to visit Iowa Legendary Rye Distillery in Carroll. Their distiller Max Poland, a 6th generation Master Distiller, gave me a tour and answered many of my questions about the distilling process used during Prohibition. I credit the authenticity of my distilling chapter to Max.

Both of these distilleries are well worth visiting; both carry on the quality of the whiskey and its history. Along with the whiskey, you can enjoy the beauty of the rolling hills and the fertile farmland of that area. We western Iowans refer to that part of the state as God's country.

Today, western Iowa residents who know a guy, who knows the guy, can still get their hands on the bootleg product. Once payment is made, a container of whiskey will appear on the porch or front step, the bottle a repurposed wine or liquor bottle, the top wrapped in duct tape to keep the cork or lid sealed. As I say often, "Only in western Iowa."

In Chapter 27, I wrote about Defiance's community hall. In my novel, I told of the hall being built in 1932. However, it was not built until 1935, opening in 1936. When I chose the location of Defiance for that chapter, I did a quick Google search to see if there was anything historically interesting. I liked the story and put it in the chapter, knowing it was the wrong year. I hope the Defiance residents can forgive me for knowingly changing their history.

I admit I'm not much of a whiskey drinker, but I may have tried a sip or two of the illegal stuff. I won't say where I got it.

ACKNOWLEDGEMENTS

Thanks to Heath Schneider, who was excited about sharing his family's stories and helping me with any questions I had about whiskey making. His help in getting the details of distilling accurate made this novel more authentic.

Thank you as well to Lisa Chase and "Whiskey" Rich. Lisa worked on the promotional pieces of the novel's release and Rich was generous with his time in reading the book and providing his approval.

Also thanks to Keith Kerkhoff for being so generous with his time. I appreciated the personal tour of Templeton Rye Distillery along with listening to his family's story.

I owe a huge thank you to the entire Hogan family: Marc, Angela, Frank, and Lucy. They allowed me to use their names and those of their children to create Frank's character once again as well as his backstory, which included the rest of his family. When Frank is old enough, I hope he enjoys a character being named for him.

Thank you to Dr. Anthony Paustain and Bookpress Publishing for getting this book out and working with me on all things book related. I always enjoy my publisher meetings.

I also want to acknowledge my husband, John Kotz, for his assistance with this novel. Usually, he helps with anything physical needed to sell books. However, on this one, he was willing to help when I was stuck on a plot point and to let me bounce novel title ideas off him.

RESOURCES

For those of you wanting more of the Templeton story, several resources are out there. These are the ones I used.

"Whiskey Cookers." Democracy Films, 2015. www.WhiskeyCookers.com.

Gentlemen Bootleggers by Bryce Bauer. 2014. Print.

NEWSPAPER SOURCES

"Mourners at the Wake of Barley Corn." *Sioux City Journal*.
    January 17, 1920.

"Iowa Jewelers Open Session." *Des Moines Tribune*. April 23, 1929.

"23 Die From Holiday Booze." *Des Moines Tribune*. December 28, 1926.

"Templeton Distillery Was Raided Recently." *Des Moines Tribune*.
    December 18, 1929.

"Prohibition As An Issue." *Sioux City Journal*. April 25, 1920.

"Carroll County Suffered Most." *Des Moines Tribune*. August 15, 1929.

"Bone Dry." Cartoon. *Evansville Press*. January 16, 1919.

"The Ku Klux Klan in Iowa." *The Des Moines Register*. August 21, 1921.

"Manufacture of Illicit Spirits Has Not Stopped." *Carroll Daily Herald*.
    April 19, 1934. (Permission by Iowa Information Media Group).

"New Law to Raise Penalty Boosts Liquor Prices Here." *Des Moines Tribune.* March 18, 1929.

"Ban Together In Local Bodies." *Des Moines Register.* October 16, 1932. *(Permission by Gannett Publishing.)*

"Coming Farm Auctions." *Des Moines Register.* August 26, 1932. *(Permission by Gannett Publishing.)*

Caravan of Trucks Photo. *The Gazette* (Cedar Rapids). January 18, 1932. *(Republished with permission © 2024 The Gazette, Cedar Rapids, Iowa.)*

"You can't fight the Devil with cream puffs." *The Daily Nonpareil* (Council Bluffs). May 6, 1925.

"$50,000 In Liquor, 22 Persons Taken in Big Booze Raid." *Carroll Times Herald.* June 1922.

"Former Coin Rum Runner Star Witness." *Quad City Times.* December 1, 1933.

"'Templeton Rye' Doomed; Plan to Distill Legally." *The McCook Daily Gazette* (McCook NB). December 9, 1933.